The Merriman Chronicles

Book Three

The French Invasion

"Dulce et decorum est pro patria mori"

Odes (III.2.13)

- Horace (Quintus Horatius Flaccus)

Copyright Information

The Merriman Chronicles - Book 3

The French Invasion

Copyright © 2013 by Roger Burnage

With the exception of certain well known historical figures, the characters in this book have no relation or resemblance to any person living or dead.

All rights reserved. This book and all "The Merriman Chronicles" are works of fiction. No part of this book may be reproduced or used in any manner without written permission of the copyright owner except for the use of quotations in a book review.

Sixth Edition – 2024

Updated by: Robin Burnage
Edited by: Katharine D'Souza

ISBN: 9798336092684 (paperback)
ISBN: 9798336093506 (hardcover)

www.merriman-chronicles.com

Books in the series

James Abel Merriman (1768 – 1843)

A Certain Threat

The Threat in the West Indies

Merriman and the French Invasion

The Threat in the East

The Threat in the Baltic

The Threat in the Americas

The Threat in the Adriatic

The Threat in the Atlantic

Edward James Merriman (1853 - 1928)

The Fateful Voyage

Foreword

Author's notes

In the spring of 1998, workmen demolishing an old nursing home to the north-west of Chester, discovered bundles of old papers concealed behind a bricked up fireplace. One of the men with more perspicacity than his fellows gave them to his employer, a builder, who, being a friend of mine and knowing of my interest in such things passed them on to me. The discovered papers were mostly in a very bad state due to the effects of dampness, mildew and the depredations of vermin over the years and many of the oldest bundles were mostly illegible. Another problem was that the papers had been by different people and some of the handwriting was not of the best. Sorting the papers into chronological order took many months of part time effort, indeed I gave up on the job for weeks at a time, but as I progressed with the work, I realised that it was a history of the Merriman family from the late 18th century to the early years of the 20th century.

The first clearly decipherable writings referred to a certain James Abel Merriman, a naval officer at the time of the Napoleonic wars, and revealed some startling facts about French activities in and around Ireland and the Irish Sea at that time. I quickly realised that I had in my hands the material for a novel or novels about a little-known part of our history. Other papers and a family tree showed that beside those serving in the navy, later members of the family were connected with the 22nd Regiment of Foot, the Cheshire Regiment.

Intriguingly, a family tree was among the papers in one of the later bundles. Armed with that and from research in local archives, church records etc. it appeared that the last male heir of the family, Albert George Merriman was killed in France in 1916 and the last descendant, his unmarried sister Amy Elizabeth, was also killed in France in 1917.

Chapter One

Homeward bound from West Indies

September 1796

Commander James Merriman was furious. He was under orders to return home "with all despatch". The ship had already taken two weeks longer than might reasonably be expected to make the voyage from the West Indies back across the Atlantic to Portsmouth. There was no possible way that His Majesty's sloop Aphrodite could make better time. Merriman's anger was felt by all aboard, from the First Lieutenant down to the lowliest ship's boy. Standing near the helmsmen, who studiously avoided looking at him in case it earned them a harsh rebuke for not attending to their duty, Merriman glowered at all about him. It did his humour no good at all to know that the damage aloft was his own fault for driving the ship too hard and all aboard knew it.

The ship had been driven back repeatedly by foul winds and late yesterday the overstrained main yard had cracked when an exceptionally heavy gust hit the ship. The yard had to be sent down to be fished, a repair which necessitated another timber being lashed to it like a splint. The carpenter, bos'un, and their assistants were sweating over it whilst the ship heaved and crashed over a quartering sea, making their task no easier. Meanwhile, the sailmaker and his mates were busy with the torn main course. After inflicting the damage the gale had eased and veered southerly, as if satisfied to have made its mark on man's puny vessel, although the skies were still covered by the dark racing clouds.

Merriman swore to himself and began to pace up and down. Of course his eagerness to make a fast passage was because he was desperately anxious to try and get home to see his fiancée, Helen. The Aphrodite had been in the West Indies for almost four years, ever since the French declared war on England, moving around the islands in such an erratic way that correspondence from home had rarely caught up with them. When it did it was always months out of date.

There had been two years of interesting and exciting secret missions to land and recover agents. These were quiet and secretive men, and the occasional woman, who were seeking to discover how far French plans had reached in their efforts to destabilise British influence in the colonies and raise the slaves in revolt. Merriman and the Aphrodite had been under the orders of a Mr. Grahame who had been sent out by the government to co-ordinate the British espionage system. But Grahame had been recalled to England and Merriman and his ship had therefore fallen under the command of the Flag Officer in Antigua, the principal West Indies station. That officer, Admiral Sir William Howarth, had never approved of the fact that Merriman with his ship Aphrodite operated virtually as a free agent in his command area, and had seized upon his opportunity to bring the ship under his control.

He had shown his disfavour by giving Aphrodite all the worst tasks. On more than one occasion, he had threatened Merriman with being demoted back to the rank of Lieutenant, something that Merriman thought to be particularly unjust as he had always obeyed orders, ran an excellent ship, and maintained a very loyal crew. Realising that it was most likely the rantings of a senior officer dissatisfied with his own circumstances, Merriman comforted himself with the knowledge that at some point he would fall under a new commanding officer. Since then there had been over a year of monotonous duty escorting slow moving convoys and of being sent hither and thither at the Admiral's whim until Merriman could have wept with frustration. It was now six months since he had received a letter from either Helen or his family and his ship had not seen English waters for years. Even the small messenger ketch which had found him and delivered his orders had no mail aboard.

Did Helen still love him, or had the long separation caused her to wonder what life would be like married to a man who could be home only rarely? Perhaps she was regretting the betrothal hastily made when Aphrodite was ordered to the West Indies. Merriman sneered at himself. It was no good taking his bad temper out on the ship's company; he had always tried to make them believe that he was above the petty moods that characterised so many officers. Where was the patience that he had learned during his years at sea? With a determined effort he threw off the black mood which possessed him and strode for'ard to where the main yard was being repaired. The carpenter stood as Merriman approached.

"Nearly done, sir, on the last bit of serving now and then there's just a lick of tar needed before we sway it aloft. The men are working as fast as they can, sir."

Merriman could see that the man was nervous, probably expecting to be rebuked for not completing the job earlier. "I know that, Mr Green. I'm pleased with your progress. Carry on." Merriman returned to the quarterdeck rubbing his hands together and, forcing a smile to his face, he addressed his officers who had been at pains to avoid his attention.

"We shall be able to get the main yard aloft again soon, gentlemen. Mr Green and his mates have done well. I expect to be able to make better progress before nightfall."

It was as though the sun had suddenly broken through the heavy cloud the way the officers brightened up at their captain's change of mood.

"Indeed, sir, and we have the wind in our favour at last instead of the incessant northerly gales we have had for so long," responded Colin Laing, the First Lieutenant.

Even the normally taciturn sailing master, Elijah Cuthbert was disposed to venture an opinion. "If the weather holds we could be off Ushant in another day or two, sir."

"Not before time, Mr Cuthbert, not before time. Mr Laing, I'll trouble you to keep the lookouts awake. We might find the odd French privateer in these waters. T'would be fine to arrive in port with a prize under our lee."

"Indeed it would, sir," replied Laing. "But we did so well in the taking of prizes during the first two years since we left England that there must be plenty to our account in the prize fund already."

"That's very true, but another one wouldn't hurt. However, I'll be below, call me when the repairs are completed."

Below in his spartan cabin, Merriman's mind turned once again to thoughts of home. He unlocked the drawer in which he kept his most personal things and took out the few letters which had reached him. The first one from his father, himself a retired frigate Captain, which was now over three years old. Apart from giving such news as there was from home, the letter informed him that the 22nd Regiment of Foot, the Cheshire Regiment in which his friend Robert Saville served as a captain, was to be despatched to the West Indies in the autumn of 1793.

This had not been news to him by the time the letter was received, of course. His meetings with Robert on Antigua had been a highlight of recent years and hearing about his betrothal to Merriman's sister, Emily, a rare delight. Merriman smiled sadly. Just as had happened to himself and Helen, so it had happened to his sister and his friend. Betrothals but no weddings.

Merriman assumed there must have been other letters from his family which had never reached him, as the next letter was dated October 1795, in which his father broke the news that of the seven thousand men in the army who went to the West Indies, barely two thousand survived. Most of the deaths were attributed to disease and the drinking to excess of rum, especially 'moonshine' rum distilled by the natives of the islands. Only a few men had died as a result of enemy action. The remains of the 22nd regiment had returned to Chester but Robert was not amongst them and Emily was distraught with worry.

Merriman had managed to meet Robert on two or three occasions in Antigua and was well aware of the terrible toll disease and alcohol took of the men in the garrisons. Fortunately the spartan life aboard a ship at sea had kept his own crew healthy and clear of such problems. Also, the ship's doctor Mr McBride, insisted that Merriman had the water barrels refilled with fresh water at every opportunity and applied himself diligently to overseeing that the men had as much fresh fruit and vegetables as they could get. That task was made easier by the Admiralty order the previous year that directed that every man should have a daily issue of lemon juice to counteract the effects of scurvy which caused a man's gums to rot and his teeth fall out.

Merriman's mind went back to the day four years ago when Helen's father, Doctor Simpson, had given McBride, a reformed alcoholic, a sheaf of notes of medical information gleaned from twenty years in India. McBride had considered the notes to be his bible and had studied them assiduously. He was now a very competent doctor and surgeon and the only alcohol he touched was the occasional glass of wine.

For a while his mind wandered back to home, his parent's country house and small estate near Burton, to the north of Chester. He pictured the hall and large reception rooms where guests would be lavishly entertained, with his mother's housekeeper and companion, Annie, producing culinary wonders from the kitchen so that nobody left the house hungry.

He wondered if his parents had had their portraits painted as they had promised. If so they would be hung on the grand staircase with other family portraits including Merriman's uncle, Nathaniel Merriman, who had died at the head of his regiment in the war with America, and Merriman's grandfather, old Elias Merriman who had been the first of the family to enter the navy and who retired as an Admiral. It was his grandfather's tales that made Merriman long to be a naval officer and there had always been something of a mystery about him. It was known that he had married a woman from a noble family who had objected to her marrying an almost penniless young officer and refused to acknowledge the marriage. His grandmother never saw her family again.

Infrequently Merriman had received letters from Helen, the last over six months ago, in which she gave him news of herself and her father, expressed her love for him and prayed for his safe return. Merriman was trying to visualise her face, her dark hair and shining eyes, tugging at his ear as was his habit when concentrating, when a knock on the cabin door brought him back to the present. It was Midshipman Oakley.

"Mr Laing's compliments, sir, and the repairs are completed."

"Very good, Mr Oakley, you may tell Mr Laing that I shall be up directly."

Fully canvassed again, Aphrodite made good time, but regardless of their hopes no French vessel was sighted nor even an English one until the ship approached the waters of the English Channel. Ushant was to the south-east when they passed and saluted a stately ship of the line and a frigate with a convoy of supply ships heading out to join the blockading squadrons off the French ports.

Soon afterwards, when Merriman had only just arrived on deck, the foretop lookout yelled out, "Deck there, ships ahead, one sinking and another hull down to starboard. There's a small boat, sir, off the larboard bow."

"Alter course two points to larboard please, Mr Andrews; we'll see what it is."

Lieutenant Andrews issued the necessary orders and it was not long before the Aphrodite was close enough to see that it appeared to be a small brig, well down for'ard, which even as they approached it lurched forward and down with the foredeck down to the water level. Another lurch forward and the doomed ship lifted her stern in the air and slipped beneath the waves with only a belch of air and bubbles as the last bulkhead gave way to show where she had been.

The boat which the lookout had reported could now be seen with the occupants waving wildly to attract attention.

"Heave to, Mr Andrews, and give them our lee."

There were five wet and shivering men in the boat which was clearly cast adrift, very soon they were all safely aboard Aphrodite. One of them, a short man with a long neck and a beaked nose which gave him the look of a bird of prey, stamped over to where Merriman, obviously the captain, was standing.

"Thank Heaven you came, Captain. I thought we were finished. I'm captain and owner of the Lucy, a merchant brig contracted to the Navy's Victualing and Stores Department. Damn it, I was, until that blasted privateer caught us. I thought we were lost until we saw your topsails. They put us in the boat and we've been adrift for hours, watching the bloody French plunder my ship and then they blew a hole in the bottom…"

Merriman held up his hand. "Enough for the moment, Captain. Mr Andrews, have these men provided with warmth and food right away. Captain…?"

"Griffin, sir. George Griffin."

"The Captain will join me in my cabin. Mr Andrews, you have the deck. Now, follow me, Captain Griffin."

Below, Peters, Merriman's servant, appeared and was ordered to bring a hot toddy.

"Now then, Captain, tell me what happened."

"Well, sir, we were on our way to take supplies to the fleet off Brest when this God-damned privateer came out of the dark at dawn yesterday morning and we were boarded. We tried to fight but we weren't prepared and they killed two of my crew. Bloody French, they took what they wanted then set us adrift and sank my ship. Damn them all to hell."

"I'm very sorry, Captain. What were you carrying?"

"Oh, barrels of salt pork, water, cordage, spare blocks, all the usual stuff. The ship was mine and now my family's livelihood is threatened 'cos it'll take the Navy months to pay compensation for the loss." The man was nearly in tears.

"What can you tell me about the privateer, sir? You're certain she is French I take it?" asked Merriman.

"All black she was, painted black and with the sails dark grey. We never saw her until too late. Schooner rigged and very fast too if I'm any judge. French? Oh yes, no doubt of that, I know enough of the lingo to know what they were jabbering about."

"And what would that be, Mr Griffin?"

"That they were going from Ireland to France, Sir. One of them said that our stores would bring a pretty penny in France if they got through our blockade. I think the captain and them were all for slitting our throats and throwing us overboard, but a man who seemed to be in charge stopped them."

"The man in charge? Not the captain then?"

"No, a man in black and with a long scar on his cheek. He persuaded them to set us adrift in our little boat with some food and water. Seemed to be a cut above the rest of them, a gentleman I think, very courteous he was." Griffin drained the last of his toddy with relish. "Ah, that's better, frozen we were."

"Well, Mr Griffin, I can do nothing about your ship, and the privateer is well away, possibly even in some French port by now if she avoided the blockade. I can at least provide you with another hot toddy. Peters, see to it please."

Peters nodded and Merriman continued, "We're bound for Portsmouth so you can report there. I suppose that your men all have certificates of exemption, Captain?"

"Aye, that they have, so you can't press 'em and one of them's my son."

At that time, men working in necessary jobs around the dockyards and in small ships contracted to the navy were supposedly exempt from being taken by the press gangs sent ashore by captains desperate to find men for their ships. In practice, with the expansion of the Navy, if a captain thought he could get away with it, he would take any man he could.

"Have no fear, Mr Griffin, I have a full crew, though what may happen to them once ashore I cannot say. And now, sir... Peters. Peters, my compliments to the First Lieutenant and will he find accommodation for Mr Griffin and his men until we reach Portsmouth."

Left alone, Merriman's mind was racing. A Frenchman, all in black and with a scarred face, surely it must be Moreau, the French agent whom he had encountered in the Irish sea nearly four years ago. With that description it could be no other. Well, he was out of reach now.

Nearer to the English coast there were all manner of small trading vessels passing up and down the channel and the entrance to Portsmouth harbour was alive with small craft as Aphrodite crept in under topsails and jibs. Once the business of saluting the Admiral's flag was concluded, a string of flags was seen to soar up a signal mast ashore.

"Our number, sir, captain to go ashore immediately," reported Shrigley, the signal midshipman.

"Very good, Mr Shrigley. Mr Laing, have my gig made ready."

Merriman dived below to his cabin where his servant Peters already had his captain's dress uniform laid out. Rapidly changing out of his shabby, sea-going uniform of trousers and salt-stained coat, Merriman looked ruefully at the white breeches and stockings and the coat with the stained lapels. His best uniform displayed rank with a single gold stripe and buttons on the cuff and not the more decorated cuff that he had noticed newly promoted officers wearing. Every piece of his uniform was showing wear after so long away at sea, but there had simply been no chance of replacing them.

Shrugging his shoulders, Merriman grabbed his hat and sword and returned to the deck.

Whist he had been below, the ship had been safely anchored and all sail neatly stowed. Under the watchful eyes of the Port Admiral and any other critical watcher on the other ships around, Mr Laing could be relied upon to ensure that every detail of the ship was perfect. The gig was waiting alongside. Owen his cox'n could equally be relied upon to see that the gig's crew was as smart as new paint.

As Merriman stepped down into the boat the officers saluted and the bos'n's whistles accompanied the slap and stamp of the marines presenting arms. The boat was under way almost before he had time to sit and settle his sword, with Owen urging the oarsmen to greater efforts.

Stepping ashore at the base of the slippery steps leading up the harbour wall, Merriman was surprised to see marines with bayonets fixed to their muskets, looking down at the boat. At the top a lieutenant stepped forward to meet him.

"Lieutenant Williams, sir. I'm ordered to take you directly to the Admiral. I'm sorry, sir, but the marines are to ensure that none of your crew come ashore and I have a written order here for your First Lieutenant to that effect. May I suggest that your gig returns to your ship at once, sir."

Merriman looked about him at the other ships at anchor, surprised to see that marines, obvious in their red coats, were present on every one. The lieutenant quailed a little at the fierce glare Merriman directed at him. "Damn it, man, what's the reason for this?" demanded Merriman angrily. "Tell me, now."

"I'm sorry, sir, but the Admiral... the Admiral is waiting." He leaned forward confidentially. "If I may recommend, sir, the Admiral has a short fuse, sir."

"Oh very well then. Owen, take the boat back to the ship and give this order to Mr Laing, and tell Mr Griffin he'll have to stay aboard until I know what the problem is."

Admiral Sir George FitzHerbert, a tall thin man, did indeed have a short fuse. His first broadside was barked out before Lieutenant Williams had finished announcing Merriman.

"What kept you so long, Commander? You were expected weeks ago. And take a look out of the window at your main course. Like washing on a line, never seen worse. Having to re-furl it, not got it right first time, I suppose. A sloppy ship, sir."

Merriman endeavoured to explain that the sail and yard were being taken down so that the fished main yard could be replaced, but the Admiral carried on without listening.

"Your crew must be kept aboard, Commander, incommunicado as they say. You won't have heard of the mutiny, I suppose. No, how could you, it only happened two weeks ago. The officers, marines and some loyal seamen managed to gain control but not before the mutineers had killed two of the warrant officers, the first Lieutenant and the two marine officers, and extensively damaged the ship. The frigate anchored ahead of you there, Thessaly, is the one, and I have to have it fit for service without half I need for the job. The dockyard is stretched to the limit."

As the Admiral drew breath, Merriman ventured, "What has happened to the crew of the frigate, sir?"

"The mutineers are in chains in the prison hulk across the harbour. We held a court martial and most of them will hang and some flogged. The captain was cleared, but I don't think he will be given another command. The incompetent fool has gone to London for examination and other officers have been moved elsewhere. The loyal men are still confined aboard the ship with the midshipmen."

"What in heaven's name could have driven them to it, sir?"

"There was talk of the captain being a drunkard and leaving all control of the ship to first officer who was too fond of the use of the cat, but that's nothing unusual."

"No, sir, I'm afraid not." Merriman paused. "I was ordered to bring my ship here, but I have no idea what for. Have you orders for me, sir?"

"Yes Commander, I have. You are to make your way to London, to the Admiralty and report to Admiral Edwards there as soon as you can. I'm to send a signal when you arrive here, which has already been done and the expense has been authorised for you to travel by post chaise. Someone wants you there in a hurry so I suggest you leave immediately."

"Aye-Aye, sir. May I submit that my First Officer Mr Laing is a thoroughly reliable officer and should be made aware of where I am and why nobody may leave the ship, and there is another matter, sir."

The Admiral's bushy eyebrows came together in a frown, "What is it now, Mr Merriman?" he said tetchily.

Merriman went on to tell the Admiral about the loss of the Lucy and the presence of the French privateer. "I have Captain Griffin and his crew aboard my ship, sir. He is desperate to know how soon the Admiralty will recompense him for his loss. The ship was his livelihood and home.

"It will be done. We'll probably give him another ship as we're so short of good seamen for the Victualling Service. They all have exemptions, I suppose, so we can let them go ashore in due course. Now go and get yourself ready to travel to London."

Chapter Two

Promotion and news of Irish rebels

As Merriman stepped into the waiting room at the Admiralty he smiled wryly to himself. The scene was practically as it had been last time he was there almost four years ago to the day when he had been promoted from Lieutenant and given command of *Aphrodite*. A collection of officers, several lieutenants but mostly post-captains, all waiting anxiously to be called in to face whatever may be awaiting them. For some a new appointment, maybe promotion, for some a possible reprimand or something more serious.

Merriman took a seat, acknowledged by one or two with a nod, but ignored by most of them. As time passed he reflected that the last time he had been in the Admiralty he had been ushered into the inner sanctum ahead of all the other officers waiting, and he had left with a promotion and a new command. Also, Lord Stevenage had proved to have an interest in his career.

But as time dragged on and the other officers were summoned to their interviews in turn, including a few who arrived after him, Merriman resigned himself to a long wait. It was interesting to speculate on the fate of those officers. They passed through the waiting room on their way out and some were clearly pleased whilst others left with heads down, not meeting the interested stares of those still waiting. The last one to go in, a captain whom Merriman had noticed to be sweating freely, left with his face the colour of ashes, staring ahead of him with unseeing eyes.

There is one career finished, thought Merriman as he watched the wretched man leave. The next to be called was Merriman himself, and as the admiralty clerk called his name he drew a deep breath to prepare himself for what might happen next.

The clerk ushered him into the same room as on his previous visit, in time for him to hear the words, "Damned fool, should never have been given a command, but by God I'll see to it that he never has another," spoken by none other than Admiral Edwards who had been Merriman's captain when he first went to sea as a midshipman.

"Commander Merriman, gentlemen," announced the clerk, discreetly closing the door behind him.

"Commander, a pleasure to meet you again. You remember Captain Edgar, I trust?" said the Admiral, advancing to meet him with a hand outstretched.

"Indeed I do, sir. I could hardly forget our last meeting in this very room."

"Yes, we sent you away with a promotion and a new ship on that occasion didn't we, what, four years ago now isn't it?"

"Yes, sir," agreed Merriman, trying to conceal his impatience to learn what was expected of him now.

"Sit down, Commander." The Admiral turned to Captain Edgar. "Jonathan, please tell the other gentlemen that we are ready."

"Yes, Sir David," said Edgar rising from his chair and going towards a door at the far end of the room.

"Sir David?" echoed Merriman. "If I may offer my felicitations, sir. I had no idea, when did you..?"

"Oh, it was last year when His Majesty bounced the sword on my shoulder, nearly cut my ear off too. I almost fell over trying to kneel," said the Admiral, dismissing the whole affair with a smile and a casual wave of his hand.

The far door opened and Captain Edgar ushered two gentlemen into the room. One was Lord Stevenage who, four years previously had become interested in Merriman's career and been instrumental in obtaining for him the command of the sloop *Aphrodite*. He was followed by a tall, lean, hawk-faced man whom Merriman immediately recognised as Mr Grahame, the Treasury agent who had been with Merriman when they foiled the French plot to kidnap the Lord Lieutenant of Ireland on the high seas and whom Merriman had not seen since he left Merriman's ship in Antigua.

After the usual polite greetings, bowings and handclasps, Lord Stevenage brought them down to the business at hand. "Mr Merriman, I'm sorry you have been kept waiting so long. I was with the Prime Minister and was unable to leave when Sir David's messenger told me that you had arrived. I wanted to meet you again and take the opportunity to commend you for the admirable way you carried out those duties entrusted to you last time we met. Mr Grahame here has told me far more about what you did to save the life of Lord Westmorland, the Lord Lieutenant, and indeed to save his own life, than we read in your reports. It seems that our faith in your abilities was well founded."

"Thank you, my Lord, you are too kind. It is Mr Grahame and his agents risking their lives who deserve most of the credit."

"Nonsense, Mr Merriman," broke in Grahame forcefully. "I was out of action and unconscious most of the time. No, the credit is entirely yours."

"Perhaps, Sir David," said Lord Stevenage gently, "we could now look to the future and enlighten Mr Merriman about why he has been summoned here in such haste. He must be eager to hear."

"Of course, my Lord. It pleases me immensely, Commander, to tell you that their Lordships are giving you a frigate and to go with it you are to assume Post rank immediately. There, what do you say to that?"

Merriman gasped. "I'm grateful to you and their Lordships, Sir David. What else can I say, I'm so taken aback."

"Should have happened sooner," said the Admiral gruffly.

"Would have too if you'd been in home waters and not under Admiral Howarth. You have been held back too long. The country needs its best young officers pushed forward. But unfortunately there is one aspect of this that will not be so pleasant. Had you arrived earlier you would have been given a frigate which was completing a refit at Chatham, but with every ship desperately needed by the fleet, that one is already at sea with another officer in command."

He paused and cleared his throat. "You have heard of the mutiny aboard the frigate *Thessaly,* I suppose?

"Yes, sir, my crew is confined aboard *Aphrodite* because of it."

"Couldn't be helped, we can't risk the infectious notion of insurrection spreading. Anyway, that's the frigate you are to take under your command. The fellow who just left here was her captain, he won't get another ship if I can help it. The entire crew of your *Aphrodite* is to be transferred over to her."

Merriman nodded.

"To make up the extra numbers you will need you can have your pick of the men who remained loyal to their officers during the mutiny. They are still aboard the ship under a marine guard. You can dispose of those you don't need to other ships, I've no doubt their captains will be glad of them and you'll need some of the marines as well. Apparently *Thessaly* was badly damaged by the mutineers and is still in need of some refitting."

The Admiral turned to Lord Stevenage. "Now, my Lord, will you tell Captain Merriman what his next commission entails?"

Captain! Of a frigate! He had finally achieved the rank he coveted. True he was used to being addressed as Captain, as was any officer in command of a King's Ship or merchantman for that matter, but now he held the rank with all the benefits that went with it.

Merriman's mind was awhirl with conflicting thoughts and it was with difficulty that he dragged his mind back to hear what Lord Stevenage was saying.

"… involved with Mr Grahame again, you see. The Irish are as fond as ever of hatching plots against the Crown and for some time our agents have been aware of further stirrings there. This time we know more, thanks to Mr Grahame's network of spies. You may remember the Society of United Irishmen which was founded by an Irish lawyer named Wolfe Tone. That is only one of many rebellious societies in Ireland, all fired by admiration for the ideals of the French revolution. Their avowed aim is to unite both Catholic and Protestant factions of the Irish population in a popular movement to gain political and religious freedom by the overthrow of English rule."

Lord Stevenage paused and refreshed himself with a sip of water, then continued, "In 1793 the British government passed the Catholic Relief Act, which granted Catholics the vote and the opportunity to hold civil office and even to attend the University of Dublin. In spite of this and other measures to allow Irish goods into British markets, this fellow Tone and his friends are a constant thorn in our flesh."

Lord Stevenage paused again and indicated to the Admiral that he should continue.

"Fortunately for England, these various factions in Ireland cannot agree amongst themselves, the old difficulty about religion you see, Mr Merriman. Why, only last year there was a pitched battle between two of these groups or societies; on the one hand The Defenders, the Catholic lot and on the other hand the Protestant lot who for some strange reason call themselves The Peep o' Day Boys. The Defenders were soundly beaten and the Peep o' Day Boys are absorbing all the fanatics and the intolerant among the Protestant and Presbyterian people and beginning to call themselves The Orange Society."

"I'd no idea that things were so bad, Sir David," remarked Merriman. "Bits of news reached the West Indies, of course, but no details."

"That's not all, Captain." Lord Stevenage broke in, "The aim of the United Irishmen to try and join Catholics and Protestants together was perhaps a laudable idea from their point of view, but it won't work and the French are involved again in Irish affairs. Mr Grahame, perhaps you are the best person here to tell the Captain what you have learned in that regard."

"Yes, my Lord. If I could go back to 1794 when France sent yet another agent to England. That one was a Protestant clergyman, the Reverend William Jackson, an Englishman of Irish descent who had lived in Paris for many years and favoured the revolution. It seems that his purpose was to travel to Ireland to see if there would be support there in favour of a French invasion."

"You will realise, Captain, that here is an echo of the business we were involved with four years ago," put in Lord Stevenage.

"I certainly do remember, my Lord. And that Frenchman Moreau seems to have appeared again."

"Moreau, you've seen him again?" exclaimed Grahame with excitement.

Merriman went on to recount the events leading up to his fortunate rescue of the men in the boat, repeating Captain Griffin's description of the privateering ship and the man with the scarred cheek.

"I think it must be Moreau, sir. He was involved with the rebels in Ireland four years ago to try and bring about an invasion even then. Griffin said that he believed the ship was coming from Ireland so perhaps Moreau is dipping his fingers in there again."

"Well I can tell you that he is, quite definitely involved. My people in Ireland have reported several sightings of him. However, to continue, this fellow Jackson wasn't suited to the job. As soon as he arrived in London he visited an old friend and rather foolishly told him why he was here. His friend, a solicitor by the name of Cockayne, is a loyal Englishman and he immediately informed Mr Pitt, who in turn informed us. We asked Cockayne to travel to Ireland with Jackson, to observe his activities and obtain incriminating evidence."

Merriman wondered at this Jackson's poor choice of confidantes.

"In Ireland they met with Wolfe Tone and some of his cronies, MacCracken, Neilson and Russell to name but three, and Tone was asked by Jackson to go to France on behalf of The United Irishmen. But Tone was already walking on thin ice with the authorities and declined to go at that time. All this took several months. Finally Jackson was arrested and charged with treason. With Cockayne giving evidence against him he was doomed. He was found guilty and condemned to death in April last year, '95. He cheated the executioner by committing suicide in prison, poisoned himself, I believe."

"What about Tone and the others you mentioned, sir?" asked Merriman.

"After Jackson's arrest the United Irishmen faded away for a while. As for Tone, although his known activities were not enough to send him to the scaffold, he was a marked man and with the aid of powerful friends he escaped to America in June of last year, arriving in Philadelphia in August. You will appreciate, Captain, that most of what we know has been discovered by our agents well placed in Paris and elsewhere in France, and also in America and Ireland. Any whisper in the wrong place about their activities could put their lives in jeopardy."

"Of course, sir, I realise that only too well. You may depend on my silence in that respect."

"I know, Captain, I know. My remark was not intended to show doubt over you, I know you too well, but I feel that we cannot be too careful. The French have their own spies, you know. However, to bring the story up to date, you must know that Tone left America on January the first of this year armed with letters of introduction from the French Consul in Philadelphia. He arrived in Paris in February and with little delay he met the French Foreign Minister, De La Croix, General Carnot, and a rising young general by the name of Lazarre Hoche. He also made a speech to the French Directory. Apparently they were mightily impressed with his zeal and ability and we know that they have approved a plan to send a large expedition to Ireland. He must have convinced them that the Irish people will rise in revolt *en masse* when the French arrive."

"Do you think, sir, that many Irish will rise against us?"

Lord Stevenage answered him, "We don't believe they will, but there may well be enough hotheads willing to stake their lives on a French invasion succeeding, and it is difficult to blame them. The peasantry live in abject poverty as tenants on short term leases from corrupt landowners. When those leases expire the rents are increased. It is called rack-renting and as most of the landlords are absentees from their land the whole system is run by their agents, most of whom are as unscrupulous as anyone can be, lining their own pockets at the expense of the tenants."

Grahame nodded. "However, we learned that in July, General Hoche submitted a plan to the Directory for a landing in Ireland and has been appointed commander of the expedition. We don't know exactly when the French will attempt this landing, but the vague reports we have suggest that it will be no later than December. As it is now coming to the end of October there may not be much time left to us. It seems certain from the recently observed activity there that the port of embarkation will be Brest, but we think that it will take them some time yet to assemble the men and prepare the ships for the venture. Sir David?"

"Thank you, Mr Grahame. Now, Captain Merriman, you see why we wanted you back here in a hurry. You have worked very successfully with Mr Grahame before and he requested your services."

Merriman looked his thanks to Grahame.

The Admiral continued, "The home fleet is keeping the French ports blockaded as best it can and as there is every likelihood that Spain will turn her coat and join the French, the Mediterranean fleet will have its hands full coping with that new threat. In fact we may be forced to withdraw from the Mediterranean altogether. As far as the Admiralty is concerned, Captain, the fleet is so stretched by the tremendous demands on it that your ship will be the largest one in the waters south of Ireland for some time to come, although more might be found if we have news from Mr Grahame's man in Brest. Sir Edward Pellew in the frigate *Indefatigable* has a small squadron patrolling the approaches to the Channel between the Lizard and Ushant, but the area is so vast that it is difficult to cover it adequately."

Merriman considered the complexity of this.

Before he could ask any questions, the Admiral said, "So in addition to co-operating with Mr Grahame, you'll be expected to patrol those waters. If the French are going to attempt an invasion of Ireland, we think that the far south west is where they will do it. There must surely be some traffic of small boats carrying spies between the French and the Irish insurgents. Your intelligence about Moreau confirms it. Is the situation now clear to you, Captain?"

"Yes, Sir Edward, it is. May I ask, is it certain that the Spanish will join the French?" asked Merriman?

"Almost certain. They haven't done so yet but from the intelligence received from our people in Spain, it could happen at any moment. With France now so powerful the Spanish are frightened of an invasion by this brilliant new general of theirs, Napoleon Bonaparte. Under this fellow's command the French army has enjoyed amazing success in Europe and Italy. It is worth remembering that some people say that the General Hoche in command of the proposed French invasion of Ireland is as good a general as Napoleon."

The Admiral stood, drawing the meeting to a close.

"So, Captain, you will return to Portsmouth and ensure that your ship is made ready for sea as soon as possible. Mr Grahame will follow you down there and let you know what he wants you to do. Admiral FitzHerbert in Portsmouth has instructions to give your ship priority. After that you will put yourself at the disposal of Mr Grahame as before."

"Aye-aye, sir."

"One other thing, Captain, we must rename the ship. *Thessaly* will always remind men of the mutiny. Any ideas?"

Merriman gulped. It was not often that a captain was given the privilege of naming his own ship, then he had a flash of inspiration. "Would it be agreeable to you, my Lord, if she was named *Lord Stevenage*?"

"Capital," cried the Admiral, "we haven't got a ship with that name."

Lord Stevenage beamed. "Thank you, Captain Merriman, I take that as an honour. Mr Grahame has told me that you have hopes of marriage, perhaps the Admiralty can allow you the time to return home before your ship's refit is complete?" He turned to the Admiral with his eyebrows raised in query.

"Would that it could be so, my Lord, but I fear that there will be insufficient time. It will be only a few days before the ship is completed and we need it on station as soon as may be."

Merriman knew the Admiral had little choice really, though a word from a man in Lord Stevenage's position could make or break even an Admiral.

"A pity. Captain, it seems that you must postpone the wedding. However, if in due course you can inform me when your wedding will be, I would be pleased to receive an invitation."

An hour later, after more instructions and information had been given to him, a dazed Merriman found himself standing on the steps of the Admiralty, clutching his commission and new orders, hardly daring to believe his good fortune. He was a post captain at last, the next rung on the ladder to higher things. If he lived he would eventually become an Admiral as more senior captains died off or were killed in action. And Lord Stevenage even wanted to attend his wedding. He grinned. *That'll put Mother in a tizzy.*

He became aware of the half dozen beggars surrounding him, mostly old seamen by the look of them, all with some form of mutilation, an arm or leg missing or badly scarred features. One poor devil with no legs at all was pulled along in a small trolley by a one armed man. God alone knew how the man had survived the amputation of both legs. All were unemployable by a navy that desperately needed whole men to man the fleet stretched round the world.

One man, standing in a peculiar hunched up kind of way, looked vaguely familiar. "You there, don't I know you? Timmins, is it?"

The man drew himself up as far as he could, dragged off his tattered hat and knuckled his forehead. "Aye, Commander, sir. Tomkins, sir. I was captain of the maintop in the old *Argonaut,* Captain Edwards, when you were a midshipman, sir. I stopped you falling off the main yard one time, sir."

"I remember that. But what happened to you, Tomkins? I see you still have all your arms and legs."

"Two years gone, sir, I was on Black Dick Howe's flagship the *Queen Charlotte* at the battle off Ushant. You know, sir, the one they are calling the Glorious First of June. Well I was a gun captain on the middle deck an' a French shot upended my gun, sir, an' I finished up underneath the carriage. Broke my ribs an' Lawd knows what else, sir. Got paid off 'cos of me injuries, sir, can't do anything heavy, the left side o' me chest is caved in."

"Can't you get another job, Tomkins?"

"No, sir. Lawd knows I've tried, but there are too many like us, sir." Despairingly he indicated the human wreckage around him. "All we can do now is beg for a few coins to keep us alive."

Merriman privately cursed the system that could so easily discard the brave men who had given so much for their country. He looked round at them, despite himself feeling a lump in his throat. "I can't do anything for you men except give you these coins I have." He made up his mind. "Tomkins, if you want to go to sea again, I'll find you something aboard my ship."

The man's face lit up. "Will you, sir? Thank you, sir, thank you. I'll do anything I can to feel a ship under me again. I won't let you down, sir."

As Merriman walked away followed by the seaman, he was well aware that the rest of the human jetsam were looking with envy at the fortunate Tomkins. He sighed, knowing he could do no more for the rest of them.

Lord Stevenage emerged from the shadow of the doorway where he had been an interested observer. Shaking his head he said, "James Merriman, you are too soft hearted for this hard world but I admire you for it. You are a good man and a credit to your father. It's time some humanity and compassion was shown to these poor devils." He was surprised to realise that he had spoken aloud.

Chapter Three

Departure for Ireland

Merriman was in a fever of impatience to get back to his ship and arrange the transfer of his crew to his new command, but on arrival in Portsmouth there were things to do before going aboard. He would have to report to Admiral Sir George FitzHerbert and confirm with him the orders transferring *Thessaly,* now *Lord Stevenage,* to Merriman's command and then he must find a tailor to make his new uniforms.

On leaving the Admiral's offices, he looked at Tomkins who was waiting for him, still dressed in the ragged clothing he had been wearing when Merriman found him in London.

"Hmm, I'm not having you aboard looking like that, Tomkins. You need cleaning up and something better to wear."

They quickly found a shop where Tomkins was fitted out with trousers and shirts, a brass buttoned jacket, shoes and a tarred hat. Then a barber's shop was found where Merriman left Tomkins to have his hair and beard cut and he could scrub himself clean in a tin bath.

"Wait for me outside the Admiral's place when you're cleaned up," Merriman ordered him. "I have my own new uniform to see to."

There he was fortunate as he found a tailor recommended to him by a captain on the Admiral's staff. As soon as the tailor knew what Merriman required and the urgency of it he was eager to please. "If you are agreeable, Captain, I have a captain's uniform here I was making for an unfortunate gentleman who was recently killed in action. It is almost completed and I'm sure it would fit you. Would you care to try it on?"

With only minor alterations needed, the coat proved to be an excellent fit, so Merriman ordered it and a new three cornered hat to be sent out to his ship as soon as ready. Fortunately he had been successful in taking prizes over the past few years and he was able to collect money from the Prize Agent in Portsmouth. He also ordered a second hat and coat and new white silk stockings and buckled shoes. White breeches, shirts and black cravats were also needed to replace those made shabby by prolonged use.

From London, Merriman had sent a letter home to his family, with another to Helen, telling them that he was back in England and hoped to be able to come home soon. He also wrote hoping that Helen and her father could set a tentative wedding date. He told them of his promotion to Post rank and that he had been given command of a frigate. Also he mentioned that Lord Stevenage hoped to be at the wedding and should be invited.

On the journey back to Portsmouth, he had begun to regret his generous impulse towards the man Tomkins. What on earth could he find for a cripple to do on a man-o-war? The problem was solved when, in conversation, Tomkins revealed that he had a knowledge of numbers and could write.

"A bit shaky, sir, but with a bit of practice I'm sure it'll come back. Old Miss Dawkins beat it into us lads with 'er cane."

"Very well then, when we get aboard I'll see what you can do. Maybe you can be my clerk and help with all the paper stuff I have to deal with."

At the dockside a brawny waterman was found to row them out to *Aphrodite,* and Merriman climbed aboard to the salutes and ceremony used by the navy to welcome a captain on board. Acknowledging the compliments, Merriman looked keenly about him. All seemed to be in order, but then the skies would fall before Laing allowed any slackness. But he wasn't looking for anything wrong with his ship, he was looking for any sign of sullenness on the faces of the crew or any indication that they had heard of or sympathised with the mutiny aboard *Thessaly.*

"Mr Laing, gentlemen, I want all officers in my cabin in ten minutes." He turned and descended the companionway to his cabin, beckoning the waiting Tomkins to follow. Peters, Merriman's steward was waiting below.

"Peters, this is Tomkins, for the moment he is to assist you."

Apart from a small frown, Peters appeared to be quite unmoved at the thought of another man in the Captain's quarters, which had until then been his own domain, but Merriman knew him too well to be deceived.

"Don't sulk, man, I know you think you are indispensable but you *will* make him welcome. He'll be spending most of his time on duties as my clerk so he can help and not interfere with your own duties. Is that clear?"

"Aye - aye, sir" mumbled Peters.

"And mark this well, both of you, your duties as captain's clerk and captain's steward mean that you will learn much that is confidential. I know from the past that I can rely on your discretion, Peters, but you, Tomkins, must learn to keep matters to yourself."

"Yes, sir. I knows when to keep me mouth shut."

"Good, now be off with you, the officers will be here directly."

The two men left as the ship's officers filed into the cabin and arranged themselves as best they could in the cramped space. Merriman looked around at his expectant audience.

"I am leaving this ship, gentlemen." He was pleased to hear exclamations of dismay from his colleagues of nearly four years standing.

"I'm sure I speak for all, sir, if I say we have been honoured to serve with you for so long," said the First Lieutenant.

"Enough, Colin," said Merriman with a smile, "I'm teasing you. I *am* leaving this ship but so are all of you as well. Their Lordships of the Admiralty have seen fit to promote me to Post Captain, and I'm to take command of the frigate *Thessaly* which you have seen re-fitting after the abortive mutiny aboard. You, with the entire ship's company, are to transfer with me."

The men raised a chorus of congratulations.

"Thank you, gentlemen, thank you," Merriman said. "There is one more promotion. Mr St James, it seems that you are now a Captain and a Marine Lieutenant is to join us."

There was another chorus of congratulations for the marine officer and when that died away, Merriman said, "Enough, gentlemen, there is much to do and the first thing must be to board the frigate and assess the situation. The loyal members of her original crew and the midshipmen are still aboard and we can have our pick to make up our numbers, including marines. The rest will be sent to other ships."

Lieutenant Laing rubbed his hands together gleefully, "Does that mean I can get rid of those two rogues Piggott and Smith, sir?"

"Indeed it does, Mr Laing." Merriman was well aware that there were a few men among his crew, as among crews everywhere, who were the source of any discontent. The two men mentioned were a constant source of irritation to the officers. There was always a feeling that the two men had managed to do something they shouldn't that authority had not yet discovered. Capable seamen both, but always that little bit slow to carry out an order and with an attitude just short of insolence. They were constantly being punished for minor infractions, said punishments not changing them one bit.

This was an opportunity all First Lieutenants longed for, to remove such men, although the chances were that they would find one or two more among the new men.

Once aboard *Thessaly,* Merriman conferred with the chief shipwright in charge of the refitting, Mr Lathom. It appeared that the mutineers had managed to kill the marine sentry and get into one of the storerooms. There they broached a keg of rum. Rendered careless of consequences by the fiery spirit, the mutineers had then murdered the hated First Lieutenant, two of the warrant officers and some of the marines, and the two marine officers.

Before the other ship's officers, marines and loyal men had regained control, the mutineers had broken open all the storerooms and destroyed their contents. More kegs of rum had been broached and the men had rampaged through the lower decks, smashing everything they could before being overwhelmed. The damage was considerable and they had even set fire to the officers' quarters, a stupid thing to do on a wooden ship.

"Thank God they didn't get into the magazine, sir. If they had I think they would have blown the ship to Kingdom Come before surrendering."

"A terrible business, Mr Lathom, indeed it was. And now to the future, how long will it be before my ship is ready for action again?"

"Another week or two, sir, before she is seaworthy again and fit for action. I still have to change the fore topmast, it's badly sprung and some fools even set about the mainmast with axes, so that will have to be replaced. That means going alongside the sheer hulk. Even though you are supposed to have priority, sir, there are two first rates in the dockyard also with priority and we're too shorthanded to do the work faster."

"Well I think we can speed things along for you, Mr Lathom. I have my entire crew available to help if you are agreeable. The Carpenter and Bos'n and their mates are all excellent men and I will tell them to follow your directions."

Merriman and his officers then carried out a full inspection of the ship except for the main gun deck forr'ard where the seamen were confined under a marine guard commanded by a sergeant.

Re-assembling on the quarter deck, the officers, each clutching his notes, gathered round their Captain.

"Well now, gentlemen, I think we all have a good idea of what remains to be done. First we must have the ship's stores of food and water replenished so that our own men can be transferred here. With them aboard to assist the shipyard men the work should be done faster, but it will still take at least two weeks to finish. Now we must see the men below and sort them out."

He looked round for the sergeant in command of the marine guard. "Sergeant, your name?"

The man drew himself to attention. "Sergeant Gordon, sir."

"Right, Sergeant, I want all the men below assembled on deck immediately. I wish to address them."

The men shuffled aft between the lines of marines, grouping themselves below the quarter deck, blinking in the bright sunlight and looking up at the officers lined along the rail. Merriman was not an orator, had no gift of words to stir men's souls, but he knew that the men below him must be desperately worried about their fate and what he said to them now would have a bearing on the whole ship's future.

"Men, my name is Merriman and I'm now in command of this ship. You will know that your shipmates who mutinied will be flogged or hanged for their crimes, but I'm told that you all remained true men. If that is so, you have nothing to fear if you do your duty. Most of you will remain on board to join my own ship's company who will move here from the sloop *Aphrodite* you see astern. My officers will now take your names and rates so that we can see who we have. Midshipmen and warrant officers, come here to me."

A ragged cheer went up from the men and a voice said, "Thank'ee, Captain. You'll have no trouble from us."

Merriman became aware of a sailor bobbing up and down and knuckling his forehead with a big grin spread across his face, obviously trying to catch his new captain's eye. With surprise he recognized Biggins, the simple minded man who had been one of his crew in *Conflict* over four years ago. After the loss of *Conflict* the surviving men had been allocated to other warships at Gibraltar and presumably Biggins had found himself aboard the *Thessaly*.

"You there, Biggins isn't it? With me in *Conflict,* weren't you?"

"Aye, sir. Biggins it is 'an I still 'ate the Frogs, sir."

Merriman also remembered that to Biggins every enemy was a Frenchman and in *Conflict's* last fight with corsairs Biggins had saved his, Merriman's, life at the expense of a savage pike wound in the leg.

"Yes, I know you. I trust that your wound is satisfactorily healed."

"Aye, sir. Right as ninepence," said the man with a grin.

"Very good, Biggins. I'm glad to see that you have lost none of your fighting spirit."

"No, sir, just let me get at 'em."

Merriman knew that his remembering Biggins would have made a favourable impression on the men. They were used to being treated badly and for a post captain to remember one man's name was exceptional.

"Sergeant, the men may remain on deck, but you and your marines will maintain the usual harbour watch against desertion."

Some hours later, back aboard *Aphrodite,* Merriman leaned back in his chair, and surveyed his officers. They had spent the time re-organising the watch bill to assimilate as many of the new men as possible. Merriman was well satisfied; his new command would start with the unbelievable good fortune of having a full complement of men and first class officers although short of both third and fourth officers. At this stage of the war with France it was a very fortunate captain who left harbour with a full crew. He shouted for Peters.

"Ah, Peters, I believe that we still have some of that excellent claret we took from the Frenchman off Martinique. Gentlemen, I propose we drink to the future of our new ship which is to be renamed *Lord Stevenage*."

"To the future and *Lord Stevenage,*" they chorused.

"*Lord Stevenage,*" exclaimed Lieutenant Andrews. "Wasn't that the name of the gentleman we rescued from the corsairs off Africa in '92 and who spoke at your court martial after the loss of *Conflict,* sir?"

"The very same, Mr Andrews. The name *Thessaly* had to go, so when I was asked if I had a new name for the ship, the Admiralty approved of my suggestion."

The next few days passed in a whirl of activity, settling the two crews together in the new watches and assessing their capabilities. All the while the work to refit the ship continued at an increased pace. Even with the full crew transferred from *Aphrodite,* so many more men were needed to supply the needs of a frigate that there were no more than thirty men surplus to his needs. Merriman removed some of the frigate's senior warrant officers as he had full confidence in the ones from *Aphrodite.*

Tomkins proved to be a great help in sorting out the multitude of forms and reports without which it seemed that the navy could not exist. He was intelligent and quick to learn. His writing and spelling left something to be desired but it was legible and improved with practice. Very soon Merriman came to rely on him to carry out the duties of Captain's clerk. It was for him to write up the multitude of reports from lists of bos'n's stores, cordage and sailcloth used or replaced, the gunners report on his supplies and on powder and shot used, to maintain the muster book, to write up the punishment book and sick book, and copy the Captain's reports in a fair hand.

He was quick to check the inventories and actual totals of stores left aboard against the amount of stores listed by warrant officers, the carpenter, bos'n and others, and he gained the hatred of the Purser, a surly individual by the name of Grummage, by reporting the irregularities to the Captain. It was almost to be expected of a ship's purser that he would attempt to feather his own nest by trying to make money from the stores under his control and falsify the lists of condemned food. Merriman gave the man a verbal tongue lashing as a result.

As the days went on Merriman began to wonder how he had managed without his new clerk. Every day brought more problems to be solved and questions to be answered. The gunner Mr Salmon wanted to know if the two twenty–five pounder bow chasers and the two carronades could be appropriated from the *Aphrodite.*

"I've checked the scantlings under the fo'c's'le, sir, and spoken to the shipwright and he agrees that the timbers will stand the recoil of the big guns, sir," said Salmon eagerly. "And we can take the nine pounders and the two carronades from the fo'c's'le to make room for them."

Merriman pondered for a moment. It would be good to have those big bow chasers aboard and with the twenty-six eighteen pounders on the main deck and two carronades, or smashers as they were generally known, added to the two on the quarterdeck, *Lord Stevenage* would be a formidably armed ship indeed. He made up his mind immediately.

"A good idea, Mr Salmon, see to it. We'll have the two big guns but leave the two smashers on *Aphrodite* and replace two of the nine pounders on the quarterdeck with the smashers from the fo'c's'le. Ask Mr Laing for a working party and the use of the longboat. And see to it that the appropriate size of shot is transferred. You can tell the purser not to fill the fore hold completely until we see what the extra weight forr'ard does to her."

"Aye-aye, sir." Mr Salmon knew his job and didn't need his captain to remind him of what to do. "I'll send the spare guns over to *Aphrodite,* sir."

"Very good, Mr Salmon, carry on."

Then the bos'n was complaining that the dockyard workers had skimped on the parcelling and serving of some of the new standing rigging.

"Mr Brockle, if we complain to the dockyard about every little fault, we'll never get to sea. You have enough men so put them to work."

Amongst all this confusion Merriman had sent Midshipman Oakley ashore to take the opportunity, with a board assembled, to take his examination for Lieutenant. Both he and Midshipman Shrigley had been acting Lieutenants for the past twelve months but Oakley was the senior and Shrigley was still some six months short of the age and sea time required to be able to take the examination. Oakley passed and was moved to one of the other ships needing a junior lieutenant, so Merriman was another officer short, and was waiting for new ones to be appointed.

Shrigley had matured over the last few years from the squeaky-voiced imp that Merriman first knew and would make a fine sea officer, but for the present would remain a midshipman acting fourth lieutenant. Merriman was determined to try to keep him when eventually he passed his examination.

Most midshipmen of the day obtained their appointment by influence or from a favour owed by a captain to a relative or friend, or by personal recommendation. One day when in the Port Admiral's office, Merriman was asked by Sir George FitzHerbert if he could find room for another boy.

"My sister's son, you see, she's been pestering me for weeks to find the boy a place. In confidence, Captain, he's a bit wild and needs discipline, his father died some years ago and now there's a bad business involving a female servant. Thinks no end of himself he does and needs to be brought down a peg or two, so if you could…"

A suggestion from an Admiral was tantamount to an order and Merriman had no choice but to accept the boy, although to be fair, the Admiral had given him warning and freedom to deal with the boy as he saw fit.

Two midshipmen had been aboard the *Thessaly,* one fifteen years old, Alan Hungerford, a rather sullen, pimply-faced lad, and one of barely thirteen years, Gideon Small, a slight youth but with a bright, alert look to him. When the Admiral's protégé arrived on board Merriman was not impressed. The Honourable Arthur Dorrington was seventeen and the possessor of an aloof manner as if everybody and everything was beneath his notice.

Merriman decided to have Shrigley to bring all three to his cabin to assess their nature as far as possible and to tell them what he expected of them. The two younger ones stood stiffly in front of him but Dorrington promptly sat down without being told.

"On your feet, boy, you're in front of your Captain. NOW," shouted Shrigley as Dorrington made no immediate effort to rise. The arrogant youth coloured and slowly took his place with the others, staring idly about him, as if trying to show his complete indifference to what was happening.

Looking them over slowly, Merriman said, "You boys are on the lowest rung of the ladder here and you must understand that I expect nothing less than complete dedication to your duties and studies. You must learn to take orders from the warrant officers as well as the ranking officers. In time you may become of some use and be valuable members of my ship's company, but until then, remember that you are now training for a career in the king's service."

He let his gaze travel across them.

"Now then, Mr Small, you're the youngest so we'll start with you. How old are you and how long have you been at sea?"

"Twelve years old, sir, and I came aboard less than six months ago."

Merriman thought the boy seemed keen to please and would become useful very quickly. "Very good, you have a lot to learn. And you, Mr Hungerford?"

"Fifteen, sir. I've been here for almost two years, but I know I've still got a lot to learn too, sir."

"You have indeed." Merriman already knew that the lad was willing but slow to learn and easily confused.

"Remember, both of you, if you have a question at any time don't hesitate to ask any of the officers, petty officers or even members of the crew who will be pleased to help you. Is that understood? Now you two may go."

"Yes, sir, thank you, sir," they replied and left together.

"Now, Mr Dorrington, stop fidgeting and tell me about yourself."

'I'm seventeen… sir." The 'sir' came out slowly, as an afterthought.

"You are older and making a later start than is usual for a midshipman, Mr Dorrington, so you will have to be even more assiduous in your studies if you wish to succeed."

"I don't want to. I'm only here because my mother and that damn fool uncle of mine made me. As soon as I can, I'll be gone. As the son of an earl I expect a cabin of my own and better treatment than the others."

"Well you won't get it. You are all equal and don't you forget it. There will be no favouritism here. And by 'that damn fool of an uncle' I assume you are referring to Admiral FitzHerbert. You need to find more respect for your elders and betters, my lad, or you'll be in trouble. Now get out," said Merriman keeping his temper with an effort.

Soon change that attitude when he's kissed the gunner's daughter a few times, he thought. Kissing the gunner's daughter was naval parlance for a flogging, but in the case of a midshipman was usually only the humiliation of a few strokes of the bos'n's cane on his backside.

As Mr Shrigley was the senior midshipman, Merriman advised him to keep a sharp eye on the juniors, especially Mr Dorrington.

Admiral FitzHerbert had given orders that the spare men and spare marines should be moved over to *Aphrodite* as soon as officers were appointed and a day came when a boat pulled alongside and two lieutenants climbed aboard. Merriman was on the quarterdeck at the time and greeted the two men.

"Good day, gentlemen. What can we do for you on this fine morning?" Merriman was in a good mood; pleased with the way the repairs were progressing and confident that his ship would be ready for sea very soon.

"Lieutenant Withers, sir, and this is Lieutenant Gorringe. We are appointed to *Aphrodite,* sir. Admiral FitzHerbert told us that you have some men here to transfer. With your permission we are to take them and start preparing the ship for sea."

"Are you to be in command, Mr Withers?"

"No, sir, to my regret. Another officer is to take command; I'm told he should arrive tomorrow." Withers paused and then said, "I believe you had *Aphrodite* before your appointment to this ship, sir."

"Yes, you'll find that we left her in good order and ready for sea except for needing a new mainyard and a crew and supplies. But, your captain should know that she has been in West Indian waters for four years and the bottom really should be checked to see that none of the copper is missing. I have informed the dockyard but I don't know what they intend to do about it. However, please inform your new captain that I'll be pleased to tell him anything he wishes to know about her."

"Thank you, sir. If you please, sir, we are ordered to move the men as soon as possible and get the ship ready to receive some men from the assizes."

"Very well, Mr Withers." Merriman issued the necessary orders and the men for transfer were soon climbing down to the boats, clutching their small bundles of possessions. As Withers and Gorringe climbed down after them, he wondered whether or not he should have told Withers about the mutiny but decided it would be better to talk to the new captain, whoever he may be.

The new mainmast had been set up and the final setting up of rigging was being completed when another new face appeared on board. Lieutenant George Weston was a young man possessed of an almost completely bald head and a three year seniority which made him the third officer under Laing and Andrews.

It appeared that his abiding enthusiasm was gunnery and he was soon involved in deep conversations with Mr Salmon over the best way of amending the mounting of the two twenty-five pounders on the fo'c's'le, so as to give the widest arc of fire possible.

The new marine officer also appeared, a Lieutenant Charles Goodwin, who it seemed, met with Captain St James' approval.

"Soon have him trained in our ways, sir," replied St James cheerfully when Merriman asked him how his detachment of marines was shaping up.

"As you know, sir, I kept our own marines and from the marines left aboard this ship I selected Sergeant Gordon, a corporal and fifteen men which gives me a total of thirty four. All experienced men, sir. I am well content with them."

One day in the middle of all the activity, a boat came alongside and Lieutenant Gorringe presented himself to Merriman.

"Commander Yelland's compliments, sir, and he would be obliged if you could join him for dinner this evening aboard *Aphrodite.*"

"Thank you, Mr Gorringe. You may tell Mr Yelland that I shall be delighted."

And so, a pleasant evening ensued. Yelland was a large man, no longer young, who had only recently achieved his present rank. He had been second Lieutenant aboard a three decker in the West Indies when Merriman had first met him three years before, a taciturn man not given to excitement and great imagination but a solid reliable officer. *Aphrodite* was his first independent command and he was eager to learn as much about her sailing abilities as possible.

He was still short of men even though he was under orders to leave for Antigua as soon as his new mainyard was fitted and supplying completed, and he confessed that his efforts to find more had been unrewarded apart from a mere handful found drunk in an alley.

"It's a difficult time, sir. The press gangs have been so active of late that sensible men steer clear of the town at night unless they have an exemption. The only ones we can find are old men and cripples." Said Yelland.

It was not unusual for King's ships to put to sea shorthanded with captains at their wits' end to find a crew. Once again Merriman congratulated himself on having a full complement aboard his own ship.

"I sympathise with you, Commander. Have the assizes been of no help?"

"Oh yes, sir. I've twenty men from there aboard now, but as you know they will be practically useless until they've learned enough to know one rope from another."

"I see that there's another old ship by the name of *Captivity,* moored with the prison hulks, what about the French prisoners aboard the hulks? They're not all Frenchmen, there must be some who would exchange prison for the comparative freedom of your ship." Said Merriman.

"I know, sir, and sorry I am to see that ship there. She's the old *Monmouth.* I served as fourth lieutenant aboard her many years ago. It's sad to see her reduced to this. As far as the prisoners are concerned, I thought of that, sir, but I am hesitant, not knowing where their real loyalties lie. And I don't know that the Admiral would approve."

"Well, they are probably all seamen. A few of them mixed with your other men are unlikely to cause any trouble. As for the Admiral I expect he will be only too happy to be rid of them. Also you could try sending a party ashore at night to some of the villages along the coast when you leave, there must be some prime seamen to be found. Or you could try stopping merchant ships on your way down Channel and taking a few men there."

"I'd like to," admitted Yelland. "But there would probably be complaints to the Admiralty if I did and I can't risk that. It's taken me too long to reach this rank and I'd never have another chance."

"I appreciate your concerns, Mr Yelland, but I'm certain the Admiralty will not concern themselves over much with his methods if an enterprising officer contrives to find the men he needs to fill his ship. Besides, you're off to the Indies and could be away for years. Time enough for any complaints to be forgotten before you return."

"You are right, sir, thank you for the advice. I'll do it."

Yelland had not stinted on his hospitality and Merriman returned to his ship after a fine meal of roast pork and dumplings followed by a selection of cheeses, all washed down with excellent claret.

Mr Grahame arrived when the ship was almost ready. He knew all the officers except the new midshipmen and Lieutenants so few introductions were necessary and he was soon settled into a cabin. He wasted no time in getting down to business.

"A pleasure to see you again, James, how soon can we sail? Our first destination will be Wexford in southern Ireland."

"Tomorrow, sir. The last provisions are coming aboard now and then we have only to load with powder and shot from the powder hulk and we can be off."

"Excellent. I have people all over Ireland. Some of them have been roaming all over the south of Ireland disguised as tinkers and gypsies, trying to learn something of the plans the damned Irish must be making to help the French when they land, but the difficulty is in communicating with them."

"Have we any more intelligence from France about a likely date for the French to start their expedition and where they may try to land?" asked Merriman.

"Not yet. But we know that the United Irishmen have appeared again and our information is that as soon as news of the French landing is received, they will start simultaneous risings in all the major cities in Ireland. Because of that, the army must keep its garrisons strong enough to deal with that threat and can spare only a limited number of men from each to reinforce the garrisons in Cork and County Kerry.

"It's certain that the place they will choose for the landing will be somewhere on the south west coast, but that being such a huge area it is virtually impossible to patrol it closely. Oh, the army is doing its best and has cavalry patrols out, but unless my people are very lucky and find out something, we can't narrow the choices down very much."

Merriman returned to the deck to be able to pace up and down the quarterdeck. He seemed to think better when he was walking. The frown on his face was sufficient to keep everyone away from him on the other side of the deck. His mind was working furiously on what Mr Grahame had said last about not being able to narrow the choices down.

There must be some places more suitable than others, surely? he thought, tugging at his ear, his unconscious habit when deep in thought. To unload soldiers quickly and easily the French ships have to get as close inshore as possible which means deep water close inshore. Also they would need sheltered water to allow the use of boats, water sheltered from the prevailing winds.

Merriman had only the vaguest idea of what southern Ireland was like other than what could be gleaned from the Admiralty charts, but he knew that Ireland was a wet, boggy, green and windswept country. And after landing, the French would need to find some kind of road or track to be able to move easily. *But,* he told himself, *they were sure to have Irish rebels to guide them.*

He became aware of a commotion on the larboardside gangway where stores were still being loaded under the dubious supervision of Midshipman Hungerford. A cargo net full of kegs of rum was being brought inboard and the hands on the ropes had contrived to bang a keg on the ship's rail. The grinning men were trying to ensure that the keg would spring a leak so that in the confusion they could get their hands on the spirit.

"Mr Hungerford," roared Merriman. "Have that net hauled higher before swinging it inboard."

It was an old trick played by the hands when they found themselves supervised by an inexperienced officer. Knowing that Merriman was watching, the men finished unloading the net and the kegs were quickly passed below into the care of the Purser.

Dawn was just breaking on the morning of departure when a freshly shaven Merriman, resplendent in his new Captains' uniform, with its single epaulette denoting that he had not yet served three years in that rank, nodded to the marine sentry on guard outside his cabin and climbed onto the quarterdeck. Even at that hour the ship was alive with activity. Men were scrubbing the decks, others aloft making final checks that all the running rigging was free, some men polishing brasswork with brickdust and doing the multitude of jobs necessary to prepare one of His Majesty's ships for sea.

To an outsider it must have seemed a scene of chaos, but to Merriman standing at the quarterdeck rail it was the very stuff of life and his eye missed nothing, as his officers knew all too well. In the growing light, details of other ships anchored in the huge harbour were becoming clearer, as were the buildings of Portsmouth naval dockyard.

This was it then, *Lord Stevenage* was ready, fully stored and with a complete crew. Merriman almost hugged himself with delight as he reminded himself yet again of how lucky he was and that very few captains could boast of a full crew in this the fourth year of war with France. With France, and with the whole of Europe it seemed, with Napoleon's army taking more and more territory every day. France controlled most of the west bank of the river Rhine from Basle to the sea, Belgium, Nice and Savoy were in her hands, Holland was now her ally and Spain likely to follow suit. Italy was being overrun and Prussia and Austria were ready to make peace.

My God, mused Merriman, if the French get into Ireland we'll be surrounded. Everything depends on the navy keeping them out. A cough behind him jerked his mind back to his surroundings.

"Beg pardon, sir. Signal from Flag, sir, You may proceed."

"Thank you, Mr Small. Acknowledge."

Midshipman Small was the signals midshipman under the watchful eye of Acting Lieutenant Shrigley.

"Mr Laing, let's take her to sea. Tops'ls and jibs to begin with."

"Aye - aye, sir."

Merriman stood back and watched as Laing roared out the orders and the crew hastened to their allotted stations. Topmen raced each other up the rigging to cast off the sail lashings and other hands, chivvied by the petty officers, gathered in groups round the base of each mast and by the pin rails ready to handle the myriad of ropes needed to control the sails. For'ard, seamen thrust the capstan bars into the sockets in the capstan head, then spat on their hands, ready to lend their strength to hauling the ship up to her anchor, whilst a party made ready to wash the anchor and lash it the cathead when it was hauled up.

Suddenly, after the noise and bustle there was a brief silence and every eye was on the captain, waiting for the final word.

"All ready, sir."

"Very well, Mr Laing, proceed."

The men at the capstan bent their backs to the job and slowly the ship moved forward until Lieutenant Weston on the fo'c'sle signalled that the anchor was free.

"Sheet home the jib, handsomely now," the orders came as the ship spun on her heel. "Meet her, meet her, now tops'ls, let go and haul." A few brief moments of intense activity and the ship was under control and heading across the harbour on the larboard tack. A few hundred yards, then a change of course and they were heading for the entrance.

Merriman watched as the shoreline fell away on either side until the ship began to feel the rollers beneath her. "Now, Mr Laing, I'll have all plain sail, please. Mr Cuthbert, be so good as to have the log line made ready. We'll see what she can do."

Chapter Four

Trouble arises with Dorrington

That evening, on passage to Wexford, came the first intimation that there would be trouble with the Honourable Arthur Dorrington.

Merriman had invited his officers to dinner. This time, unlike the occasion when he had taken command of the *Aphrodite* he had ample supplies of food and wine aboard for his own use. He had bought some chickens that would provide fresh eggs for him before they drowned in rough weather and were eaten, and he had a share with the officers in a couple of piglets which had caused consternation when hoisted aboard in a couple of sacks, squealing like a couple of, well, pigs.

Once free of the sacks they had escaped and provided a few minutes of amusement as the seamen delegated to catch them chased them all over the main deck before they were cornered and put in the pen made for them by the ship's carpenter. Mr Laing was cursing fit to burst as, in their panic and fear, the piglets left a trail of liquid manure behind them on his well-scrubbed deck.

Merriman's new cabin was so much bigger than his last that there was comfortable room for all, except the officer of the watch Mr Weston and the two midshipmen Hungerford and Small who had not been invited.

Merriman knew them all well from their years together. Apart from Mr Shrigley, who had matured from a mere boy into a young man with a surprisingly deep voice, they seemed not to have changed since he first met them. The ship's surgeon, Alan McBride, had lost his craving for alcohol years ago and perhaps old Elijah Cuthbert the Sailing Master had a few more lines on his face, but Merriman knew each man's strengths and few weaknesses.

He knew he was fortunate to have them. On appointment to a new ship a Captain rarely got to take any of his past ship's complement with him but he had them all. *Though not Mr Jeavons,* he reminded himself. Jeavons, his First Lieutenant in *Aphrodite* had never recovered properly from the head wound received when they had fought the Frenchman Moreau and his ship *La Sirene* in the Irish sea. The poor man had suffered more and more frequent bouts of dementia and Merriman had been forced to leave him ashore in the Stonehouse naval hospital in Plymouth. A sad end for a brave officer.

Merriman roused himself, aware that the conversation had died and his officers were watching him. "I'm sorry, gentlemen, I was thinking about other things. Mr St James, have you tried that impressive cheese yet? It is so strong you'll think it has bitten your tongue, I'll warrant. Mr Cuthbert, I know you to be a lover of cheese, perhaps Mr St James will cut you a piece. And you Alfred, your plate is empty. If I didn't know better I'd swear you must be full."

That brought a laugh for they all knew of Shrigley's appetite. Surprisingly, even the usually quiet Grahame was moved to comment that Mr Shrigley deserved a mention in despatches for his skill at making food disappear.

"I might manage a little more, sir. Thank you."

"But not fish I think," commented Merriman dryly, his remark occasioning a roar of laughter from the others. "You had enough of that when you fell into the hold of that fishing boat."

"I was pushed, as you all well know," said Shrigley resignedly. He was the butt of a standing joke amongst the officers who remembered the incident of four years ago, but he took it all in good humour and was popular with the others.

After the meal, when Peters assisted by Tomkins had cleared the table and they had all been supplied with full wine glasses, Merriman and Grahame told the others all that was known about the threat of a French expedition to Ireland and what part *Lord Stevenage* had to play.

Laing was the first to comment. "Sir, surely the Admiralty can't expect one frigate to stop the French. They will have a fleet of warships to protect the troop transports."

"First of all, Mr Laing, we are relying on the blockade by the Channel Fleet to keep the French bottled up in Brest. Secondly, there is a squadron under the command of Commodore Sir Edward Pellew, which is also covering the channel and the area south of Ireland, but well off shore. Our task, as I have said, is to help Mr Grahame contact his people ashore and to try and intercept any small craft which may be carrying messages between the French and Irish."

"But we will fight if we find a Frenchman, won't we, sir?" exclaimed Shrigley.

"Of course we will, Mr Shrigley. No opportunity will be missed, I assure you."

There were pleased smiles round the table. A successful action could bring promotion, not to mention prize money. Typically, no one thought about the possibility of death or mutilation which was also very likely.

"Fighting is all very well," remarked Grahame, "but sometimes more can be done to defeat an enemy by stealth and the skilful use of intelligence. By putting together little pieces of seemingly unconnected bits of information, one can often discover the enemy's intentions. That's how we know so much about this latest threat to Ireland. But it's a slow and often boring business. An agent can spend weeks and months, living in constant danger of discovery, before he learns something worth reporting."

"Those agents you speak of must have nerves of steel to be able to do what they do, sir. They must be remarkable people," said Captain St James, the marine.

"On the contrary, Mr St James, they are mostly quite ordinary people. Women as well as men, who are so unremarkable that they can pass completely unnoticed in a crowd. Or, by the use of disguise, they can blend in with whatever activity is going on."

"How do you find these people, Mr Grahame?" asked the Master.

"Our agents are always on the lookout for suitable people they can recruit. In France we have several who are prepared to help because they have reason to hate the Revolution. Usually because they are either Royalists or have had their family denounced and executed after a mockery of a trial."

At this point, Midshipman Dorrington, who had been listening to the discussion with a sardonic look on his face, interrupted Mr Grahame with the sneering comment, "Something damned underhand about the whole business. Not what a gentleman should be involved with though, is it?"

There was a sudden silence, and all eyes turned to Grahame whose face had turned white.

"Am I to understand that you do not consider me to be a gentleman, sir? That a whipper-snapper like you, with no experience…"

He broke off as Merriman laid a hand on his arm.

"Mr Grahame, you'll oblige me by allowing me to deal with this matter before it goes any further."

"Mr Dorrington, for that remark Mr Grahame would be within his rights to call you out, although I'm sure that he would feel that no honour would be gained by so doing. You are an impertinent boy, sir, and will be punished as such. You will go on deck and report to Lieutenant Weston. You will give him my compliments and tell him that you are to go to the main topmast crosstrees and stay there until I allow you to descend."

The red faced Dorrington rose to his feet. "By God, sir, you have no right. My father was a peer of the realm and if he was still alive you wouldn't dare…"

"I have every right and it would make no difference if your father was here at this very moment. You must learn that titles are of no value to you aboard this ship."

"Sir, I must pro..."

"Silence! If you dare to open your mouth again I will ask the Bos'n to play a tattoo on your rump with his cane. Do you understand? Now get out."

Merriman was seething, never had his officers seen their usually imperturbable Captain quite so angry.

"I'm sorry, gentlemen, that our evening has been interrupted. Mr Grahame, I hope you will consider the matter closed."

"Indeed, James, let us say no more about it and if there is some more of that excellent wine..." Peters and Tomkins hastened to refill the glasses. "...I would like to propose a toast. Gentlemen, to a successful conclusion to our commission."

As the officers prepared to leave, Merriman called Shrigley back.

"Alfred, we'll need to keep a very, very sharp eye on our Mr Dorrington. He obviously has too high an opinion of himself. I'm sure you know, and I remember from my own experiences that a character like that can cause no end of trouble for the younger midshipmen if he thinks he can get away with it. Remember the old saying – it only takes one rotten apple to spoil them all."

It was not until eight bells was struck at the end of the morning watch that Merriman allowed a miserable and half frozen, though still defiant, Dorrington to come down from aloft.

Chapter Five

Brest, France. French army and a Fleet prepare to invade

The harbour at Brest in north west France, in the area known as Finistère, was alive with activity. Men swarmed over the warships and transport ships swinging at anchor. Due to the blockade by the British Navy, the French vessels had not been at sea for months and with most of the aristocratic officers of the old navy having fled abroad or been executed, both discipline and maintenance had suffered. Now there was an air of purposefulness in the way boats and barges moved between the ships and the dockside to replenish stores and equipment.

Inland, a vast encampment of tents sheltered the soldiers being assembled for the invasion of Ireland, and from all directions the roads were filled by marching men and strings of wagons bearing more and more provisions for the enterprise.

In a field close to the river, detachments of both cavalry and infantry were exercising and drilling. Long lines of cavalry horses were waiting patiently while their masters fetched water and forage for them. It was a scene which the casual observer would have thought to be total confusion, but one in which every man knew what he was there for. The French army had not won its battles without good order and discipline and most of the men were hardened veterans.

In a large chateau overlooking the harbour, chosen and commandeered because there was insufficient room in the naval headquarters for the army of staff and clerks needed to control all the activity, General Lazarre Hoche, the General-in-Chief, and his senior officers assembled. Hoche was demanding that the senior naval commander, Admiral Villaret de Joyeuse, give him a firm time when the fleet would be ready to set sail.

"For the last time, Admiral, when will your ships be ready? We cannot delay this enterprise much longer."

"General, my people are moving as fast as possible but there remains so much still to be done. Many of the ships require fresh rigging if they are to be seaworthy enough to withstand the gales which are common this late in the year and, as you know, more than a quarter of the comestibles which arrive are unfit to eat and have to be sorted out and destroyed. Then replacements have to be ordered which all takes time. Of course everything we need has to come by land as the English blockade prevents anything coming by sea. Indeed, sir, there are so many difficulties that I doubt that the expedition can leave before the new year, and with that blockade I fear that it may take a miracle for us to get to sea at all."

"Mon Dieu," roared General Grouchy, Hoche's second in command. "You have half our soldiers helping your damned sailors and still you complain! I can see now why our own navy skulks in port while the English flaunt their flags outside in our own waters. French sailors have no stomach for a fight."

"How dare you, General? I will not sit here and listen to this abuse a moment longer. You will apologise or my seconds will wait on you later."

"There will be no duels fought over this, messieurs. I forbid it. Sit down, Admiral, and as for you, General Grouchy, I expect my generals to have more to think about than insulting our navy."

Both officers subsided, glaring at each other and grumbling under the rebuke. Hoche continued, "General Humbert, are you and General Hardy satisfied that your men are in good heart and ready?"

"Oui, mon General, there are the last few companies still to arrive but they are soldiers of France and are ready for anything."

Grouchy growled his approval of the sentiment expressed. "The army is always ready, unlike the navy," he said.

"Enough, gentlemen, enough." Hoche turned to two men sitting side by side, neither of whom had said anything so far. "Monsieur Moreau, have we any more news from your spies in Ireland? And you Monsieur Tone, are you certain that the Irish people are ready to rise against the English as soon as we land?"

The assembled officers turned to look at the man named Tone. So this was the famous Irish revolutionary Wolfe Tone. They had all heard of him but not met him until now. So much depended on his assurances of the support of the Irish people. Wearing the uniform of, and given the honorary rank in the French army of Chef de Brigade, Tone made an arresting figure.

"The Irish are ready, General. In every town we have a nucleus of armed men ready to strike as soon as word reaches them that we have landed. Their first successes will encourage all Ireland to rise and overwhelm the English garrisons." He warmed to his theme. "And then we can break the connection with England, that accursed country which is the source of all our troubles and political evils, and we can assert the independence of my country."

"M'sieur Tone is right, General, although the shortage of arms among them may make a rising longer to succeed than he believes," said the man named Moreau. "I have not heard from my people in Ireland for over three weeks now but from the content of the last despatch I had, there is nothing more to be done but for them to wait for us to arrive."

This man, Charles Henri Moreau was one of the revolution's most trusted agents. He favoured powdered hair and black clothing and carried an exceptionally long sword. A deep scar on his left cheek, acquired when he fought alongside Lafeyette and the French volunteers in the American War of Independence, made him instantly recognisable. It was not generally known that he was an aristocrat, the erstwhile Count de Treville and Beaupreau, and that his entire family, parents and sister, had perished under the guillotine. He had only survived because he had left France after a furious row with his father and not returned for several years.

He continued, "It is remarkable to me that it has taken so long for us to reach the situation in which we now find ourselves. Four years ago I had hopes of making the Irish our allies when I attempted, with some Irish rebels, to capture the Lord Lieutenant of Ireland and force the English to give Ireland her freedom. The plan was only foiled at the last minute by the presence of an English warship under the command of a devilishly lucky man. Had that plan succeeded we would have had French ships in Irish ports long ago."

General Hoche smiled. "A pity you did not succeed, m'sieur, nevertheless, gentlemen, we have a fleet of some forty three ships and an army of nearly fifteen thousand men and with good fortune this time we will succeed." He quelled the rising shouts of approval with an upraised hand.

"There is one final matter, gentlemen." He faced the Admiral. "I have now to tell you formally, that you, Admiral Villaret de Joyeuse, have been replaced as senior naval officer at my request. I have for some time considered that you had insufficient enthusiasm for this expedition and your reply to my question earlier has confirmed it. I am informed that the Directory has appointed Admiral Morard de Galles to replace you, and you are to leave for Paris immediately."

The assembled officers watched silently as the white-faced man, without a word, rose and walked out of the door. They all knew that he would be fortunate to keep his head on his shoulders.

"Admiral de Galles should arrive tomorrow. We shall see if he can make the fleet ready in time. I want, no, I demand that this expedition departs for Ireland not later than the middle of December, let us say four weeks from now. That is all, gentlemen."

Chapter Six

Grahame has news of French activities in the South West

Captain Merriman climbed on deck and regarded the Cove of Cork harbour with something less than enthusiasm. The rain was coming down as if poured from a bucket, and aboard the various trading vessels around the harbour all work had ceased. There was also no life to be seen ashore. The distant hills were veiled in curtains of rain falling from the lowering dark grey clouds. Haulbowline, a big island, was being prepared to become the new and better placed naval dockyard instead of Kinsale, and numerous fortifications were under construction on Spike Island and the surrounding cliffs. However, the work still had a long way to go. It would afford a far bigger and better harbour from which the Navy could guard the approaches to the English Channel.

Aboard *Lord Stevenage,* all the hands of the duty watch forced to remain on deck were trying to shelter in the lee of the bulwarks.

"They tell me that it is always raining in Ireland, sir," said the officer of the watch, Mr Andrews. He spoke gloomily, bending forward so that a stream of rainwater flowed out of his hat brim. "I need hardly say that I prefer the Caribbean at this time of year."

"The Caribbean has a lot in its favour, I'll grant you that," replied Merriman. "But after four years out there I would have expected you to be pleased to be back in home waters."

"Oh I am, sir, really, but we have been here in harbour for nearly three days now and the damned rain hasn't stopped once. Indeed, sir, I think it has been raining ever since we sighted the coast of Ireland nearly two weeks ago. It rained when we waited in Wexford harbour, it rained in Waterford harbour and it's raining here. I swear we shall all be growing webbed feet if it doesn't stop soon."

"Well," laughed Merriman, "it can't go on forever, and I've heard tell that the sun does shine sometimes, even in Ireland. We must put up with it. Maybe when we get further west there will be a change."

He changed the subject and gestured forr'ard to where his three surviving chickens were standing in their coop. A more miserable, dispirited and bedraggled group of birds it was hard to imagine. "I don't think those birds will survive much longer, David, it's too cold and wet for them. Besides, they have stopped laying. I think I shall dine on chicken tonight. Some of you will be able to join me."

"Yes, sir, thank you."

Nevertheless, Merriman was worried. Grahame had been put ashore in the dark to find his way into Cork which was some distance upriver from the harbour. That was two nights ago and there was still no sign of the man. He had gone ashore at both Wexford and Waterford, hoping to find one of his agents or news from them, but at both places he had returned empty handed.

It was well known to the authorities that there was much seditious activity in the city and district by the United Irishmen group who were secretly recruiting. It was a dangerous game Grahame was playing and, on a previous occasion ashore in Ireland, he had been fortunate to escape with his life when rebels discovered him to be spying. He had pistols with him but if discovered again his only real hope would lie in flight.

Merriman returned to his cabin still pondering what to do. Grahame had asked that a boat wait for him near the jetty in the harbour but he had not expected to be so long, neither had Merriman any idea where to start looking for him.

Finally he resolved to go ashore at first light and visit the army garrison to see if they had heard anything. Meanwhile a wet and miserable boat's crew must keep on waiting. Merriman had ordered the shivering men to be relieved regularly and given a tot of rum when they climbed back on board. Merriman smiled at the memory of a wet and bedraggled Midshipman Dorrington coughing and spluttering when the rum went down the wrong way. No sign then of his usual haughtiness.

Mr Grahame turned up in the early hours of the next morning, cold, exhausted and disheveled, but the bearer of news. In Merriman's cabin, with a hot toddy in one hand and a piece of meat in the other, he said, "Captain, I think we have something fairly definite at last. There are more reports of agitators going around trying to stir up the peasantry with news of a French army coming to liberate them. You can imagine the kind of thing, James: 'all men should take up arms and rally to support the cause of freedom'. Nonsense of course, the first thing the French would do is to conscript the men into their army and ship them off to fight elsewhere."

Merriman nodded his agreement with that.

"This next report will interest you. One of my people in the west of Ireland, in Galway to be exact, sent word that a stranger in the area has been seen talking with known rebels. This was five or six weeks ago, but I am sure that the description of this man will be familiar to you. He is described as a gentleman, tall, dressed in black, affects powdered hair and has a scarred left cheek…"

"Moreau, by God," exclaimed Merriman. "That damned French spy, it can be no other."

"Exactly, and there are reports of this man being seen in several other locations over the last few months, but he has not been seen more recently than two or three weeks ago. I infer from this that he was confirming with the rebels that their preparations are ready for the French to arrive and that he returned to France when you came across him in the channel. It is interesting to note that most reports of his presence originate in the south and west of the country which I feel confirms the theory that the south west is where the French will attempt a landing."

Merriman reached for his drink, saying, "I doubt not that you are right, sir. So what do you propose we should do now?"

Grahame sat quietly for a few moments, stroking his chin as he pondered. "I think we should cruise off the coast, westwards, in the hope that we may gather more information from one or two of my people who have not yet reported. I am hoping that they are still living. May we have another look at your chart?"

"Indeed, sir, I have it here." Merriman unrolled the chart and placed a few objects on it to hold it down. "I've been giving some thought to the question of where the French will try to land and I'm convinced that they must choose one of these big bays here, here and here." He indicated Dunmanus Bay, Bantry Bay and Kenmare River.

"And what leads you to that conclusion, James?"

"Several points, sir. To begin with, they will need deep water as close inshore and as sheltered as possible to enable them to disembark troops by boat. Secondly, they will need time; time to bring all their equipment ashore and time to get the soldiers, possibly men weakened by seasickness, organised properly as a fighting force. This I believe cuts out the part of the coast eastwards from Cork as it is too well populated and the garrisons of Cork and other towns would have plenty of warning in time to prepare a force to resist."

"Excellent, James, I agree with your reasoning so far. Pray continue."

"Thank you, sir. Now the coast westwards from Cork is too open for some sixty or seventy miles to allow safe anchorage for a fleet of warships and transports. There are bays to be sure, but in most of them the water is too shallow and, as I say, they are too open to the weather. There is nothing before Dunmanus Bay and that I would rule out as being smaller than either Bantry or Kenmare River."

He drew his finger across the chart.

"Of course, if we go further there is Dingle Bay, but that one is so wide and completely open to westerly winds that I think it most unlikely that any sensible commander would risk it. Further north there is the estuary of the River Shannon and then Galway Bay, but why would the French go any further than they need? No, sir, if I had to choose, it would be either Bantry Bay or Kenmare River and my preference is for Bantry."

"Why Bantry, James?"

"Simply because it has a little more shelter from westerly gales, has deeper water closer inshore and it is far enough away from Cork or any town of size to give the French ample time to establish themselves before any local force could be raised to stop them. Apart from local militia that is, part time soldiers, and from what we know of the French army they would cut through the militia like a knife through butter."

"I cannot fault your reasoning, James. I must say that I think you may be correct. None the less, I don't think we can put all our eggs into one basket and we must continue to patrol from Cape Clear at least as far as Great Blasket Island off Dingle Bay. And speaking of Dingle bay, that is where I would like the ship to go now. There are two men living near to the village of Dingle on the north side of the bay. One is a cattle and produce dealer who travels a lot in the way of business all over the south west area and sometimes collect bits of information which are of use to me. The other is a barman at the tavern in Dingle. They do it for money of course and I don't trust either of them entirely, but there is nobody else."

"Very good, sir. Fortunately the wind is fair for us and we can put to sea immediately."

And so began a long period of frustration while *Lord Stevenage* cruised off the coast, from Cork past Kinsale and Galley Head, past Cape Clear, keeping well to seaward of the notorious Fastnet rocks, then closer inshore to look into Roaringwater Bay and round Mizen Head to Dunmanus Bay. All the while it rained and the ship had to fight against rough seas and almost gale force winds

From what could be seen, the land seemed to consist of wild, windswept mountains, poorly wooded but with lush green valleys. Overall a most uninviting prospect with only occasional scattered villages and farms. The buildings for the most part appeared to be almost derelict with only the odd one or two chimneys showing a little smoke which was immediately dispersed by the wind. And it continued to rain solidly with no hint of a break.

Merriman was in his cabin going over his log entry when he became aware of voices raised in argument on the quarterdeck above his head. As the skylight was closed it was hard to distinguish the words but the deep, calm voice could only be that of Shrigley and the higher pitched one, almost shouting, must be one of the midshipmen.

"I want him flogged. He pushed me and stood on my foot, damn him!"

That was clear enough and it sounded like Dorrington's voice. Another man answered too quietly for his words to be heard, then Shrigley's voice again, followed by another outburst from Dorrington.

"I don't care, Lieutenant, he insulted an officer and I promised him a flogging for it."

Merriman sighed and called to the marine sentry outside the door to pass the word for Mr Shrigley and Mr Dorrington to come to his cabin at once.

"Now then, Mr Dorrington, what are you making such a noise about?"

"One of the men, sir, he pushed me and stood on my foot. When I called him a clumsy oaf he tried to make excuses. I told him to shut his mouth or I'd have him flogged, but he still tried to say it was my fault. Damned impudence. No respect for an officer."

"I see. Mr Shrigley, who is the man involved?"

"Matthews, sir."

"I know Matthews, one of my old *Aphrodites* isn't he? A good hand. What did he have to say for himself?"

"Hardly know, sir. Mr Dorrington wouldn't give him a chance to speak, but he's waiting outside."

"Right, bring him in."

"You're not going to listen to a common seaman, are you, when I've already told you what happened?" shouted Dorrington.

"It is customary to say sir when you address a superior officer and I will not tolerate rudeness or shouting from you or anybody else. You will hold your tongue or you'll find yourself up at the top of the mast again," said Merriman, icily calm and desperately trying to keep his own temper in check.

Matthews entered the room.

"Ah, Matthews, what have you to say? Mr Dorrington tells me that you trod on his foot and pushed him."

"No, sir, that I didn't. Well, I did tread on his foot but it were an accident, sir. I were flaking down a rope and when I'd done I stepped back like. I didn't know 'e were behind me, sir. I didn't push him, sir, honest, and when I tried to apologise and told 'im I didn't know he were there, 'e said e'd 'ave me flogged for not showing respect. I does me duty, sir, I don't go looking for trouble, sir."

Merriman studied the man in silence for a moment, taking in the sturdy frame, the weather-beaten face and wide open, honest blue eyes. With not a blemish on his record, Matthews had been one of his crew for the past four years, a first rate man and always amongst the first to volunteer for a boarding party or any difficult operation. Merriman wondered why he had not found the opportunity to promote the man.

"Very good, Matthews. You may go, you will hear no more about this."

As a very relieved Matthews left the cabin, Merriman turned to the midshipman.

"Now listen to me, boy, and listen well. You have been in the Navy for only a few short weeks but long enough to learn that you know nothing, absolutely nothing of discipline and men. Matthews is a first class seaman and worth far more to this ship than you are. If it were necessary for the good of the ship to throw one of you over the side, it would be you doing the swimming. You have the temerity to speak of his lack of respect for your uniform. Let me tell you that respect must be earned from men by the way you behave and lead them. It is not something you should expect as a right."

"Sir, I don't..."

"Hold your tongue, and don't interrupt. I tell you that I believe that man's version of events and he will not be punished. I think you have been stupidly trying to make trouble where none exists, all because of your mistaken sense of your own importance. Make no mistake, I'll have you off this ship at the first opportunity, with a report sent to the Admiral if you don't pull yourself together. Now, off you go to your duties."

When the white-faced midshipman had gone, Merriman turned to Shrigley. "Whatever possessed that boy's family to think that he would be suited to a life at sea?"

"I don't know, sir," remarked Shrigley. "Do you think he will improve after this?"

"I think it very unlikely, Alfred. He's been spoilt all his life and thinks the lower orders are there for his own convenience. The Master reports that he is probably the worst pupil he has ever had, useless at mathematics and shows no interest in navigation or in learning anything. I think we may have more trouble from that one before this commission is over."

Merriman had no idea then of how right he was.

Occasionally some small trading vessels were stopped, boarded and searched but nothing suspicious found. Once or twice they bought fish from fishing boats, but there was no sign whatsoever of French vessels.

They entered Bantry Bay, sailing into the bay nearly as far as Whiddy Island without seeing another ship. At some twenty-three miles long and seven miles at its widest, the bay would have ample room for the French fleet as Merriman had pointed out to Mr Grahame.

It was the same in Kenmare River and as the ship passed Scariff Island to starboard to turn north for Dingle Bay, Grahame remarked that they might as well look for a needle in a hayrick.

"Damn it, James, the only good thing that has come about from the last few weeks is that I seem to have overcome my seasickness at last."

Merriman remembered the first time Grahame had boarded *Aphrodite*. He had spent the first few days prostrate in his berth, expressing the wish to be left alone to die. On this occasion he had not suffered nearly so badly.

As the ship cleared Bolus Head, Merriman noticed that the Master, Mr Cuthbert, was beginning to fidget, looking from Merriman to his chart and notes and back again at his captain.

"Have you a problem, Master?"

"Aye, sir. Well, not really a problem but my notes have mention of an uncharted reef or rock between Puffin Island and the Great Skellig rock to seaward. With this poor visibility I'd prefer to shorten sail and put another one or two lookouts aloft if that is agreeable, sir."

"Very well, Mr Cuthbert, we shall do as you suggest. Mr Andrews, have the main and fore courses off her at once and send two men with the best eyes aloft. That will be Larkin and Thomas."

But in spite of the Master's misgivings, no rock was seen and very soon *Lord Stevenage* rounded Valencia Island with the huge expanse of Dingle Bay opening to starboard.

The weather was abating somewhat and the wind backing to the north so Merriman was able to bring the ship to anchor in ten fathoms in the lee of Bull's Head. The rain was now no more than a drizzle and hardly noticeable after the heavy downpours of the past few days, though it still made visibility difficult.

Later that evening, in pitch darkness, Mr Grahame was put ashore near Dingle Harbour with two seamen as a bodyguard. One was Matthews and the other was Jackson, both reliable, capable men.

"I don't need a bodyguard, James. I know where I'm going and I am armed." Grahame complained.

"Nonetheless, sir, I must insist that these two men go with you. I well remember the time four years ago when we put you ashore near Dublin and you nearly lost your life. You have yourself said that you don't trust the men you are going to find. I'd rather take no chances."

The boat was commanded by Lieutenant Weston who had his orders to keep the boat ready to bring Grahame and the others off again when they were ready.

"I would be pleased if you could do this as quickly as you can, sir," said Merriman talking to Grahame just before the latter descended to the boat. "The ship is safe enough at the present but if the wind begins to shift to the south east we will be on a lee shore and we'll have to move out to sea."

"I will, James, but as you know, these visits have to be done mostly at night to avoid compromising the safety of my people, which makes it even more difficult for me to find my way in unfamiliar surroundings. I can't say how long it may take."

Chapter Seven

Agents dead and Grahame barely escapes with his life

Mr Grahame and the two seamen following him walked as quietly as they could up to the village of Dingle, in places having to feel their way in the dark.

"We'll call on the barman first, he lives in a small house, more of a hut really, at the end of the village street," Grahame told the men. "Stay behind me when I go in."

Creeping nearer to the hut they could see that the door was ajar, with the feeble light from a small lantern glowing within. Grahame pushed the door gently and it swung open to reveal the body of a man lying on the floor with a pool of blood spreading round his head and shoulders. A muffled scream indicated that someone else was there so Grahame entered carefully, followed by Matthews. In a corner, a terrified woman huddled, dressed in little more than rags, clutching two small children to her, peering fearfully up at him.

"He's not been dead for more than a few minutes, sir," said Matthews. "The body's still warm and the blood's still wet."

Grahame approached the woman who tried to shrink further into the corner and asked her gently what had happened. She replied in an incomprehensible gabble.

"From the little I can understand it seems that two men burst in here and killed her man, then they raped her, in front of her children at that. We'd better leave here immediately and go and see if anything has happened to my other informant."

He tossed a small purse of coins to the woman as they left. "I think she will be safe enough, they could have killed her if they had wanted to, and there's nothing we can do for her now."

As rapidly as they could, they made their way to the farm where Grahame's other informant lived, but in the darkness and with the need to be as quiet as they could, it took them well over half an hour to reach it. The door and shutters were tightly fastened but a faint light escaped from cracks in the woodwork of the door.

"I don't like this," said Grahame to his companions. "It seems too quiet, not even his dog is barking. Stay close and keep your wits about you."

"There's somebody else close by, sir. Can't see 'em but I knows they're there somewhere," whispered Jackson. "I can sense it."

Grahame rapped sharply on the door. There was no reply so he knocked again, louder this time and called in a low voice, "O'Hara, it's me, your friend from Cork."

There came the sound of bolts being drawn and the door opened a little to reveal the frightened and be-whiskered face of the man O'Hara.

"Come in and shut the door. Quickly now, they're out to kill me!" he said in passably good English.

"How do you know that, Mr O'Hara?"

"I've found notes pushed under the door, with death threats in them. They say they know I've been giving information to the English. I sent my wife and children away to her mother two days ago, since when I've only dared venture out to feed my stock."

"Well, I'm afraid I have to tell you that we have just found another of my men lying in his house in Dingle with his throat cut. Perhaps it would be better for you to come away with me now."

"Can't do that, all I own is here. I've got my pistols and a musket so be damned to them. I'm staying put."

I admire your courage, Mr O'Hara, but I fear that you will suffer for it. These people mean business and you are all alone and isolated. I urge you again, come with me."

"No, sir," said O'Hara stubbornly.

"Well I thank you for your services in the past but I think we shall not meet again and we cannot stay to help you. Good fortune go with you, Mr O'Hara."

So saying, Grahame turned to the door and was just about to open it when Jackson put his hand out to stop him.

"Begging your pardon, sir, it might be safer if we put the light out first and Matthews and I will go out in front of you."

"Very well, do as you see fit."

He nodded to O'Hara who immediately blew out the lamp. Jackson cautiously opened the door, listened intently, and when nothing happened they quickly left. Just as the door was closed behind them there was a flash and a bang and a pistol ball struck the doorpost close to Grahame's head, a splinter from which struck him on the cheek.

Without ceremony Matthews promptly dragged him down into the deeper shadows by the house wall as Jackson fired his pistol in the direction of the flash. A squeal came out of the darkness.

"You winged one of them that time, Ted. Let's go, sir, you lead and we'll guard your back" said Matthews.

Moving carefully and watchfully, with weapons ready in their hands, they had not gone far when a shot sounded behind them and a sudden flare of light showed that the thatch of O'Hara's house had been torched.

"God help the poor man now," muttered Matthews as they turned their back to the sight.

They were perhaps halfway back to the beach where they had landed not four hours before, when the moon slid from behind the clouds and illuminated the path they were following. There came a hoarse shout and shadowy figures lunged towards them with the moon reflecting from the swords and knives they carried.

Grahame and Matthews fired their pistols almost together. Two of the attackers screamed, one dropped to the ground, the other clutched his shoulder, dropped his cutlass and ran off. Three more men flung themselves forward but they stood no chance against the two seamen who were ready for them. The attackers ran into blades wielded in the experienced hands of men well used to that kind of fighting. In only a few moments another of the men was down, clutching at his belly, and the others in full flight, both of them bleeding from wounds.

"There could be more of them, sir. We must go," panted Matthews, and the three men ran as fast as they could to the beach over ground now well enough lit by the moon for them to see where they were going. It seemed no time at all before they were on the beach and tumbling into the boat which Lieutenant Weston had brought close in on hearing the shots.

"Back to the ship, if you please," gasped Grahame. "My God, I'm getting too old for this kind of excitement." As his breathing eased he turned to Matthews and Jackson and shook them by the hand. "Thank you both. I would be a dead man now if it weren't for you two."

Chapter Eight

Youngest Midshipman found beaten and in great pain

Perhaps it was an hour after the first watch came on duty, about nine o'clock, when the marine sentry knocked on the door of Merriman's cabin. "Lieutenant Shrigley, sir."

The door opened at Merriman's reply to reveal an agitated Shrigley. "I'm sorry to disturb you, sir, but we seem to have lost Midshipman Small."

"Lost him, what do you mean, lost him?"

"Just that, sir. He didn't appear on watch. The other midshipmen say that they haven't seen him for two or three hours. I've had the word passed round to see if anybody knows where he is, and we had a quick search made, but so far he hasn't been found. Of course we haven't searched the hold and storerooms yet, but I can't imagine why he would go down there."

"Neither can I, but he must be found and found at once. Surely he hasn't gone overboard, someone would have seen or heard him."

On deck, Merriman found the First Lieutenant organising groups of men to search below.

"An officer or warrant officer with each party please, Mr Laing. I want a thorough search made. If he is still aboard he'll be hiding somewhere. Remember, a small boy can creep into a very small space."

The men dispersed and Merriman returned to his cabin to wait and to wonder why the boy should disappear like this? He tried to cast his mind back over the last few days. Had there been anything wrong with the lad, had his behaviour been different in any way? There was nothing he could think of but Merriman had the uneasy feeling that he had missed something.

Half an hour later, Lieutenant Laing announced that the boy had been found in the sail room. "He won't say anything, sir. I don't know what is wrong with him but he seems to be in pain. Mr Shrigley is outside with him."

"Right, bring them in and then pass the word for Mr McBride to come here."

When Shrigley brought him in, it was immediately obvious that there was something wrong with the boy. He was shivering violently but holding himself as stiffly as he could. His face was unnaturally pale and from the blood smeared on his chin it was evident that he had bitten his lip.

"Now, Mr Small," said Merriman quietly, "I want you to tell me why you were hiding in the sail room."

"S-s-sir, w-w-with respect, I wasn't hiding, I f-f-fell asleep."

"Maybe so, but why were you there, are you ill?"

The boy looked about him with a look of desperation. "I w-w-was t-trying to find s-somewhere quiet to sleep, sir," he mumbled through chattering teeth, "and I t-t-tripped and fell, sir. That's all."

"I don't think that is all, Mr Small. What do you think?" Merriman directed his question to Laing who was watching the boy with a frown of concern on his face.

"I agree, sir. There is something else the matter here, but what is it?"

"Perhaps Mr McBride can tell us when he examines the boy."

Waiting for the ship's doctor, Merriman tried to encourage the boy to tell him what the trouble was but to no avail, the lad stuck to his story and even when told to sit down he simply said that he should stand before his captain.

"Ah, Mr McBride, here you are. Examine Mr Small if you would and see if you can tell us what is wrong with him."

McBride looked at the boy's white face and felt his forehead, then grasped him by the shoulder. Small uttered an involuntary moan of pain and winced at the doctor's touch. McBride glanced at Merriman, then said, "Right, my boy, off with your coat and shirt."

"Please, sir, must I? I'll be alright."

"Do as I say, laddie, and don't argue."

Carefully and with reluctance, Small eased off his coat. Shrigley, who was standing behind him gasped in surprise.

"My god, sir, look at this."

He turned the boy round so that his back was towards the captain. His shirt was spotted with blood, most of it dried. Gently McBride tried to remove it but the shirt was sticking to the boy's back.

"I'll need some water and some things from my dispensary, sir. Meanwhile, if he could lie down on the bench under the stern window?"

The doctor was back very quickly and began to moisten the bloodstains to release the shirt. As he did so, Small writhed and gasped with pain.

"Easy, laddie, I'll be as careful as I can." The doctor gently removed the shirt then turned to the others. "This is not the result of a fall, sir. This boy has been savagely whipped."

He stood back so that they could see clearly. The boy's back was covered in weals and bruises. Several of the wounds had split and were oozing blood. McBride eased the boy's breeches down over his hips to reveal that his buttocks were likewise lacerated and bruised.

"Hell's teeth, no wonder he wouldn't sit down. By God, I'll find out who did this to him and why." Merriman was coldly furious. "Doctor, your opinion of his condition?"

"No bones broken, sir, and most of the wounds will heal in time but some of the bruising is extensive and it appears to have been inflicted over a period of time as some of it is not new. Besides which the boy has a high temperature and a chill. I hope it won't develop into a fever."

Merriman looked down at the small, battered body lying face down. The boy was sobbing quietly in spite of his earlier resolve to be brave. "Well then, Mr McBride, he is in your hands now. Look after him well."

"Yes, sir. I'll put him in my own berth for the time being. Come on, laddie, come with me."

The boy climbed slowly and painfully to his feet and, followed by the doctor, left the cabin. Before the door closed, the three officers heard the marine sentry's oaths when he caught sight of the midshipman's back and they knew that the news would be all over the ship inside five minutes.

"Gentlemen, we must get to the bottom of this and without delay. Somebody has repeatedly beaten that boy and I have an idea who it might be. I don't think it can be one of the men, none of them would dare to lay a hand on an officer even one as young as that, besides, most of them would be more inclined to be protective of the boy. No, my suspicions fall on the other midshipmen. Surely you as the senior, Mr Shrigley, should have some idea of what goes on."

"Well, sir, we know that there is always a certain amount of bullying in the midshipmen's berth, and it is quite usual that the most junior has to act almost as a servant to his elders and is beaten occasionally, but that is to be expected. We all went through that in our turn."

"Yes, I remember it well, but this has gone beyond normal."

"I had noticed that he was not as cheerful of late and on one occasion he was slow to move to an order, but I'd no idea he was in such a state, sir."

"Well you should have," Merriman told him bluntly. "I know that you spend more of your off watch time with the other officers than in the midshipmen's berth, but as only acting lieutenant you are still the senior midshipman and it is up to you to keep an eye on them."

Faced with the evidence of his being found wanting in his responsibilities, Shrigley could only mutter a shamefaced, "Yes, sir."

"It is up to all the officers to take note of anything unusual and we didn't. We are all to blame, yes, I include myself in this."

Lieutenant Laing spoke for the first time. "Sir, from what I know of the Honourable Arthur Dorrington, I would imagine that with his arrogance he has elected himself the leader of the others and expects them to do his bidding. Would you not agree, Mr Shrigley?"

"Yes, sir, I had noticed that Hungerford always agrees with Dorrington, but I think Small has too much spirit to toady to anyone. Perhaps that is why he has been beaten. But if it was them to blame, they must have been sly about it to be able to keep Small quiet and prevent anyone outside the midshipmen's berth from knowing of it."

"I think we have the answer, gentlemen," said Merriman. "We'll leave it until the morning, but I want you, Mr Shrigley, to go to and have a word with Mr McBride. The boy may be more willing to talk to you now that his problems have come into the open, but I think he may be more inclined to confide in the doctor. Report to me anything you may learn."

Left on his own, Merriman sat, thinking hard about how best to resolve the matter. That Dorrington was guilty he was certain, but certainty was not proof. Unless Small or Hungerford would admit what had transpired, there was no proof beyond the boy's injuries and without proof Dorrington could not be punished.

"Pass the word for my Cox'n," he called, hearing the message passed for'ard from the marine sentry.

A few moments later, Owen arrived. He had been Merriman's Cox'n for over four years and had saved his captain's life more than once. If anyone knew what was happening in the crowded conditions aboard ship it was Owen.

"Sit down, Owen, you may be able to help with a problem."

Merriman proceeded to tell him what he suspected was happening in the midshipmen's berth. "Do you know anything about this?"

"I know Mr Dorrington is a nasty piece of work, sir, begging your pardon. He never tires of taunting the men as if e's tempting them to strike 'im, and e's fond of threatening a flogging for any man that upsets 'im. We know 'im and the other one 'ave been seen teasing Mr Small and pushing 'im about, but that's probably only skylarking, sir."

"Very wel,l Owen. If you hear of anything else be sure to let me know."

Later, approaching dawn, the boat was sighted bringing Grahame and the others back to the ship.

Once he was seated in Merriman's cabin, the strain of the past events clearly showing on his face, Grahame said, "Things are bad ashore there, James. The first man I wanted to see was lying dead in his own house with his throat cut and his terrified wife said that two men had burst in and killed him. Apparently it had happened only shortly before we arrived."

"Doubtless somebody knew or suspected that he was one of your agents, sir," said Merriman. "And what of the other?"

"When I called he was reluctant to open the door. When he did he held a loaded musket and a brace of pistols was lying ready on the table. He was in fear for his life which had been threatened but he wouldn't leave his home. I think the fellow was frightened to stay and too frightened to move. Nothing I could say or offer him would induce him to talk. I told him of the fate of my other informant and even offered to bring him back here with me, but he would say nothing other than that he'd rather stay on his own land. I don't think I'll see him alive again."

"Undoubtedly, sir. Did you see no sign of the men who killed your man?"

"Oh indeed we did. Somebody was following us. Jackson said he knew they were there but we couldn't see them until they suddenly attacked us. I'll tell you, James, those two, Matthews and Jackson are first class fighting men and I was grateful to have them with me. I doubt that I'd be alive now but for your forethought in sending them with me. I really can't thank them enough and I trust you will prefer them when you can."

"Jackson was a poacher once and used to the dark, sir. Anyway, I'm happy to see everybody back unharmed."

"Well, James, I can see no way of learning more. Assuredly there must be somebody who knows something but our chances of finding them or intercepting a messenger ship in this appalling weather are very poor."

Since leaving Cork, the ship had encountered high winds and erratic seas, but the rain had hardly ceased. Conditions below for the crew were unspeakable. With their clothing permanently cold and damp, many were suffering from chills and fever. Merriman had authorised extra rum rations for each off going watch and the ship's cook was ordered to keep a sort of broth hot for the men as best he could.

"Well, it's now the middle of December and all the information we have indicated that the French would make the attempt before Christmas," said Grahame. "Although that is far from certain. Even if they have managed to get their ships ready and the troops assembled, they still have the blockade to consider."

"True, sir, but remember that a strong offshore gale could scatter our ships and be ideal for the French to leave harbour. They could sail without a King's ship seeing them."

Merriman would never have thought of himself as having second sight, indeed in his usual hard headed way he considered all such to be stuff and nonsense, but unknown to him, he was exactly right.

On December 17th the French fleet sailed. It was a formidable force with several massive ships of the line, including *Les Droits de L'Homme, Revolution, Indomptable, Courageux* and *Surveillante*. Wolfe Tone was aboard *Indomptable* and Moreau aboard the corvette *La Sirene*, with the soldiers crammed aboard the warships and transport ships.

The blockading English ships under Sir John Colpoys were blown off station by an offshore gale which allowed the French to escape without hindrance. The only English warship to see them was Pellew's *Indefatigable*. The French fleet was now loose in the Atlantic and Pellew headed south, believing that they were going to Spain and hoping to warn the English fleet

When the gale abated, a thick fog descended which had the effect of scattering the French ships, although most managed to rejoin the main body. On December 20th, in relatively calm weather, thirty four out of the original forty three approached the Irish coast and entered Bantry Bay. There they anchored, making their preparations for landing the troops.

The flagship, which had not been seen since the fog enveloped the fleet, carried the Admiral and the commander in chief, General Hoche. General Grouchy, aboard one of the ships at anchor, made the worst decision possible from the French point of view. He decided to wait for them to arrive before ordering the troops ashore.

That same morning, *Lord Stevenage* began to retrace her movements along the Irish coast. Merriman was on deck, pacing up and down as was his habit when thinking. As yet, young Small had revealed nothing. The doctor had confirmed that the boy would be stiff and sore for a time but would recover from the beating, though not fit for duty for a few days. At eight bells of the morning watch, Merriman reached a decision and spoke to Lieutenant Andrews who had just come on watch.

"Mr Andrews, my compliments to Mr Laing and would he bring Mr Hungerford to my cabin and ask Mr Shrigley to bring Mr Dorrington down but wait outside."

Laing ushered in a pale and trembling Hungerford who stood before the table looking nervously from one officer to the other. Neither spoke but simply stared at the youth who became more and nervous as the moments passed. Merriman finally broke the silence.

"Mr Hungerford, I know all about what has been going on in the midshipmen's berth. Mr Small has been badly beaten and..." here he paused, stood up and leaned forward until his face was close to that of the terrified midshipman and roared, "I WANT TO KNOW WHY YOU DID IT."

"No, sir, I didn't. It was Mr Dorrington, sir. He made me."

"But you helped him, didn't you. Why?"

"Yes, sir, I held him down on a sea chest while Mr Dorrington beat him with a riding whip he has, sir. He said he would beat me if I didn't and would have his family throw my parents out of their shop. He found out that his family owns the property my father rents, sir."

The boy was openly weeping now. "What else could I have done, sir? My parents scraped together every penny they could to give me this chance of a career, and they would be destitute."

"Very well, Mr Hungerford. Tell me how long this has been going on."

"Almost from the first, when Mr Dorrington came aboard, sir."

"And do you know why he picked on Mr Small?"

"Y-Yes, sir, he wanted Mr Small to do some of his duties for him, and he wanted to do things to him and Small wouldn't let him."

"What things? Come on, boy, speak up."

"To him, sir, you know," and the boy pointed vaguely to his groin.

"Ah-h-h, I see. Thank you, now stand over there. Mr Laing, I believe we have the truth at last. We'll have Mr Shrigley and Dorrington in now."

Dorrington attempted to keep a supercilious sneer on his face when the officers stared at him in a silence broken only by muffled sobs from the other boy.

"We know what you have been doing, Mr Dorrington. How you have been beating Mr Small, literally the smallest and weakest of you, because he won't fall in with your depraved wishes, and bullying Mr Hungerford into helping you."

"It's a lie! If Hungerford told you that, he lied. You can't take the word of the son of a shoemaker above mine. He was the one doing the beating. I tried to stop him but..." his voice trailed away before the fury on Merriman's face.

"The Honourable Arthur Dorrington, that is your title I believe, isn't that so?"

"Yes, you know it is," replied Dorrington.

"Then your title is a sham. There is neither honesty, manhood or anything honourable about you. You are arrogant, a liar, a sadistic bully and a shirker. No gentleman would force another by means of threats to help him ill-treat another, and a boy a mere twelve years old at that. Your behaviour is despicable and not that expected of an officer in the King's service. You will be punished, oh yes! You will be punished. Keep quiet, boy, and I've told you before to say sir when you address an officer."

"Mr Shrigley, kindly pass the word to the Bos'n that he is needed on the quarterdeck with two of his mates and to bring his cane. We will join him there."

"Aye – aye, sir. With pleasure."

"Sir, what are you going to do?" cried Dorrington in a panic. Gone was his arrogant pose. He was looking wildly about him as if looking for a means of escape, but there was none.

"Do? Why, nothing you don't deserve. I'm going to have you beaten as you beat little Mr Small."

"No you can't, you can't, I couldn't stand it. I've never been beaten."

Merriman was a stern disciplinarian but not a cruel man and he felt a pang of regret that he was being forced to subject the youth to this punishment, but he hardened his heart.

"Then you should have been. It may have curbed your temper and arrogance. Mr Laing, please take the two of them on deck and hand them over to the Bos'n. If Mr Dorrington causes you any difficulty we'll have a couple of marines drag him up there. I will follow."

The other officers and Mr Grahame had gathered on the quarter deck and Mr Brockle, the Bos'n, with two of his mates was standing apart with the two midshipmen between them. Temporarily the rain had ceased and *Lord Stevenage* was swooping and rolling in a quartering, confused sea.

"Mr Brockle, these boys are to be punished. I think you will know what for."

"Aye, sir. We all know what they've done to Mr Small and we 'eard of the state of the lad's back."

It was amazing how word travelled round a ship. Only those in Merriman's cabin had heard all that had been said but already the watch below and other hands had appeared on deck to see what was happening.

"Right, Mr Brockle, start with Mr Hungerford. He is not the main culprit so I think six strokes will do, six of the best, mind. Bend him over that gun."

"Aye – aye, sir."

As the Bos'n rolled up his sleeve, Merriman was pleased to see Hungerford walk to the gun and bend over it without being told, his face set determinedly. *May be hope for that one*, mused Merriman as the Bos'n administered the six stinging cuts with his cane without a sound coming from the boy's lips.

"And now for Mr Dorrington. He is to have twenty strokes, and laid on with a will, Mr Brockle. If your arm tires, one of your mates may continue the punishment You may need to hold him down," warned Merriman.

When he heard the sentence, the midshipman broke free of the bos'n's mates and attempted to run forr-ard, but Owen thrust out his foot and the two men were on him in a flash, dragging him kicking and screaming back to the gun. There they spread him over it and hung on to his hands and feet.

"Lay on, Mr Brockle." Merriman watched with a face like stone while the youth writhed and bawled unavailingly. At twelve strokes Merriman called the doctor to look to the boy.

"He's well enough, sir," McBride reported with a grin. "He'll stand the rest."

"Very good. Continue, Mr Brockle, if you please."

After the last eight strokes Dorrington struggled to his feet. His sobs and screams had finished and when the doctor made to attend him he snarled, "Keep your filthy hands off me, damn you." Holding himself stiffly erect he looked round the watching officers, his face scarlet with fury and humiliation.

"I'll see you dead for this outrage if it's the last thing I do," he almost spat the words out, looking directly at Merriman as he did so.

"You'll keep your mouth shut and get below before I ask the Bos'n to give you another ten strokes," replied Merriman. "And if I hear of any more of your bad ways, you'll find yourself bending over a gun again. From now on you will not lay a finger on Mr Small and I want that whip of yours given to Mr Shrigley to throw over the side."

For the time being nothing more would be heard from Dorrington, but that he had not accepted his beating would soon become dreadfully apparent. Merriman had made himself a vengeful enemy.

Chapter Nine

French corvette and three troop transports in Ireland

The next day a lookout sighted a sail which turned out to be a naval cutter. Both ships hove to and the young lieutenant in command of the cutter climbed aboard, wet to the waist having badly misjudged the movement of his boat relative to the frigate in the heaving sea.

It seemed to bother him not one bit as, to the ill-concealed amusement of the officers and men on deck, he squelched across the quarterdeck to where Merriman was waiting. "Lieutenant Heatherington, sir, the cutter *Tiny*. I have despatches and letters for you, sir, and one for a Mr Grahame."

"Thank you, Mr Heatherington. Perhaps you will join me in my cabin for a glass of something to warm you while I read these despatches. My servant will find you a towel. Mr Grahame, will you join us?"

The despatches contained little of use except the news, now several days old, that the French fleet was expected to try to break the blockade at any time. "That means that if they have succeeded, they could arrive off this coast at any moment," exclaimed Grahame after Merriman had passed the despatch to him.

"Exactly so, sir, they may have arrived already."

"Mr Heatherington, dry or not, back to your ship at once. There is a French invasion imminent and we could have French cannon balls about our ears before the day is out. Have you been given any further orders?"

"Only that I should go back to Portsmouth after finding you, sir."

"Good, well then my orders are that you sail eastwards ahead of this ship but remain within signalling distance. Any sign of enemy ships and you'll signal so and then make your fastest time to Cork to alert the garrison there. Try and stay out of trouble. If you do sight the French, keep away from them. It is more important that the army is alerted than that you test your popguns against a French warship."

"Aye – aye, sir. Are the French really going to invade Ireland, sir?"

"Indeed, they are going to try, Mr Heatherington. They have much to gain if they succeed. Another thing, if you can discover where Commodore Pellew's squadron is, you must make haste to find him and warn him, after you have been to Cork."

Heatherington practically hurled himself down into his boat and, almost as soon as he was aboard his little ship, it was under way again.

Merriman called his officers together. "You know what this means, gentlemen. If the French succeed in their purpose and wrest Ireland from our control, then England will be ringed about with the enemy. If we sight the invasion fleet we must avoid the warships and endeavour to attack and sink as many transport ships as possible. Those ships will be carrying cannon and powder and the bulk of the army's equipment, not to mention hundreds of soldiers. Every one we sink means fewer troops for our garrisons to fight."

"It seems like a David and Goliath situation, sir," said Lieutenant Weston. "Just us against a fleet. Long odds, I would say."

"Quite right, Mr Weston, but the navy thrives on long odds. When we get among the transports I'll be looking to those big twenty-five pounders and the smashers to speak well for us."

"Oh they will, sir, I have no doubt. Mr Salmon and I have paid special attention to the crews of the big guns. They are the same men that stood to them aboard *Aphrodite*."

Speed was impossible with the two ships sailing into the teeth of rising winds which made progress slow. The cutter made better time with her fore and aft rig than the big frigate with square sails and Heatherington was forced to reduce sail so as not to leave *Lord Stevenage* behind.

The wind increased and Merriman was forced to shorten sail even more whilst *Lord Stevenage* rolled and pitched without cease. Mr Grahame groaned, turned green, and bolted below. Midshipman Dorrington, who regardless of his soreness still had to stand-to with the ship at action stations, was crouched in the scuppers retching his insides out to the amusement of the officers and men on the quarterdeck.

Merriman went below to read the letters delivered by Lieutenant Heatherington. It became obvious that his hastily scrawled letters, sent from London, had reached home very quickly and just as quickly the replies had reached him.

The naval postal service has excelled itself for once, he thought to himself as he read one from his father congratulating him on his promotion. Apart from giving him all the family news, the letter also told him that his friend Captain Saville had finally returned home from the West Indies and would be at the wedding. Another piece of news was that a man named Robinson, a lawyer from Chester who had been helping the French agent Moreau in the affair of the Viceroy of Ireland, had at last been traced to America where he had vanished, probably in Boston or New York. Robinson was wanted not only for his traitorous activities but also for the murder of his wife.

The authorities will be lucky to catch him now, mused Merriman. But maybe Moreau will appear again and we can catch him at least.

The other letter, which he read over and over again, was from his fiancée, Helen. She missed him terribly, she couldn't wait to see him again, the wedding was all arranged, only the date to be set, but that could be done at short notice. She closed the letter with endearments Merriman would not have wanted anyone else to read. She still loved him; even after four years away she still wanted him.

Merriman was still basking in the glow of that knowledge and lost in memories and thoughts of the future over an hour later. The ship had Scariff Island just in sight ahead on the port bow, when the boom of a cannon and a hail from aloft startled him out of his dreams and sent him back on deck, alert to the possibility of action.

The cannon fire was from *Tiny* to draw attention to her flag signals.

"Up you go, Mr Shrigley, see what you can make of it."

Merriman would have been reluctant to send the signals midshipman Gideon Small up the wildly gyrating mast, even if he had been fit. The boy would have had his work cut out to hold on, never mind identify a flag hoist. Shrigley however was like a monkey aloft and he was back on deck in no time.

"Can't see the signal clearly, sir, it's blowing almost directly towards us, but I think it is "Enemy in sight". *Tiny* wouldn't fire a gun if it wasn't important, and she's shortened sail and hove to, sir."

"Thank you, Mr Shrigley. I think you are right. Gentlemen, you know what is expected of us, so pass the word to the men and clear for action but don't run out the guns just yet. Mr Laing, if we have time, see that the men get some hot food inside them before the galley fire is doused. Jack always fights better on a full stomach. You can release each division in turn."

There was instant rush and bustle as the ship was made ready to fight. The decks were sanded to provide more grip for the men's bare feet, partitions were knocked down and cabin furniture taken below. Chain slings were fitted to the yards in case the halliards were shot away, nets rigged to prevent falling blocks and tackle striking down men on deck, and Merriman was pleased to see gun captains carefully selecting the truest ball for the first carefully aimed broadside.

The Master, beside the men at the big double wheel, started to swear quietly. "The devil and all his minions must be sending us this bad weather." He raised his clenched fist to the skies. "I want some sunshine, damn it."

The helmsmen looked at the old man in amazement as, as if in response to the Master's shout, the rain ceased and visibility suddenly improved, but there was no sign of any other vessels. It was not until *Lord Stevenage* cleared Scariff Island and Kenmare River began to open that there was a hail from a lookout, "Deck there, four ships inshore beyond *Tiny.*"

"Up you go again, Mr Shrigley."

Only a few moments later Shrigley was back. "Looks like a corvette with three other vessels, sir. Can't be certain but it looks like the corvette we fought in the Irish Sea four years ago. What's her name? The Siren or something like it."

"*La Sirene,* the Mermaid."

"Yes, sir, that's it. She has an odd shaped patch on her main tops'l, but they are definitely Frenchies and they are sailing close hauled on the starboard tack, well up into the Kenmare River."

"That's it then, gentlemen. The French are here, but there will be more than four of them somewhere. This must be only a small part of their fleet, perhaps separated from the rest in a storm."

"Yes, sir, what do you intend to do?" asked the First Lieutenant.

Merriman took a few steps up and down the quarter deck, thinking furiously and tugging at his ear. The rest of the French force must be nearby, probably in Bantry Bay if his earlier deductions had been correct. Even now the transports could be unloading, screened by the warships. He could go and look for them but it was no part of a frigate's role to try conclusions with a squadron of French three deckers. *Lord Stevenage* would be blown to kindling long before she got anywhere near the transports.

No, he must rely on Lieutenant Heatherington in his handy, fast little cutter avoiding the French and reaching Cork to sound the alarm. Merriman's own task must be to destroy the four ships in Kenmare River. His mind made up, he turned to the officers waiting for his decision.

"Mr Laing, we'll go in after these four ships and try to sink or take them all. Alter course to follow them, if you please."

Broad smiles broke out on their faces. Here was a definite promise of action and action could mean promotion and prize money. The French ships were trapped in the long narrow estuary and could not escape without meeting *Lord Stevenage.*

Merriman had been aware of Mr Grahame standing quietly with the officers and as they dispersed about their duties he approached.

"I'm pleased that's your decision, Captain. I didn't want to influence you but if that French corvette is *La Sirene,* the one that we encountered all that time ago, then it is quite possible that fellow Moreau is aboard her. I'd dearly love to get my hands on him. If we can capture him, that alone would be a bigger blow to the French than sinking a few transports."

Captain St James, the marine, overheard Grahame's remarks and joined in.

"If he *is* there, sir, I hope our practice has improved our swordplay enough to be able to match him."

St James was a far superior swordsman than his captain and he was referring to the fact that for the last four years, when time and weather permitted, he had spent at least an hour a day practicing with and tutoring Merriman in the finer points of fencing and taught him a few unusual tricks as well.

"A bit underhand and not considered to be a gentleman's way by the so called fencing masters, sir, but after all, the whole purpose is to get your blade into your opponent before he gets his into you," St James had said grimly when teaching Merriman a particular move. "I learned that one off a Spanish officer some years ago and it has saved my life on more than one occasion."

Merriman's swordplay had improved remarkably but he was far from being as good as the marine captain. However, remembering the Frenchman's skill with his exceptionally long blade the last time they met, Merriman had his doubts about the outcome.

"I hope so too, Edward, but he is quick, damnably quick. Still, we'll worry about that if we catch him. Meanwhile, when the time comes I want your marines to concentrate their musket fire on the enemy officers and crew. With them out of action their ships and the soldiers in them will be helpless."

The frigate had drawn close to the *Tiny* and Merriman could see Lieutenant Heatherington watching, doubtless wishing he could join in the coming action. Merriman pointed vigorously to the eastward and Heatherington waved and turned to give his orders. The cutter rapidly got under way again and headed south by west to clear Dursey Island and the Bull rock before the run eastward to Cork.

The frigate clawed her way slowly into Kenmare River, as close hauled as she could go under topsails and headsails, fighting against the wind which was still increasing and blowing almost directly out to sea. Violent squalls brought more rain to obscure visibility again. As the ship progressed in a series of tacks, Merriman and Mr Cuthbert anxiously watched the shoreline and listened to the leadsman in the fore chains shouting out the changing depth. Despite his protective leather apron, the man was soaked to the skin, as were most of the crew from the rain and spray. It was a condition they were well used to after their years at sea.

The estuary was perhaps twenty miles long and three to four miles across at the widest but the chart showed shoals and shallows on the larboard side past the halfway mark which abruptly narrowed the navigable water. Merriman desperately needed to know what the French corvette was doing. That the French would fight was expected, and if it were indeed *La Sirene,* she would fight hard. So much he knew from the action of four years ago which had ended inconclusively, but now he was commanding the bigger of the two ships and, although the corvette was like a small frigate, he should have no great difficulty in defeating her.

"Aloft again, Mr Shrigley, see if you can see better from up there."

Shrigley was back almost at once, sliding down a backstay as the quickest means of regaining the deck. "I caught a glimpse of her, sir, about a mile away on the starboard tack and heading our way."

"Thank you, Mr Shrigley. Mr Laing, I'll have the guns run out now."

Merriman's mind raced. *Lord Stevenage* was on the larboard tack struggling to make headway, but with the wind at her back the corvette would be on them in an instant. He had to at least cripple the corvette so that he could deal with the transport ships before they could put too many troops ashore.

A shout from Laing near him on the quarterdeck, "I can see them, sir, the rain is easing again."

It was so, Merriman could see the French ship clearly, on the larboard bow and closing rapidly, still on the starboard tack and with all gun ports open and guns run out.

Merriman's decision was instant. "Mr Laing, when I give the word I want the ship to go about like lightning, we'll cross his bow and give him our starboard broadside as we pass and then we'll tack again to cross his stern. Have all the guns at full elevation. Mr Hungerford, forr-ard with you, tell Mr Weston that we are going about and I want the big twenty five pounders to fire as soon as they bear, see if he can hit their bowsprit or foremast."

As the boy sped away, Merriman knew that from the heaving and pitching deck they would be lucky to hit anything with the two shots which were all that Weston would have time for as the ship turned, but it was worth the chance.

"The transports have anchored on the north side of a large inlet and men are already ashore, sir," reported Shrigley.

Watching keenly, Merriman was juggling figures in his head, the relative speed of the two ships, the decreasing distance apart, and the speed with which *Lord Stevenage* could tack. And the imponderable, would the French captain hold his course?

The ships were approaching each other at an obtuse angle and there was every chance that the Frenchman would not want to wear ship if he could avoid it, especially with such a wind behind him. No, he would expect to veer to starboard a little so that the ships would pass larboard side to. Well, too late now to change his plan.

The men at the sheets and braces were poised and ready, the men at the wheel looking expectantly at Merriman, all waiting for the moment.

"Now," he shouted. The wheel was hard over, the spokes flying through the men's hands as the ship spun round. Forr-ard the men waited for their moment, leaving the headsails sheeted in as they were to allow the wind to reach the other side and push the ship's head round before loosing the sheets and hauling madly on those on the other side, while equally frantically other men were hauling on the sheets and braces controlling the topsails.

The two big bow chasers roared out one after the other as the ship's head passed through the wind and pointed at the enemy, but with no discernible effect apart from a cloud of splinters from her rail.

"As you bear," roared Merriman and the starboard guns erupted in a ragged broadside as each gun captain decided the moment to fire.

The result was devastating as the hail of iron struck *La Sirene* on her bows, mostly on the starboard side. Merriman saw two gun ports beaten together into one and the guns behind smashed backwards. A cheer went up from the British seamen as the bowsprit dissolved into a mass of fragments, and the headsails, loosing their supporting stays, blew into a tangle of torn canvas and flailing ropes.

Now it was the frigate's turn to stand the French broadside. Merriman had just enough time to order the ship brought back on to her original course, to swing round the Frenchman's stern, before the side of the corvette disappeared in the flame and smoke of her own broadside.

"For what we are about to receive…" intoned Laing before the air was filled with flying iron and splinters of wood.

Merriman felt his coat twitch as something tore through the air past him and he saw the crew of one of the quarterdeck carronades fall in a confused welter of blood and smashed flesh. Miraculously neither the men at the wheel or anyone else on the quarterdeck was hit but down on the main deck men were dragging the dead to the base of the mainmast and carrying the wounded below.

Amongst the carnage, Lieutenant Andrews, in command of the starboard battery, was yelling like a fiend at his men to finish reloading. The dead and wounded had already been replaced by men from the larboard side battery which had not yet fired.

"Mr Andrews," bellowed Merriman. "Hold your fire till we pass her stern, then rake her as the guns bear."

Andrews waved to indicate that he had heard and then ran forr-ard to see that each gun was properly laid. Again the frigate's cannon thundered out and the iron hail crashed into the corvette's stern.

"Caught 'em, sir, two broadsides to their one, and only... Oh look, sir, their fore topmast is going," shouted Laing excitedly.

It was true, as *La Sirene* fell behind, the mast, deprived of the support of the forestays from the smashed bowsprit, and with some shrouds parted by cannon shot, was seen to lean over, slowly at first but increasingly quickly as the remaining shrouds and stays parted under the strain. Then it crashed over the side in a tangle of rope and canvas. The ship was immediately unmanageable and it disappeared behind them into the murk.

"Well then, she won't bother us for a while, although we have only scotched the snake not killed it," remarked Merriman calmly to hide his inner turmoil. He knew that if the Frenchman had decided on a similar move the boot might have been on the other foot and his own ship in a similar state.

The frigate had lost almost all steerage way due to the sudden turn to starboard before sufficient momentum had been achieved after her turn under the bows of the corvette. It took a few minutes to get her moving again, heading further up the estuary to where the transport ships were anchored.

The three of them were anchored in line in the lee of the headland which also protected a miserable huddle of cottages. Boats were transferring soldiers ashore to join a substantial number already there.

"The French have made good use of their time, sir. They have a good many ashore already," commented the Master, Mr Cuthbert.

"Indeed they have. There must be a very energetic officer in command there, but it's time for us to put a stop to their activities, Mr Cuthbert. We have no reliable chart of these waters so we'll keep the man in the chains with his line if you please."

Mr Cuthbert passed the order on.

"Mr Laing, when we are in range I want a broadside of canister concentrated on the French soldiers already ashore and only afterwards aim at the transports."

Canister shot was musket or pistol balls tightly packed into a tin cylinder which split apart when fired, releasing the balls and causing fearsome damage to flesh and blood.

As *Lord Stevenage* drew nearer and nearer the shore, the soldiers there, perhaps not realising the destruction a ship of war could create, stared curiously at the English frigate. When the smoke of the broadside cleared, Merriman could see the carnage that the hail of musket balls had created. Scattered blue-coated bodies were lying on the beach while the survivors were running wildly about, looking for cover.

Aboard the French ships, men could be seen looking nervously over their shoulder at the menacing appearance of the approaching frigate. Two of the captains lost their nerve, cut their anchor ropes and tried to make a run for it. However, before their ships could be brought under control, the wind drove them ashore where they immediately began to break up. The third ship, the captain obviously deciding that resistance or flight was useless, promptly hauled down the flag and a white cloth was waved on the stern.

"Three of them and not another shot fired," exclaimed Laing delightedly.

Merriman was watching the doomed men on the two shattered ships clinging to the rigging, or the more courageous of them jumping into the sea in an attempt to swim ashore as some of their fellows had already done.

"And a lot of men drowning, Mr Laing. The poor devils have little chance in that sea."

A worried looking Mr Cuthbert stepped in front of Merriman. "The water is shallowing, sir, and the gale is worsening. I really must urge you to make for the open sea immediately."

"You're right, it is worsening, Mr Cuthbert." Merriman looked at the skies and the nearby land for a moment. "We must anchor, there where the other two transports were anchored. We must keep our eye on the French. Mr Laing, I am determined to anchor, two anchors if you please, the larboard one well offshore in case the wind backs more to the north."

This meant a difficult sequence of operations had to be carried out. First the ship had to be manoeuvred into position to drop the larboard anchor and then sailed crabwise across the wind to drop the second one. It took time in the teeth of what was by then a howling gale with more lashing rain, but with arduous work by the men and brilliant seamanship, the ship was finally anchored. Meanwhile the work of repairing the damage carried on.

Laing and Cuthbert anxiously compared their bearings before announcing to Merriman that the ship was making no leeway and the anchors were holding firm.

"Very good, gentlemen, there is nothing more we can do about the French before the gale blows itself out. I'd like a prize crew aboard that that ship as soon as the weather abates enough, but I won't risk men's lives in a boat in these conditions. This ship will remain at action stations as the French will be a desperate lot and we don't know what they may attempt in the night. However, have the men fed and rested by turns. Such repairs that are still to be made must wait for daylight, but I am confident that the ship is ready for action at a moment's notice. Meanwhile I am going below to see the wounded."

Below on the orlop deck was a nightmare scene. In the middle, the surgeon, Mr McBride, was busy fastening a bandage round a man's head and his assistants, the loblolly boys, were moving the bodies of those who had died. Merriman was surprised to see a pale faced midshipman Small going round the men with water.

"Thank'ee, lad, that's good," he heard one man say after taking a drink, and many of the men reached out to touch the boy as he passed. "He's a good lad, that one, not like that bloody Dorrington," commented another. "No, that un needs a good flogging 'imself. Sorry, sir, didn't see you there. Didn't mean any offence, sir."

"Never mind, rest easy." Merriman raised his voice, "Men, I think you will be pleased to know that we have dealt a hard blow to the enemy. The corvette is badly damaged and most likely aground and two of their transports are also aground and smashed. The third one has surrendered. All we have to do tomorrow is round up the Frenchies that got ashore. Well done, all of you. Mr McBride, a word on deck if you can leave here."

As Merriman turned to leave a hoarse voice called out, "Sir, I told you the men wouldn't let you down, if you'll pardon the impertinence, sir."

He recognised one of the men from the original crew of the frigate. He smiled and replied, "Nor have you, any of you."

On deck, the surgeon reported the numbers of dead and wounded. "Not too bad, sir, there are six dead and ten wounded. They should all recover except one who has a splinter through his stomach. He won't see the dawn, sir."

"No, not too many, but more than I like to see. Carry on, Mr McBride. We'll bury the dead at sea as soon as we can."

He became aware of Peters and Tomkins hovering round, "Yes, what do you two rogues want?" His irascibility had no effect on either of them.

"If you please, sir, I've got a hot drink for you and the last of the chicken too, sir" said Peters.

"And here's a chair for you, sir," said Tomkins eagerly. "And I've rigged an 'ammock too, with a curtain in your cabin, sir, seein' as 'ow all your furniture is still below."

Merriman realised that he was bone weary and he hadn't eaten or drunk since his sparse breakfast. The thought of a hot drink, food and a comfortable hammock was almost too much but there was one more order to issue before he surrendered himself to such luxuries.

"Mr Laing, as soon as the weather permits I want a prize crew sent across to secure that transport ship."

"Aye – aye, sir, I'll see to that." Laing found himself almost ushering his captain below. "You have a good rest, sir. We'll need you wide awake tomorrow."

Merriman descended to his cabin, or rather the space where his cabin would be if the furniture and partitions had not been sent below, to find the hammock suspended between the guns which normally shared the cabin. In spite of the noise, the howling and demonic shrieking of the wind, the groaning and creaking of timbers, and the pitching and rolling of the ship, he fell asleep almost as soon as he climbed into it, never noticing Peters gently covering him with his boat cloak.

Chapter Ten

Moreau and French marines manage to get ashore

After the disastrous fight against the *Lord Stevenage,* seamen aboard the crippled *La Sirene* were frantically working to rig a staysail from the remains of the foremast fighting top to bring the ship under control again.

"We must anchor, M'sieur Moreau," shouted Captain Ferrier above the howling of the gale, "before we are driven ashore and the ship is lost."

"Very well, Captain, you must do whatever is necessary, but try to get as close to the shore as you can."

"Close to shore, do you say? We'll go only as close as we must to find an anchorage, M'sieur, and that will not be easy."

"We must endeavour to get the marines and myself ashore to support our men from the transport ships. From the cannon fire we heard, that damned English frigate must have attacked them and there must have been a lot of men killed. We have no idea how many have survived but the survivors will try to cross the hills to join our main force in Bantry Bay."

And so, with great difficulty and good seamanship, the French corvette closed the shore and Captain Ferrier ordered anchors to be dropped and sails taken in. But there was to be no rest for the weary crew working feverishly in the dark, wind and rain to make their ship seaworthy again. The work was progressing well and in the early hours of the morning the captain was beginning to allow himself the luxury of hope that the ship would survive.

The gale was abating and the seas going down when suddenly, with one final effort, the wind increased in force and a violent gust swept over the ship before dropping away almost completely. That last blow was too much for one of the ship's overstrained anchor ropes which parted with a bang. The other rope held but it was quickly realised that the anchor was not holding. Before anything could be done the ship crashed onto a rock, lifted to a wave which carried her aground and came to rest with a slight list to starboard.

Captain Ferrier raised his arms in despair. "I'm sorry, M'sieur Moreau, we can do no more. The ship is holed and aground, my crew is exhausted and it could take days to repair and re-float her."

"Very well, Captain, I can see that you have done the best you can, but as I said earlier, those of us who can, must get ashore to support our men from the other ships."

Eventually, Moreau, Major Marmont, an army officer, and fifty marines managed to get ashore with nothing worse than wet feet.

Moreau, Marmont and the marine officers looked about them in the pale light of the dawn.

"I think the best thing we can do is to climb to the summit of these hills and advance along them until we can see the fleet and see how much of our army has already been landed," said Moreau. "We should also be able to discover how many people have got ashore from our own few ships. Do you agree, M'sieurs?"

It took them several hours to reach a position from where they could see into Bantry Bay and there they were shocked and bitterly disappointed to see no sign of the French Fleet.

"B'but where are they?" stammered Marmont. "They should have arrived yesterday."

"The gale has kept the fleet out to sea I expect, sir," replied the marine Lieutenant.

"That will be it. We shall see them soon enough, I imagine," said Moreau as cheerfully as he could, although there were doubts creeping into his mind even then. "Meanwhile let us proceed and find our survivors."

After an hour's hard marching, one of their advance scouts came running back to report. "We can see our people, sir, perhaps three hundred of them further on and down below us near an old farm."

"So few? Did you see any sign of the English?" asked Major Marmont.

"No, sir, but we did hear what might have been shots."

Marmont looked at Moreau. "I think we had better join our comrades, M'sieur."

Chapter Eleven

Merriman ashore, determined to follow French survivors

Merriman gradually became aware of a hand shaking his shoulder. Petulantly he tried to ignore it and let sleep overcome him again, but the hand persisted and as full wakefulness returned he realised that it was Lieutenant Laing beside the hammock. The sound of hammering and sawing testified that work on the repairs was continuing.

"I'm sorry to wake you, sir, but its dawn and the weather's better. No more than a stiff breeze blowing now."

"The ship, man, how's the ship?"

"Still at anchor, sir. She took the gale well and we managed to get the prize crew aboard the transport an hour ago."

Merriman realised that Laing was red eyed from lack of sleep and looked desperately tired.

"Damn it, Edward, you should have called me earlier." Merriman tried to get to his feet and had perforce to clutch at Laing's arm as the boat cloak wrapped itself round his legs and nearly brought him down.

Regaining his composure, he grabbed his hat and ran up on deck to find that the wind was now no more than a strong breeze and the sea had abated considerably. The rain had also ceased. Of the two transports which had gone aground, only a few timbers protruding above the waves showed where they had been and on the shoreline a tangle of rigging, torn canvas, shattered timber and the corpses of both men and horses testified to the fury of last night's gale.

The third transport vessel lay to anchor between *Lord Stevenage* and the shore and members of the prize crew could be seen moving about her deck.

"Who is over there, Mr Laing?"

"Mr Weston and Mr Hungerford with ten men and a bos'n's mate, sir. They sent the boat back with the marines I sent as they found the ship completely deserted. The crew and soldiers must have managed to get ashore when the weather eased."

"The ship lies closer inshore and has more shelter in the lee of the headland than we do, so they would have had time before dawn, nonetheless it shows that there is a determined officer in command. Anything else?"

"Somebody had tried to set her on fire, sir, but unsuccessfully, fortunately for us, as there is a large supply of powder aboard. Also field pieces and shot."

"That was probably panic on some Frenchman's part, wanting to get away from the ship before it blew up, so he didn't wait to see that the fire had caught properly I expect."

"Yes, sir, apparently they left a hatch open to allow more air to reach the fire but that allowed water over the deck to get below and it put the fire out. There were horses too, sir, but the heathen French cut the throats of most of them before leaving, and there are only three left alive."

"And the corvette?"

"A mile or so further down the coast, sir, either aground or anchored, it's difficult to be sure from here. You can just make her out with the glass." Laing passed his telescope to his captain and waited for his reaction.

"Well she may be aground, she seems to have a slight list but as you say it is difficult to tell. We know she lost her fore topmast as well as her bowsprit and in that gale she would be difficult to handle without her headsails. At this distance I can see no sign of life. Looks deserted to me but she hasn't been set afire, I wonder why?"

"I wondered that, sir, and I can see no sign of men ashore though we can't see the part of the shore hidden behind that small headland. There could be some there as well as the men over here."

Laing pointed to the beach beyond the wreckage of the two transports. A number of men were making an attempt to light a fire of damp timber but only a few pathetic wisps of smoke rose to show their efforts.

"There must be more French ashore than we can see there," exclaimed Merriman.

The other officers had arrived on the quarter-deck by then and were huddled in a group, rubbing chilled hands together to warm them, and discussing the situation.

"Gentlemen, to work. Our duty is clear. We must go ashore and find out what the French are doing. Captain St James, I'll have all your marines in the landing party, and we'll take most of the men with us. Mr Andrews, Mr Shrigley, you'll go with me. Mr Laing, Mr Cuthbert, and you Mr Hungerford, you will remain with the ship with enough men to defend her or move her if necessary. The repairs will continue. All seamen to have a cutlass or pike and the more reliable must have a pistol or musket. Now, select your men and let's be about it. Oh, one more thing, Mr Laing. Send word to Mr Weston. I want one of those French field pieces out of that ship and ashore with powder and shot, especially canister or grape. And the horses. We'll likely be outnumbered and may need it. Mr Salmon should go with it. Oh, and I want my clerk, Tomkins, to go over with O'Flynn and make a list of her cargo."

"Sir, please sir, can I go ashore too?"

Merriman turned to find a chastened looking Dorrington behind him.

"Yes, of course. It'll be good experience for you. Now pass the word to Mr McBride that I need him ashore too."

Dorrington disappeared below while Merriman wondered if the lad was beginning to show some improvement. Amid the hustle and bustle of preparing the boats, men arming themselves and being sorted into groups, Merriman stood alone on the quarter-deck, staring at the shore, mulling over the problem of what the French would do. That a good number had been put ashore before *Lord Stevenage* arrived was certain, and together with those from the third transport and any able bodied survivors, they would make a formidable force.

"If I'm right and these four ships were separated from the main force, then where are the rest of them?" Unaware that he had spoken aloud, he was startled when a voice answered.

"If you are right, James, they'll be in Bantry Bay and that's where the French from these ships will have gone, overland," said Mr Grahame, who had been a silent bystander while Merriman issued his orders. "And I'm going ashore with you."

The landing party gradually assembled on shore. The two marine officers with their thirty four men, along with the other officers with some seventy or so seamen and petty officers. The men were all chattering like so many monkeys, excited at the prospect of a shore excursion and the chance to deal another blow to the French.

Weston's party was rowing the longboat ashore with the French cannon balanced on planks laid athwart ships to another boat. It was slow work and the load was precariously balanced, but eventually the gun was run ashore and the boat sent back with a relief party of seamen to bring powder and shot. The horses were swum ashore and fitted with harness for pulling the gun.

In accordance with Merriman's orders, the marines had landed first to secure the beach and low hills behind and already they had rounded up the French left on the beach.

"A poor lot, sir," reported St James when Merriman landed, "Only forty of them, mostly soldiers and a few seamen. They're wet, cold, exhausted and thoroughly miserable and some of them are suffering from broken bones and near drowning. They have no weapons, sir, so what do you wish me to do with them?"

"We can't bother with them now, they will need nourishment and warmth but we can't spare the time. I don't think we will need to guard them, with no weapons and nowhere to go they pose no threat. Have the able bodied of them drag the bodies of their countrymen to the far end of the beach for burial. They'll have to stay on the beach until we return. Meanwhile I'll speak with them. Mr McBride, come with me."

Not for the first time was he grateful for keeping on his ship one Anton O'Flynn, a Frenchman of Irish descent, captured four years ago, who had betrayed French plans to Merriman, albeit in fear for his life. Since then O'Flynn had taught both Merriman and Shrigley to speak French. He approached the woebegone prisoners.

"Who is the senior man here?"

A lanky individual, his clothes mostly rags, stood up. "Me, sir. I am an under officer, what you call a petty officer. My name is Pierre Cabette."

"Well then, I know that many more men landed from your ships last night, where have they gone?"

Cabette waved his arm inland, to where the red coats of the marine pickets could be seen on the hills.

"All the men able to walk left us, sir. Most of us were too weak to follow and besides, I couldn't leave the wounded behind."

He gestured to where the ship's doctor was already examining the wounded Frenchmen.

"How are they, Mr McBride?"

"They'll survive, sir. Some broken limbs and two of them with cracked ribs but what they need now is warmth and food."

"Oh, very well then... Mr Shrigley, have four men take a boat over to the transport and bring back the means of lighting a fire and some of their provisions. Then send the boats back to the ship. No point in leaving them here to tempt the prisoners. Mr McBride, you can attend to the wounded men and then follow us."

He turned back to the Frenchman. "We'll leave you some food and the means of lighting a fire, M'sieur Cabette, but that is all I can do for you now. I repeat, do you know where the others have gone, why, and how many are there?"

"Yes, sir, I know but I will not tell you. We are enemies, are we not?"

But it was obvious which way the French had gone. The tramping of many feet had left a clear pathway from the beach leading up to a valley in the hills where the wet ground had been churned to mud. Merriman called his officers together.

"It seems that the French are trying to join their countrymen who I believe to be landing in Bantry Bay, over these hills in front of us. Where they go we must follow, and now that Mr Weston has managed to get this gun ashore we must take it with us." Andrews eyed the long uphill slope unhappily.

"I know Mr Andrews, it will not be easy but the horses will be a great help. Sort out the men into three groups. One to haul the gun, one to carry the shot and the third to carry the powder cartridges. They can change round at intervals. Mr St James, apart from skirmishers, your marines must help with the gun."

"Aye – aye Sir. I'll take ten of my men ahead to keep an eye open for the French."

"Very good, but when you reach a point from where they can see the French, you must stop, keep out of sight and send a runner back to tell me."

In spite of a cold wind, the exertion of climbing the hills soon warmed every one up and that and the appearance of a watery looking sun behind thinning cloud raised their spirits considerably and the men were soon singing a sea shanty to help them with the hauling of the cannon, but that quickly died away as they reached the steeper slope. Shipboard life with its lack of exercise was not conducive to great physical fitness and it was not long before Merriman and the other officers were sweating freely beneath their heavy uniform coats. The seamen were more used to an active life especially the lean and fit topmen who were used to scrambling up the rigging and along the yards, but even so, the harsh physical effort of dragging the heavy gun uphill began to wear the men down, even with the horses to help.

Progress became slower and slower until Merriman halted the column. Rocks were hastily pushed behind the wheels and the men, gasping and blowing, collapsed on the ground.

"This is taking too long Gentlemen, we must change our tactics. Leave half the shot here and send the other half ahead with all the powder. That will spare more men for the gun. The men with the lighter loads of powder will make better time if they don't have to wait to change places with the gun pullers and as soon as they reach the top of these hills they can find a dry place to leave it and then come back here. The men with the shot will take a bit longer but they too can deliver their loads to the top and then come back. Eventually all the men will be pulling the gun."

He turned suddenly as the pop-popping sound of musket fire from higher up the slope told that the marine detachment was in action.

"Mr Goodwin, Advance at once with your marines to support Mr St James and send a man back to tell me what you find. We shall follow as fast as we can."

They were moving in an extended column, following the path up a valley which was covered in small, wind distorted trees and scrub, up to a pass through the mountains. Merriman estimated that they must have climbed to over two thousand feet already and his new arrangements were working well. The cannon was moving more quickly with more men on the ropes even without the marines. His lungs were heaving as he gasped for breath and Mr Graham was in no better condition. Determined not to show weakness before his men he struggled on gamely though he was amused to see his cox'n Owen at his back, ready to help him if necessary. So it was with relief that he saw the red coated figure of a marine hurrying downhill towards him and he had a good reason to halt the column and take a breather.

The sweating marine approached. "Mr St James's compliments Sir an' 'e encountered some French. We lost two men and the French 'ave retreated down the hill on the other side. We can see the main party from the top Sir".

"Thank you. Well Gentlemen, we shall soon see what we have to contend with. Mr Andrews, you and I will move up first following the marine. Mr Shrigley and Mr Dorrington, you follow on with the gun. Mr Grahame, do you wish to join me?"

Another few hundred feet up, the path levelled off and he found the marines waiting. Captain St James was waiting to report.

'We were surprised by a small number of French Sir. They opened fire from ambush and killed two of my men and wounded two others. We returned fire and killed one of them and I think wounded another before they ran to join their main party which has disappeared into that valley ahead, leading to the coast."

"From where the ambush was, could the French see the cannon we are bringing up?"

"Unlikely Sir, I think it was too far back. You will see that it is only just emerging from that gully and those few trees would have screened it as well. Before that it would be hidden by the slope of the ground."

"Sir, if you will follow me, I've found a good vantage point from which we can see the enemy. I've put guard pickets out to protect our flanks but It seems that there are no more French up here."

A hundred yards further on some of the marines were behind some scattered boulders, from the cover of which they could keep an eye open for enemy activity. Merriman peered round the side of a big boulder. From his position, most of the wide expanse of Bantry Bay lay before him and he immediately spotted the French far below, hurrying through the trees in a valley and obviously making for the beach of Bantry Bay.

"Well, they know we are here so there is no need to conceal ourselves, gentlemen. And there is something else, or perhaps I should say nothing else."

"What do you mean by that cryptic remark?" asked Mr Grahame.

"If I may." For answer Merriman opened his small telescope and proceeded to study Bantry Bay, or at least as much of it as he could see.

"No ships, sir. Either I am wrong in suggesting that this is where the French fleet would attempt their landing or else they have not yet arrived."

Merriman was not to know that he had been right all along, but that the French fleet had arrived but already gone. Having anchored in the bay while the weather was still relatively fine, the fleet waited for their missing ships including the flagship to arrive and not a man had been landed. Had they done so, the French plan could have succeeded as their force was one and a half times that of the total of British troops in Ireland at the time. General Grouchy's indecision and the gale saved England that day. As the time passed, the wind increased by the hour and became the violent gale with squalls of sleet and snow which had overtaken Merriman and his ship in Kenmare River.

Fifteen of the thirty-five French ships had anchored close inshore and the rest scattered about the bay. The wind was blowing directly offshore and the twenty ships in the bay were unable to maintain their position. They were quickly blown out to sea. The remaining ships closer inshore had some six and a half thousand men aboard and, belatedly, Grouchy determined to land them.

Admiral Bouvet refused to obey, saying that a landing from boats was impossible in the conditions and that more men would drown than would reach the shore. In vain Grouchy argued, but Bouvet was adamant that he would not risk the lives of their men in such an impossible enterprise.

The ships were dragging their anchors and finally Bouvet ordered that they cut their cables and stand out to sea. They never assembled together as a fleet again.

By the time Merriman and his men arrived overlooking the bay, not a single French ship was to be seen and the only sign that the French fleet had been there were the topmasts of the *Surveillante* showing above the water close to Whiddy Island. The ship, being too damaged to sail back to France, had been scuttled.

Grahame took a look through Merriman's telescope. "Well, Captain, whatever the main force is or is not doing, our duty is clear. We must attack this force and take them prisoner. Maybe Moreau is among them, though I can't see him. Please tell your men that he must not be killed. He could give us much valuable information."

"Very good, sir. Mr St James, this is now a land engagement which is your sphere of expertise. You heard what Mr Grahame said about Moreau, what do you suggest?"

"If I may, sir, I would suggest that with the daylight going we cannot go further. The men and horses are exhausted and must rest and have some food. We could bivouac here and make a fresh start at daylight. I shouldn't think the French can go further either, sir."

"Yes, you are right, that is what we will do, Mr St James. But have your men stand sentry so that we are not surprised."

A heavy frost had fallen overnight and when the officers woke the men in the dark. many of them had ice on their clothing and were shivering violently. Fires had been lit and soon they were all having hot drinks and a chew of ship's biscuit. Merriman waited until it was possible to see and then started the men and the cannon moving again. Eventually, having climbed another mountain pass, they descended into a valley and, still following the tracks of the French, they came to a small, almost derelict village with only a few bedraggled and half-starved inhabitants.

Merriman halted the column and called the officers to him. "We can't go on like this, gentlemen. The French are probably travelling faster than we can with the cannon and shot. I suggest we send a scouting party ahead, no red coats, to see if they can find them. Send Jackson with them, he was a poacher and should be able to find them. We'll take a break here."

The men were back very quickly and Jackson doubled up to Merriman. "Found 'em, sir. Over the next rise you can see the sea again and they are heading for it. They're strugglin', sir, some can hardly walk and are bein' 'elped by others, sir."

"Good man. Right, gentlemen, everybody up and we must advance as fast as possible. Mr St James, your marines in advance."

"Sir, sir," a call came from an obviously agitated Lieutenant Andrews, "there are more French coming. There, sir, coming round that bump of land sticking out below us to the right."

He pointed to where Moreau's small force was moving lower down the hill to join the main party of French, obviously unaware of the English above them.

Moreau had arrived in view of his main party at about the same time as Merriman had his first sight of the French, but their relative positions hid them from one another.

Merriman pulled his small telescope from his pocket and tried to control his breathing. He was able, after a few moments, to keep the lens focussed on the men below and, as he did so, he drew in his breath sharply. Lieutenant Andrews, the marine officer, and Mr Grahame were behind Merriman eagerly waiting to hear the news.

He beckoned to Mr Grahame and as the man approached he handed him the telescope.

"I believe we have sighted our quarry, sir."

Grahame took the glass and moved himself into a position from which he could see. A grunt signified that he too had identified at least one of the men below, a man dressed in black, with a scarred face and with a long sword suspended from a plain leather baldric.

"You're right, James. Moreau himself, it can be no other. We must make certain of him this time," and he turned back to peer through the telescope again, watching the larger French party welcoming the new arrivals.

The marine officer had a look, thought for a moment and then said, "Well, sir, they know we aren't far behind them and there is no possible way that we can advance without them seeing us, sir. They know we are here and the sight of red coats will keep them worried, not knowing what we are going to do. We'll keep our main force out of sight for the time being. When everyone is rested and fed, we will determine our actions, with your approval of course, sir."

"Very good, Mr St James. Have your men keep watch on the French and keep us posted as to their actions, but let the French see them."

"Yes, sir. When we are ready, may I suggest that the marines advance in the centre with your people spread on either side. The men with muskets together on the right flank and the others to the left. The marines will fire volleys at intervals when near enough and if your musketeers could fire a volley when my men are reloading that would enable us to keep the enemy well occupied. We are outnumbered, sir, but as always it will be sword and bayonet at the last."

"Not so hasty, my friend. I'm sure that the men dragging that confounded cannon up here would be mightily disappointed if they didn't see it used."

"You're right, sir, I had almost forgotten. That cannon could give us the advantage."

"It must, so we'll wait here until the men have brought it to the top."

Chapter Twelve

Moreau slips away

"And I tell you, we can find a way out of this situation," shouted Moreau, "if we keep our wits and think clearly, instead of wringing our hands and bemoaning our misfortune."

"What more can we do, Monsieur," retorted Major Marmont. "Only half of my men are properly armed and equipped, the others were lucky to get ashore with their lives. We have no cannon and only a limited amount of powder and shot for the muskets, and now the English have followed us even here."

"I can't believe I'm hearing an officer of France proposing to surrender without a shot fired."

"I am no coward, Monsieur, if that is what you are insinuating, I'm a realist. We marched here hoping to find our ships had arrived, but instead what do we find? Nothing except one ship sunk and no sign of the fleet. Our own ships have been destroyed or taken by the English, our men are exhausted, and by now the alarm must have been raised."

"Truly I think you may be right," answered Moreau. "It seems hopeless, but maybe we..."

He broke off as a sergeant shouted the alarm, pointing to the hills above. The red coats of the marines could be seen advancing down the hill with English seamen in two groups with their officers in front of them.

"Merde! The damned English are advancing already. I was hoping we would have more time." Moreau looked swiftly about. A small nearby farm was the only place within reach which might be defended.

The men raced over the ground towards the buildings where the trained soldiers quickly took up positions behind the low wall surrounding the farmyard. They crouched, watching the English as they advanced slowly and then stopped beyond musket range. The marines formed up in two ranks with the two groups of seamen extending the ranks on either side. Moreau could see their officers in a separate group in front, obviously discussing their next move.

"What do you make of it, Mr St James?" asked Merriman.

"We are too weak to attempt a frontal assault, sir. There must be nearly four hundred of them behind the cover provided by those walls, but the cannon..."

"Yes, the cannon, but we'll keep the cannon a secret for the moment. Mr Andrews, what do you think?"

"Mr St James is right I think, sir, but they are perhaps not such a strong force as first appeared."

"How so, David?"

"Well, sir, when they ran to the farm I could see that less than half of them were carrying muskets and only a few men were carrying more than a small knapsack. Of course, the second lot seemed to be properly equipped."

"Hmmm! And what do you deduce from that?"

"The men with the muskets and knapsacks are the ones who have just arrived and probably some of the men landed early this morning from the last transport ship, and the rest are the survivors from the wrecked ships who would have been able to save only their own lives, sir."

Merriman studied the French position through his pocket telescope. The wall between the three small buildings enclosed a space only about forty yards by thirty, but was nowhere higher than four feet or so. The soldiers lined up behind it looked to be well disciplined and in full uniform with their bayonets fixed and a purposeful air about them. By comparison the bulk of the men were wearing no more than shirts and trousers and were a bedraggled lot.

"I believe you're right, David. They aren't as strong as their numbers indicate."

"Then we have them, sir. They can't get away from us."

"Maybe not, Mr Andrews, but remember, 'The man that once did sell the lion's skin while the beast lived, was killed in the hunting of him.'"

"That sounds like a quotation, sir."

"It is, from Henry the Fifth. Shakespeare."

Even as Merriman watched, he saw two scrawny cows being dragged out of one of the low roofed buildings and their pitiful bellowing travelled clearly to his ears as their throats were cut. The smoke from fires set up for cooking drifted towards the English.

"It appears, gentlemen, that we have a problem. I agree that any frontal attack would be very costly in lives as we are outnumbered. Any French soldier who falls can have his weapons taken by another and be replaced, whereas our numbers are limited. They have fresh meat and the stream passing in front of the farm gives them water."

It was true. A small stream, crossed by a rough bridge leading to what was evidently a gateway, flowed just in front of the wall. The French had managed to choose a strong defensive position.

Ideas and plans passed through his mind one after another, each to be as quickly discarded as impractical or hopeless. Merriman, as usual when faced with a problem, paced up and down tugging at his ear, his mind in a ferment and conscious that every man's eye was on him as the officers waited for him to come up with a plan.

A plan! He almost stamped in frustration. So much for the infallible Captain Merriman, he had no plan. This was where his reputation would be lost ... unless ... As another idea crossed his mind, he stopped pacing and looked up to where they had crossed the hills, his eye searching for obstacles. *It might work. If it could be done then...*

His thoughts were interrupted by marine Lieutenant Goodwin. "Sir, a horseman is coming this way."

Riding round the French position, well out of musket shot, a man on a mud-splattered black horse was urging his mount towards them waving madly the while. Unerringly picking out the group of officers, he pulled his blowing horse to a halt, slid down from the saddle and addressed Merriman, the obvious leader as marked out by his captain's uniform.

"White, sir, Richard White. I'm very glad to see you and your force, we had thought to be alone to face the French."

Merriman quickly assessed him. The man was obviously a gentleman and English.

"Captain Merriman, sir. My officers..."

After the civilities of introductions were done, Merriman asked, "May we know the reason for your haste?"

"The French fleet, Captain. They were here yesterday and anchored but nobody came ashore. Then the storm came and by this morning they had all gone except for a frigate and another ship that was sinking. I think they blew the bottom out of it and then the last ship left. Over there, sir, you can just see the top of her masts sticking out of the water. We have been expecting them to come back now that the storm has blown itself out. I have the militia assembled and when I saw the soldiers come over the hills, I thought they were back."

The words tumbled out in a torrent, but when the man had to pause to draw breath, Merriman quickly interrupted. "Militia, Mr White? Did I hear you say militia? Where are they and how many?"

"Yes, sir, local militia, about four hundred of them. Willing enough but not professional soldiers, I'm afraid. I called them together at the head of the bay when the French ships first appeared. We wanted to make the French think we were the vanguard of a larger force and were pleased with ourselves when we saw they had gone, but I don't suppose we really succeeded in frightening them off," he said despondently.

"And where are the militia now, sir?"

"Marching this way, as I said, expecting to confront these Frenchmen on our own. I rode ahead to assess their strength. You can imagine what a relief it was to see the red coats of your men coming down the hill."

"Indeed, sir, your arrival is most timely. My ship is in Kenmare River and we followed the survivors of four French ships we encountered yesterday. My party is as you see it, only about a hundred of us as I had to leave sufficient men behind to safeguard the ship. We are badly outnumbered by the French but your militia will address that problem when they arrive."

White's face fell. "So few, sir! I had hoped you were the vanguard of a larger force. Well, as I mentioned, my men are willing but most of them have never heard a shot fired in anger. They have been trained well enough in marching and drill and handling their muskets, but how they will stand against experienced troops, I can't tell."

"They may not need to, sir," said Merriman slowly as the plan, half formed in his mind before Mr White's arrival, took shape. "Gentlemen, I have an idea. Bluff and deception may be our best allies today. This is what I intend to do. Please be good enough to wait here, Mr White, while I go and speak with the French."

Moreau and the French officers, keenly watching the movements of the English, had been aware of the man galloping up on a lathered horse. They watched the huddle of men and then watched as a party of men started to climb back up the hill to the pass through which they had all come. After that, they saw two men approaching the farm.

The light was fading but Moreau could see that one was definitely an officer and the other was carrying a stick to which a white cloth had been attached. The English wanted to talk.

Merriman walked steadily towards the farm, Midshipman Dorrington one pace behind carrying the flag of truce. The rough gate was dragged aside and two of the French men emerged to walk slowly towards them. Merriman instantly recognised Moreau, the other was a French officer. All three men and the youth bowed to each other.

"Monsieur Moreau, I believe. Four years since our last encounter, is it not? I had not thought to meet you again, especially in such a dramatic setting," said Merriman.

He waved his arm to encompass their surroundings, the expanse of grey water flecked with white where the waves broke on the shore on the one hand and the gloomy green and brown hills frowning down on the other, with hardly a tree to be seen. The entire scene was illuminated by the weak sunlight struggling to shine through gaps in the scudding clouds.

"That is so, Captain. It appears that you and I are fated to meet in difficult times. May I compliment you on your seamanship, sir. However, you have the advantage of me. Regrettably I have not the honour of knowing to whom I am speaking."

"My apologies, sir, my name is James Merriman, captain of His Majesty's frigate *Lord Stevenage*. This is Mr Dorrington, Midshipman."

"A pleasure to make your acquaintance, gentlemen. This is Chef de Battaillon Henri Marmont, the rank you would call Major."

All bowed again, and both principals regarded one another in silence for a few moments before Merriman began.

"Monsieur Moreau, you must see the hopelessness of your position. I ask you to surrender so that there may be no unnecessary loss of life on either side."

"Surrender, sir? Hopeless position? You misjudge the situation entirely. You are in the weakest position. You have what, a hundred men? You see before you five hundred soldiers, well-armed and in a good defensive position. What can you do against us?"

He indicated with a gesture the line of grim, moustached faces watching from the farm, weapons held ready.

"That may be mostly true," said Merriman mildly. "But you do not number five hundred. You have three hundred and fifty or four hundred at the most and only a few of your men are armed. You are feasting on roast beef now, but two scrawny cows will not feed so many men for long and I think you have little else but water. Beside which, even if we fought and you won, where can you go? Your fleet came here but has now gone. The weather is fair and, if your ships were going to return, we would have seen some of them by now. No, monsieur, it seems you have been abandoned to your fate. There will be no invasion."

"They will be back. Frenchmen do not abandon their own."

"Then consider this. There is a force of militia marching here, expected within the hour. The alarm has been raised and men of the British Army also will be on the march. And cavalry will be here sooner than you think, monsieur."

"Militia? Poof!" sneered Moreau. "They will not stand up to soldiers of France. They will scatter just like that," and he snapped his fingers with a flourish to emphasise the point.

"Nevertheless, I repeat, Where will you go? Your ships may have escaped from Brest if the blockading fleet was scattered by the weather, but you may be certain that the British ships have followed them and will bring them to action. I repeat again, there can be no invasion of Ireland."

Of course Merriman did not know where the British ships were, but it must be as obvious to the French as it was to Merriman that there would be no help coming for this isolated detachment. Up to that point, the conversation had been conducted entirely in English but now an agitated Marmont broke into a torrent of French, addressing Moreau. Merriman had purposefully avoided letting the Frenchmen know that he spoke their language and he kept his face immobile whilst learning all he could.

Marmont was repeating all that Merriman had said and emphasising that they were abandoned, with nowhere to go. He also confirmed what Andrews had observed earlier, that half the French were unarmed. It was clear that Marmont was pleading with Moreau to surrender. Moreau silenced the man with an abrupt motion of his hand and turned back to face Merriman.

"We will consider what you have said, Captain. You will have our answer in the morning."

Merriman looked directly into Moreau's face, looking for any sign of treachery. "Very well, monsieur, until the morning."

The four separated to return to their own comrades. Merriman's mind was awhirl with ideas to amend his earlier plan. By the time he had returned to where his officers and Mr Grahame gathered about him, his mind was made up.

"Gentlemen, I believe that the French will fight. They are fully aware of their situation and Moreau, and it is indeed the French agent we have encountered before, said he would give me his answer to my surrender demand in the morning. However, I think they may well attack us before then. Remember, gentlemen, 'Bees that have honey in their mouths have a sting in their tails.'"

He looked around at his men, assessing their reactions before he went on, "In the early morning, shortly before dawn, is the most likely time. They will be expecting us to be unprepared, so we must be ready for them. They cannot go further inland so their only hope is to get past us and reach their ship. However, I have ideas for a few changes to my original plan. Listen carefully."

The men drew closer.

"Mr White, your militia must be made to look like a thousand. This is what I wish you to do."

As he explained what he wanted, their faces broke into broad smiles and Mr White was as enthusiastic as any of them.

"Captain, my militia won't let you down. It's an excellent plan and I know we can carry it off."

"Is all that clear, gentlemen? Are there any questions?"

He received none.

"No? Good. Mr White, I look to you to organise your people right away."

White mounted his horse and sped away while the sailors and marines made a show of preparing to spend the night in the open. Fires were lit and provisions distributed.

As darkness fell, Merriman remarked to the officers, "I see that Mr White and his militia are already carrying out their part of the plan."

Indeed, from their position on the hill they could see beyond the French position, to where the militia were lighting camp fires. As more militiamen arrived, the number of fires increased, spreading round in an arc beyond the farm. It was Merriman's hope to convince the French that a large force was encamped there, far more than the four hundred militiamen. As each group arrived they lit campfires and then slipped away to light more, with a few men left behind to move about and show themselves in the firelight. So far Mr White and his men were doing well. The French would see the fires but now that night had fallen they could not know how many men there were.

"Now, gentlemen, see to your men and remember, as little noise as possible. We don't want the enemy to become aware of what we are up to."

It was now completely dark with not even the odd twinkle of starlight to relieve the blackness. Merriman shivered and pulled his cloak closer about him. His mind wandered to his recently acquired book of Shakespeare's plays, and he muttered, "'Tis now the very witching hour of night, when churchyards yawn and hell itself breathes out contagion to this world.'"

"That quotation is from Hamlet, I believe, James," said a voice behind him.

Merriman jumped with surprise. "Mr Grahame, I didn't know you were there, was I speaking aloud?"

Grahame smiled and nodded.

"Why yes, the quotation is from Hamlet. You are familiar with Shakespeare's works?"

"Not all of them, but I have a passing knowledge of Hamlet, Henry Fifth, Macbeth and Julius Caesar. I didn't realise you were interested, James. Since when have you been reading Hamlet?"

"Only a short while, sir. I also have Henry the Fifth which I obtained the last time we were in Antigua. I bought them from an army officer, he strongly recommended them. And in my cabin aboard ship I found copies of Macbeth and the Merchant of Venice. The previous captain must have left them."

"You must find them interesting then."

"Yes, I do. I haven't had time to read them all yet and I'm trying to remember quotable lines from some of the more notable speeches, but it isn't easy."

"No, it isn't, but you're right there are some inspiring quotes from the plays. Perhaps I might borrow The Merchant of Venice from you when I have time to read it?"

"Of course, sir. My pleasure."

"Thank you. I will look forward to that pleasure, but now I'll go and try to get some sleep, although that won't be easy either with this cold and miserable dampness. Goodnight, James. Oh, by the way, have you remembered that it's Christmas Day tomorrow?"

"Haven't given it a thought for days, there's been with so much else to think about. I don't think I shall sleep too well either. Goodnight, sir."

Chapter Thirteen

Attacked in the dark

In the miserable conditions of the small, dirty, earth-floored farmhouse, Moreau and Major Marmont stared gloomily into the poor fire of peat which smouldered sullenly in the hearth and did little to warm them.

"The Englishman was right, Monsieur Moreau, where can we go? The longer we stay here the more force will be raised against us and, with barely half our men armed, we cannot resist for long."

For a while Moreau did not answer. His fertile mind was looking for a way out for himself, regardless of what happened to the rest of them.

"Whatever we do, Major, I must not be captured. The English already know I am an agent of the Assembly and I know too many secrets the English would dearly love to beat out of me. However I have an idea. If you will call in your lieutenants and the other officers, I will explain."

When the men were settled as best they could in the cramped conditions, Moreau looked round the dispirited, cold and shivering officers.

"As you all know, our situation is desperate. It seems unlikely that we can expect help from our own fleet simply because they do not even know we are here. Apart from the fact that our four ships arrived in the wrong place, they would assume that we are still somewhere at sea after we were separated in the fog."

One of the naval officers began to defend the events, but Moreau hastily added, "I apportion no blame for the wrong landfall. The weather was foul and we were fortunate to be able to anchor. The real misfortune began when we were seen by the English ships. Had they not done so we would all have anchored safely, a scouting party would have discovered the absence of our fleet, and we could have put to sea again when the gale abated. Then *La Sirene* was dismasted by the frigate and could not continue to fight."

He held up his hand as another of the officers tried to interrupt. "What has happened is past, messieurs, what we must do is plan what we are going to do from now. I will tell you what I suggest, you will listen and comment afterward."

Moreau spoke in clear terms, trying to convince his listeners that there was one good chance of success and only one. "We expect no help; to move deeper inland would be folly, merely putting us further into the arms of whatever force may even now be marching to oppose us. To stay here will only prolong the inevitable."

A storm of protest arose from the officers. Moreau sat silently until the clamour died down.

"No, messieurs, there is only one way we can go - back to sea. I know all the difficulties, but the inescapable fact remains that the English have the advantage and we are too few in number to continue with the original plan. If we are to see France again, we must try to reach *La Sirene*, which as you know, is but a few miles away with the crew making repairs. Do you not agree with me so far, Major?"

"Oui, monsieur, I must agree with you so far. But how can we manage to reach the ship? We are surrounded and outnumbered. And perhaps you have not considered that the English frigate may have attacked our ship since we left her," said Major Marmont.

Murmurings from the others showed that most of them agreed.

Moreau smiled with more confidence than he felt. "As to being outnumbered, I don't believe we are. The militia are only part time soldiers and won't stand, although they appear to have more men than we thought. Apart from them there is only one English ship and that would have a crew of no more than two hundred or so men. Add to that the marines we have seen, then I calculate a force of what? At most two hundred and fifty. Some will have been killed or injured already and there are no more than a hundred and twenty or so in front of us. How many will have been left behind to guard the ships and those of our men who have been captured?"

The men began to mutter between themselves as Moreau's words sparked their interest.

He continued. "I'll tell you. A hundred at most and probably a lot less. Not enough to adequately sail the ship and man the guns. And of course, *La Sirene* still has a full crew. Finally, we are more than three times the number in front of us. I do not count the militia."

A knock sounded on the door and a sergeant appeared.

"Yes, what is it, Sergeant, why the interruption?" asked Marmont testily.

"Thought you should know, sir, we have lost our water supply. The English must have dammed the stream or diverted it."

"Thank you, Sergeant," said Moreau dismissing him with a wave of his hand. "There you are, messieurs, that is another reason why we cannot stay here. We must make a move as soon as we are ready. Obviously the first thing we must do is to move out of here as fast as we can at the first glimmerings of daylight, or even before. The English will be expecting my reply to their demand for surrender and may not be prepared for an assault so soon. A surprise attack in the dark may give us the advantage over them. If we can get round the English and through the hills the way the Major and I and the marines came, then we would have an excellent chance of reaching the ship."

During Moreau's discourse the officers had brightened up considerably and they all started chattering at once, with ideas as to the best way to outwit the English and planning their route to the ship, as though their escape from the farm was a *fait accompli*.

Moreau watched them with ill-concealed contempt. He knew, and he was certain that Marmont knew, that the English would not be so easily defeated.

"Major, that is the only plan I have. If our soldiers who still have their muskets and bayonets make a surprise frontal attack while the unarmed men and marines move as quietly as possible round the enemy, most of us could get away. In the confusion and darkness many of the soldiers could also escape. The marines could then provide a disciplined rear-guard if the English rally quickly enough to follow. It could work and I leave the organising and execution of it to you and your officers."

"I think you have a good plan, m'sieur. As you say, it could work. I myself will lead the attack."

Speaking quietly so that only Marmont could hear, Moreau said, "I wish you success, Major. I regret that I cannot be with you. As you know, I cannot risk capture and must make my own arrangements."

He slipped out into the darkness which was relieved only by the flickering light of the campfires made from some poor sticks of furniture and the timbers of the byre lately inhabited by the unfortunate cattle. Most of the men were sitting or lying on the wet ground round the fires. Pacing round the farmyard wall, past the sentries spaced at intervals, he studied the positions of the enemy camp fires. Movement could be seen as vague figures passed in front of the fires, so it was certain that the English had their own sentries on watch. Moreau thought for a few moments, then, making up his mind, he approached a man asleep in a corner and roughly prodded him into wakefulness.

"Come, M'sieur O'Rourke, my friend. We have things to do."

Chapter Fourteen

Moreau and some Irish found

Merriman wakened with a start as a hand touched his shoulder. He hadn't really been asleep, had he? He remembered wrapping his boat cloak about him and sitting down for a few minutes to rest his back against a rock while he went over his plans for the umpteenth time. Damn it all, he must have gone to sleep. What would they all think of him? Then he smiled to himself in self-satisfaction, perhaps it had done his reputation as captain some good after all. He imagined the word spreading round the men. "Fast asleep he was, sleeping like a baby, had to be woken by his cox'n. If he can sleep like that I reckon we don't have much to worry about."

He became aware of the bos'n's mates rousing the men. One in particular making his presence heard in loud whispers. "Up, you lazy buggers, d'you want to sleep all day? Greene, you idle bastard, you'll feel a rope's end round yer arse if you don't move yerself smartish like."

He looked up at the bulk of his man Owen.

"Sorry to wake you, sir, but the French are moving. All's ready as you ordered and the men are in position, sir."

"Very good, Owen, thank you. Where are Mr Andrews and Mr St James?"

"Here, sir." Both men appeared as dark shapes in the dark.

St James reported. "Sir, we sent a couple of men out beyond our sentries and they just now came back and reported that the French are forming up outside the farm. One of them was Larkin, he can see in the dark like a cat, sir, so I'm sure he's right."

"I don't doubt it. So, they hope to take us unawares do they? We'll see what they make of our little subterfuge. Fall back to our places, gentlemen."

The first tentative paling of the eastern sky had appeared before they could hear the sound of the French troops advancing.

Grahame murmured in Merriman's ear, "'But look, the morn in russet mantle clad, walks o'er the dew of yon high eastern hill.' More Hamlet, Captain."

As the French advanced in typical formation, with bayonets fixed, Major Marmont allowed himself the luxury of hope. Still no sign of movement from the English and he could just see the forms of the sleeping men huddled in their blankets round the remains of their campfires. His voice rang out and the sole bugler sounded the charge. With a cheer the men rushed forward to plunge their bayonets into the sleeping men.

But what was this? The soldiers stopped, irresolute; there were no men beneath the blankets, only stones and brushwood. And then Marmont realised that they had been fooled as the unmistakeable shouts of command rang out in English.

"Marines, present, take aim." A brief pause, then, "Fire."

The crash of the volley rang out and men fell, either shrieking with pain or dead before they hit the ground.

"En avante," roared Marmont, "En avante, at them before they reload."

But even as the French rallied and began to move forward, another volley of musketry flailed at them from either side of the marines and more men fell. Undaunted, the French came on like the brave men they were, clambering over the bodies of the living and dead piled in front of them.

The light was improving and Marmont could now see the ranks of marines and seamen before him. "On, on," he shouted, waving his sword aloft. "They are breaking before us."

Indeed it seemed to be true, the marines in front were falling back, but too late Marmont recognised the trap the English had laid. Aghast he saw the cannon revealed and the last thing he ever saw was the flash from its mouth before he and at least thirty men round him were smashed by a hail of musket balls. Merriman had ordered the cannon double shotted with canister and the execution it wrought was terrible.

Before the French could recover, another blast of musketry tore into the men still standing. Flesh and blood could stand only so much and the French began to give ground. The men at the front, the real soldiers, did so reluctantly, facing the English lines with their bayonets at the ready, but the men at the rear turned and fled back to the farm and the illusion of safety it gave them, only to recoil in horror from the sight which awaited them.

The militia had advanced and occupied the farm and the wall was lined with muskets presented ready to fire. It was too much and the demoralised French flung up their arms in surrender.

Merriman was amazed that the French had not fired a shot and, reluctant to order more slaughter, he shouted to his force to hold their fire. The order was repeated out to the wings where the seamen were.

"By God, gentlemen, I believe we have them. Mr Dorrington, where is our white flag?"

"Here, sir," replied the midshipman. "My kerchief, sir. I lost the other one."

"No matter, this will do." Merriman raised the rag over his head, stepped forward and called out in French, "I would speak with Major Marmont or Monsieur Moreau."

"The Major has fallen, sir," replied a voice. "I am Lieutenant Gautier. Monsieur Moreau is not with us."

"Very well, Lieutenant, I ask that you surrender. Your position is untenable and as you see my men and the cannon are ready to fire again." He gestured to where the lieutenant could see Mr Salmon the gunner with a smouldering slow match held ready to plunge onto the touch-hole.

In the growing light, the lieutenant looked round at the remains of his little army and sighed.

"Will you assure me that my men will be treated according to the usages of war, sir?"

"I so assure you, Lieutenant. If you lay down all your arms you will be treated as honourable prisoners of war."

The Lieutenant took his sword in both hands and, in a theatrical gesture, snapped the blade across his knee and threw the pieces to the ground. He then gestured to his soldiers to relinquish the rest of their weapons which they began to do, slowly and reluctantly.

"Mr Andrews, have a working party of seamen collect those weapons and stack them securely well away from the French. Mr McBride, please attend to the French wounded if you will. Mr St James, keep your men alert for any treachery although I doubt we need to worry on that score, and have Lieutenant Gautier brought here to me. But there are more French than we have here. Where are they?"

"I think they slipped past us in the confusion and darkness, sir. There are two of our men dead over there and some odd bits and pieces the French must have dropped."

"Can you see which way they went?"

"Along the shore, sir, maybe they are hoping to regain their ship."

"Yes, that would be likely, there is nowhere else they can go."

Merriman turned to look at the cannon. "Mr Salmon, you will please me by staying by the gun until the French are completely disarmed."

"Aye – aye, sir," replied the grinning gunner.

"Congratulations, James," said a voice behind him. "Your plan succeeded brilliantly. Not a man of ours so much as scratched apart from those two unfortunates. But I don't understand why they didn't fire a shot."

Merriman turned to see that Mr Grahame had joined him.

"Because Major Marmont ordered the men not to load their muskets, sir," said the French lieutenant bitterly in surprisingly good English. "He thought to take you by surprise and he was afraid a clumsy soldier would discharge his piece and warn you we were coming."

"Lieutenant, can you tell me where Monsieur Moreau and the rest of your men are?" asked Grahame

"No, sir, I cannot. He disappeared during the night together with his tame Irishman. As for my countrymen," he gestured vaguely around. "They have gone."

"Damn and blast the man," cried Grahame. "I thought we had him. He's as slippery as an eel, but he can't have gone far. We must find him, James, before he goes to ground somewhere with his rebel friends."

"Well, sir, we must have horses if we are to catch him. Mr St James, you will oblige me by keeping a watch to our rear for the missing French. Now, Mr Grahame, perhaps Mr White can help in the matter of horses. Here he is now."

Mr White arrived, smiling all over his face. He flung himself off his horse, seized Merriman's hand and shook it vigorously.

"Congratulations, Captain, a wonderful outcome to your plan. You have won a famous victory and my militia were part of it. There will be some tall tales flying about soon, telling of this day's work, I'll warrant. You and your officers must join me at my house for some refreshment when the prisoners are secure."

"Gladly, Mr White, but there is a more urgent matter to be resolved before we can avail ourselves of your hospitality."

Merriman proceeded to tell him about Moreau and how important it was that he should be apprehended.

"What can I do to help, do you know where he might go?"

Grahame answered him, "He will try to find refuge with Irish rebels somewhere, possibly in Kenmare or Killarney or even Killorglin. We know that there are underground, rebellious groups in most of the towns and villages in Ireland. Any of them would hide him in an isolated farm somewhere until he can be smuggled out to France."

"Very possible," said Mr White.

Merriman cut in, "We need horses, sir, to be able to send out search parties in various directions. We have three, captured from the French, but they are used to pull the artillery and are not good saddle horses, even if we had saddles for them. Could you and your militia friends supply some?"

"Of course, I have ten or more in my stables and there are plenty more at the houses of my friends," said White eagerly. Then his face fell. "But it will take time to gather them, Captain. The nearest are those of mine at the house you see yonder at the end of the bay. We can send one of your men on this horse with instructions to my stable hands to saddle them and bring them here for you, if that is what you want."

"Thank you, sir, please do so at once and then perhaps one of your people could ride out to see if he can find an army patrol."

Merriman called Captain St James to him. "Edward, I think it would be easier to watch the prisoners if they were put back in the farmyard where the wounded will have some shelter. Lieutenant Goodwin can see to all that."

After sending a man away for the horses, Richard White had returned to the group.

"Mr White, I trust we can leave your militia to guard the prisoners until the army arrives? Good, I must send most of my force back to the ship. If the French who escaped get back to their ship, my own will be in danger."

"Yes, of course," replied White. "I quite understand, and if those French return I believe my militia are confident enough now to cope with them."

"Well, I'll leave Lieutenant Goodwin with half a dozen marines with you and I'll also leave that cannon with you as a souvenir of this occasion, Mr White. Something more for your men to boast about."

Mr White smiled.

"Mr St James, when the horses arrive I'd like you to ride with me after Moreau, and we must find some of our men who can ride to go with us."

"I can ride, sir," called out Midshipman Dorrington, "and I can shoot."

"Very well, Mr Dorrington, if we have sufficient horses you may come."

Owen was the next to put himself forward. "I can stay aboard a horse, sir. I'd keep up."

"Be glad to have you, Owen. With you, and with you, Mr Grahame, that makes five of us. We need more."

"You'll need a guide, sir. I know all the roads and byways, I must go with you," said Mr White.

"Thank you, sir, your help will be invaluable."

In the end two marines were found who could ride and the party was made up to ten with Jackson, a seaman who had once been a poacher before choosing the navy in preference to a spell in prison, and one other seaman by the name of Brown.

The officers fell to discussing the most likely route taken by Moreau and his companion.

"As I said before, I believe he would head for the nearest town where he might find rebels to help him. That would almost certainly be to the north and west," said Grahame. He turned to Mr White, "What do you suggest, sir?"

"Well, the nearest place is Kenmare, though it's not much more than a large village. Depending on how much start they have they might be nearly there by now."

"There is something else to consider, gentlemen," said Merriman quietly, tugging at his ear in concentration. "We understand one of them is an Irishman. He is likely to know the best and fastest way to go to find help. Besides, Moreau is very cunning and would probably not go to Kenmare, thinking that we might expect him to go there, being the nearest place."

The others nodded in agreement and Grahame, pale with fury at the prospect of losing his quarry, almost shouted, "We must start somewhere and make an effort to catch them!"

Merriman continued as if there had been no interruption. "Moreau would not want to be afoot longer than necessary. I think it more probable that they would be looking for a house or farm not too far away where they might steal horses. With most of the local men gathered to form the militia, who could stop them?"

"James, you are likely right," replied Grahame. "Mr White, where do you suggest?"

White raised a small telescope to his eye.

"Well thank God, not my place, Bantry House, although that is nearest. I can see across the bay to where my man is leaving there with our horses. Apart from that the nearest are Dunmore House or Crusheen House."

"Then let us head for there as soon as the horses get here, gentlemen," said Merriman. "In the meanwhile, I suggest we all snatch a bite to eat and check our weapons."

He called Lieutenant Andrews over. "David, I want you to take our seamen and marines back to the ship as quickly as you can. My compliments to Mr Laing and he is to endeavour to seize or destroy the enemy corvette. Mr McBride, you can stay here with the wounded until I return. I must go with Mr Grahame to try and apprehend this elusive Frenchman although I'll be back as soon as I can. This cannon and the captured weapons can be left for the militia."

"Aye - aye, sir." Andrews began issuing orders to the men, who very quickly prepared themselves for the arduous journey back to the ship, but a journey made easier without the burden of the cannon and shot.

It was not an easy decision for Merriman to make. He was under Mr Grahame's orders but still totally responsible for his ship. To leave his ship behind whilst he chased a spy round the Irish countryside would not be looked on with favour by his superiors at the Admiralty, especially if that ship were to be lost when he was not aboard.

The groom eventually arrived with ten horses. Sensibly the man had not galloped them and, although it took longer, trotting meant that they were still fresh.

The party mounted and set off with Mr White in the lead and the seamen and marines last. Merriman was pleased to see that all appeared to be fairly competent riders although Owen's style left a lot to be desired. Nevertheless, he hung onto his horse with grim determination and managed to keep up.

The ground was sodden from all the rain and the horses hooves sank deep into the mud and turf, making it hard going and slowing them down.

There was nobody at the first house the party stopped at, but at Dunmore House they found the lady of the house, an overweight, middle aged person with a large wart on her chin and the thin sprouting of a moustache, with two flustered female servants gathered round a man lying on the ground near the stables. Mr White dismounted and approached them.

"Richard White, ma'am, from Bantry. We are after two felons who may be after stealing horses."

"They must have been here, sir. My stableman has been attacked and the carriage horses are gone. It must have been some hours ago."

"Did anyone see which way they went, ma'am?" asked Merriman.

"No, sir. Patrick here may have done, but as you see the poor man has not yet regained his senses."

"Sir, sir!" An excited shout from Jackson caused them all to turn to face him.

"Sir, two 'orses went this way, you can see fresh tracks in the mud 'ere. They're headed towards the hills yonder." He kicked his horse in the ribs and led off to show the way.

"Good man, well spotted," cried Grahame and they splashed off after him. St James paused briefly to raise his hat to the lady. "Good day, ma'am. Captain St James at your service. I hope your man will recover and that we can catch and return your horses."

The lady smiled up at the handsome marine. "Thank you, sir. I am Mrs Charnock. I hope we may meet again." St James kicked his horse and chased off after the others.

Two hours later and the light was fading as fast as were their hopes of catching the fugitives. The rain had started again, not the heavy rain that had fallen for the past days but a fine drizzle which veiled their view and soaked into their clothing. None of them had oilskins or cloaks with them and soon they were chilled and half frozen.

The horses were almost finished, and the pursuers had strung out into a long line with the better riders to the fore and the others, the two marines, and Owen far to the rear, his huge frame being too much for his poor horse which was near to foundering. Jackson, who had proved to be a surprisingly good rider, was still well ahead of the rest of them and had disappeared into the gloom.

"It's no good, sir!" shouted Merriman to Mr Grahame. "We must rest the horses or we shall be on foot before we have gone much further."

"Damn and blast it, Captain. The man's getting away as we dawdle here."

"He can't go far, sir. In these conditions, his horses must be in no better condition than ours."

Slowly the group closed up again, Owen the last to arrive, and they set off again leading their horses. Scarcely twenty minutes had passed before a figure materialised out of the darkness.

"Stop there and identify yourself," shouted St James.

"Jackson, sir. I've found them."

Chapter Fifteen

Moreau plans anew

Charles Henri Moreau looked about him at the filthy hut and the three scruffy men who had arrived to share it with him and O'Rourke, the disgust he felt plainly written on his face. His thoughts were chaotic. *To think that I, who once lived in luxury as the son of an aristocratic family, should be reduced to this: a fugitive being chased around this God forsaken country and sharing this appalling food with peasants.*

He turned to O'Rourke, the man who had crept away with him in the middle of the night hours before the desperate sally from the farm by the French soldiers. "M'sieur O'Rourke, have any of these fellows seen anything of our pursuers since darkness fell?"

"No, and I don't believe they will. The last time we saw the English from the last hill we crossed they were far behind, and don't forget we changed direction in the dark."

"That is so, but they will not give up easily and the outcome of a fight must be in doubt even though we are nearly equal in number."

"That also is true. These are good stout lads but how well they'll fight I don't know." O'Rourke paused. "You know, M'sieur Moreau, neither of us will survive capture. I'm too well known to the English and all I can expect is a rope round my neck if I'm caught, and as for you, you are a Frenchman and a spy, what better fate awaits you?"

Moreau roused himself from the despair he felt at his companion's words. It was true, he would be lucky not to face a firing party. Briefly he considered the situation. If they could slip away from their pursuers, then maybe O'Rourke could find a boat to take them to France. And then what? It was not his fault that the French fleet had not carried out the planned invasion, but the Directory in France would want to find a scapegoat. Even though he had only been involved in organising the Irish rebels, Moreau had the uneasy feeling that the scapegoat might be him especially as he had been in disfavour in some quarters since his failure in the affair with the Viceroy four years earlier.

No, he dare not risk a fight and possible capture, nor did he dare return to France without some kind of success to speak for him. What then could he do?

In the poor light afforded by the rush candle, he stared at the men in the hovel with him. Even O'Rourke had fallen asleep with the rest of them and there was nothing but their snores to keep him company. In spite of his tiredness, Moreau could not sleep and his thoughts overwhelmed him again. What alternative was there for him instead of returning to France? Vague and useless ideas drifted through his head, only to be instantly rejected as ridiculous. He had almost fallen asleep when a new thought came to him with such forcefulness that he was instantly wide awake.

But there was an alternative, wasn't there? But no, it was unthinkable, not to be considered for a moment, totally out of the question ... wasn't it? He knew that there were many French aristocrats living in England and hoping for a restoration of the monarchy. He was an aristocrat and by blood he was closer to them than to the France of the revolution. Perhaps he could contrive to join them? What he knew would surely be of value to anyone hoping to overthrow the revolutionary government. Doubtless there were many who would say he was a traitor, but surely he was more a traitor to his own kind by working for that government. No, it seemed that his only reasonable hope of life would be to leave his present companions and strike out on his own. By giving his parole to the English officer he might save his life.

His mind working feverishly on the problem, he felt the need to escape the foulness of the air in the small room and breathe fresh air to clear his brain. Carefully stepping over the sprawled bodies, he lifted the piece of greasy cowhide that formed the only door and quietly eased himself outside into the darkness of the night. Deep in thought, his steps led him without conscious volition to the two horses tied in the meagre shelter of a rough lean-to in the company of two scrawny donkeys. A man fond of horses, he was absentmindedly stroking the muzzle of one of them when the animals raised their heads sharply and pricked their ears. Moreau immediately melted into the deeper shadow between them and stood silently listening.

"I found them, sir," repeated Jackson as the others gathered round. "It was my 'orse that told me. He started pulling to the side. They'd changed direction an' he must've smelled them an' tried to follow. I let 'im go, sir, and after a while I saw a light. Only a quick flash it were but I left the 'orse and went on foot and found one of them rough buildings that pass for 'ouses. There was voices inside and some 'orses tied in a sort of lean-to, sir."

"Good, anything else?"

"Yessir, I think there are more men there than the two we was following, and there's another two smaller 'ouses not far away with people inside. I didn't go too close, sir. Thought I should report what I found."

"You've done well, Jackson; I don't know how you can see anything it's so dark. Gentlemen, we must decide what we must do next."

"Well, if they are inside the buildings, sir, we have them trapped," said Captain St James. "We can surround the huts and order them out one at a time."

"And if they won't surrender?" asked Grahame.

"Burn them out, sir. The roofs are thatched, I presume, Jackson?"

"They are, sir, an' the doorway's only narrow, so they can't rush us, sir."

Merriman was tugging at his ear as he listened. "Jackson, did you see anyone posted as a guard, or any dogs."

"No, sir, but I didn't go right round the huts."

"Right then. There are three huts and only ten of us, so I think we should proceed with caution as we do not know how many we face. How are the huts placed with regard to each other, can we see all three doorways at once?"

"Two of 'em, sir. The other, the one with the 'orses by it, is apart from the others and faces the other way."

"Very well, this is what I propose, gentlemen. We must assume that Moreau and the Irishman who escaped with him are in the hut with the horses outside. They would not want to be too far from them in case they needed them in a hurry. That is the one we must concentrate on. The other huts may contain rebels or they may not. I consider it more likely that there are just ordinary country people inside who will offer no opposition. Nevertheless we cannot ignore them."

He looked around to check the men were in agreement.

"Jackson will lead us to a point where we can leave the horses. Then we must investigate further to see if there are any guards posted that he did not see. Jackson, you go round behind the two smaller huts and I will look round the bigger one."

"Can I go with you, sir?" asked Dorrington. "I can move quietly."

"Very well, Mr Dorrington."

"Me too, sir, what about me, sir?" asked Owen. "I must stay with you."

"Not this time, Owen, You are too big to move quietly. You must stay with the others until we get back. Then we can devise a plan to capture the men we want. Right, Jackson, Mr Dorrington, are you ready? Good, then let us proceed, quietly, on your lives."

The two men and the youth disappeared into the darkness, leaving Owen cursing softly to himself. In all the years since being made his captain's bos'n, he had always been close to him to guard his back. Owen looked round at the others. As far as he could see in the darkness, nobody was looking in his direction. He slipped quietly away in the direction taken by Merriman.

Moreau, still in hiding in the stable, saw two shadowy figures move cautiously round the side of the house. All of a sudden, the smaller of the two stuck a violent blow to the back of the head of the leading figure who collapsed. Before Moreau could move, a third, larger figure lunged from the darkness and charged at the smaller man who raised a pistol and shot him. Dorrington, for it was he who had struck Merriman on the head, stood dazed for a few moments, looking down at Owen's body, long enough for Moreau to slip behind him and fell him with a blow to the back of the neck.

The shot had woken the men in the hut who came piling out of the doorway with weapons raised. Moreau quickly told what had happened and ordered a lantern to be brought. He immediately recognised the unconscious bodies of Merriman and Dorrington. Seeing the hated uniforms, some of the Irishmen wanted to kill the prisoners at once. Moreau argued against doing so. His decision managed to save Merriman coming to further harm but he could not stop them kicking and beating Dorrington rather badly. Finally he prevailed upon them to tie the prisoners up. Owen was left for dead.

"M'sieur O'Rourke, we must leave here at once. The rest of our pursuers cannot be far away. We will take these two with us, they may be bargaining counters to buy our freedom at a later time."

The Irishman grinned evilly. "We can kill them later then, painfully I hope."

The two unconscious bodies were thrown over the backs of the two donkeys and, with Moreau and O'Rourke riding the horses and the remaining Irishmen trotting behind, the party disappeared into the darkness.

Jackson moved carefully down to the house. He had not seen Dorrington shoot Owen, but had heard the shot and managed to work his way close enough to recognise Owen's body in the light of the lantern. He watched helplessly as the prisoners were taken away. Feeling his way, Jackson found Owen lying where he had been shot. He was relieved to find that the man was still breathing but his questing fingers soon discovered that Owen was bleeding from a head wound and could not respond to a vigorous shaking.

Jackson squatted beside Owen, trying to gather his thoughts together. Obviously things had gone wrong. Should he go and fetch help for the badly wounded man or should he follow the Captain and see where he was taken? Maybe he could then go back to report to Mr Grahame or Mr St James. Making his decision, he patted Owen sadly on the shoulder and left him, not expecting to see him alive again.

Moreau and his party could only move slowly in the darkness and it was not long before Jackson, who had eyes like a cat, caught up with them. Staying well back, he followed them for no more than a mile before they arrived at a farmhouse. Creeping closer he was able to see a little of the interior through a dirty window and he watched Merriman and Dorrington carried into a side room, with the door locked. It seemed evident that Moreau and the others were settling down for the rest of the night, so he withdrew slowly and then set off at a run to find his comrades.

Chapter Sixteen

Merriman's party attack

Consciousness was black, a blackness that bore down on Merriman like a smothering blanket. It was so black that his eyes ached with the strain of trying to see and his head throbbed with pain. There was no sound. He discovered that he couldn't move, he was tied hand and foot and half frozen. As his confused mind struggled to comprehend his situation, his over-riding emotion was fear that he was blind. He rolled his head to one side and immediately a ray of light struck his left eye like a needle. Tentatively opening his eyes again he realised that the blinding light was in reality a glimmer through a keyhole. He stared at it with the desperation of a drowning man clutching at a floating plank of wood. It indicated a place of warmth, of people, of …? Something passed in front of the light. His brain instantly assessed that it was between himself and the keyhole, but there was no sound. Oh God! What was in there with him?

In spite of the cold, Merriman found himself sweating freely but he couldn't move a finger to help himself. Something touched his shoulder and he almost screamed aloud. His fears were instantly soothed as a voice whispered, "Captain, sir, are you awake?"

Jackson, it was Jackson, thank God. He felt the cold steel of a knife against his wrists as Jackson cut the rope there and then cut the rope round his ankles but he had been tied so tightly that his limbs refused to answer the commands his brain sent out.

"Jackson, where are we? Where are the others? How did you find me?"

"Sir, please be quiet. We're in a small room in a farmhouse, and that Frenchman and 'is men are asleep on the other side of that door," whispered Jackson. "I got in through the roof, sir, it's only rotten thatch. I saw them bring you in here."

"What happened to Mr Dorrington, he was with me?" asked Merriman as he tried to rub some life into his hands.

"He's here, sir, but he's still unconscious. He's been badly beaten and they shot Owen, sir. He was still alive when I found him but I don't know if he'll live. I had to leave him, I thought it my duty to follow you and then report back to Mr St James."

Merriman's mind was working feverishly to absorb what Jackson was saying, but he knew that unless they could escape there would be no mercy shown to any of them if Jackson was found to have cut them free.

"Have you reported to Mr St James? Where are they?" whispered Merriman.

"Mr St James and the others are outside waiting for me to signal that I've found you, sir."

"Good, is there a plan?"

"Yessir, Mr St James asked me and Brown to move their 'orses from the stable to stop them escaping and we managed to do that without the alarm being raised. We knew that if we attacked they'd probably kill you before we could reach you, so Mr St James suggested that I should try to get in here and release you first. We didn't know if you or Mr Dorrington would be able to help so I've got four loaded pistols 'ere, sir, all wrapped up in Mr Grahame's coat, and I've got my cutlass, so if they tried to come in after you when we attack I could hold 'em off."

"You've been busy, Jackson, by God, well done. However, I don't think I am in a fit state to climb out of here without making a noise and anyway we cannot leave Mr Dorrington behind."

"No, sir. Can you hold these two pistols, sir? If you are ready, I'll signal that they can start the attack."

"Right then, I'm up to firing a pistol if I can see a target, so let's get on with it."

The seaman tied a piece of white rag to the end of a stick and thrust it up through the hole he had made to gain entry through the thatch. "Part of Mr St James' shirt, sir. It's dark out there but they'll see this alright," he whispered.

The two men stood side by side, waiting with their pistols cocked for whatever might happen next.

There was silence for a few moments and then there came a thunderous knocking on the door of the house and a voice shouting, "Open up in the name of the King. Come out without weapons and surrender at once or we shall put a torch to the roof."

It seemed that all hell broke loose as Moreau and the rest were so rudely awoken. Men shouted at each other, picked up their weapons and looked wildly round for an escape route. One of the Irishmen pulled the rough leather covering off one of the windows and tried to climb out but a musket shot rang out and he fell back choking on the blood filling his throat. A final struggle and he was dead. As his friends looked on in horror, Moreau was the first to act.

"O'Rourke, have the prisoners dragged in here, we can bargain our way out with them."

The door to Merriman's prison slammed open and two men burst in. Two pistols exploded as one and both Irishmen were thrown back by the impact of the shot and were dead before slumping to the floor.

Merriman and Jackson, with their second pistols ready, peered cautiously round the doorframe. There were only two men left standing, Moreau and O'Rourke.

"It's over, m'sieur. Your men are dead and the house is surrounded. Surrender before there is any more killing," shouted Merriman. "We have your horses so there is no escape."

"I cannot do that, Captain," Moreau smiled sadly. "My life is forfeit anyway." He turned to O'Rourke, "What do you say, M'sieur O'Rourke?"

"Surrender, to the damned bloody English? Never, I'll die first." He ran to the front door, flung it open and dashed out. Almost immediately musket balls slammed into his body. A man of immense animal strength, he staggered back inside, bleeding profusely from his wounds, drew himself up and shouted, "God save all Ireland," before crashing to the floor, dead.

"Mr St James," bellowed Merriman, every syllable causing his head to throb painfully. "Don't shoot. There's only Moreau left now, you can come in."

The red coat of the marine officer appeared in the doorway. St James' first thought was for his captain, "Are you alright, sir?"

"Apart from a bad headache I am well enough, Mr St James. As you see, we have M'sieur Moreau here."

Moreau had retreated to a corner, the long sword held before him glittering in the lantern light. "You'll have to take me, if you think you can."

Sword in hand St James moved further into the building, his two marines with fixed bayonets following him. Then Mr White appeared behind him with Mr Grahame peering over his shoulder.

"I believe I can manage that," said the marine, advancing on Moreau. "I've learned a bit since we last crossed swords."

There was a brief and rapid clash of blades and Moreau clutched his arm and stepped back.

"My compliments, s'sieur, you *have* improved since our last meeting." Moreau remembered his thoughts earlier that night. He was caught and there was no other course open to him unless he was prepared to die there and then. He looked across at Merriman. "Captain Merriman, will you accept my parole if I surrender to you?"

"Indeed I shall be happy to, sir."

Moreau bowed and handed his sword, hilt first, to Merriman.

"I look to you, sir, as an officer, to safeguard my interests as a prisoner of war. I have much information which may be of use to you but please understand that I will do nothing against my country, only those who presently govern it."

Merriman accepted the weapon. "This is a fine sword, sir. Should we be fortunate enough to survive this war, I shall return it to you."

"Thank you, Captain, it was my father's and I should not like to lose it."

"Captain Merriman, I must protest." The angry voice was Mr Grahame's. "This man is a spy and is involved with these damned Irish rebels. He is a prisoner and deserves to face a noose."

143

"I am aware of that, sir, but he has surrendered to me and given his parole, which I have accepted. That makes him my responsibility. In all honour I cannot surrender him to you."

"Damn it, Captain, you know what he's done. He was involved in that devilish plot to seize the Viceroy of Ireland four years ago, not to mention other things we know little of. I insist, I must be allowed to question him." The normally calm and unflappable Grahame was beside himself with rage. "I don't know what Lord Stevenage will have to say about this when I report this to him. He won't be pleased I can tell you. You'll find yourself without a command I expect. This man is an enemy of our country, Mr Merriman, and you are allying yourself with him."

"Sir, Lord Stevenage is a gentleman as I know you are. When you have time to think about this and discuss it in a calm and reasonable manner, I am sure that you will see that I have taken the best course. This man would have fought to the death if I had not accepted his parole. A live Moreau is of more use to us than a corpse and a corpse he most certainly would be. Am I not right, m'sieur?"

"Yes, Captain, you are. I would have fought," replied Moreau sadly.

Merriman staggered over to a rough chair, sat down and gingerly felt the back of his head. There was a matt of congealed blood and hair and as he touched it he tried to remember what had happened before he received the blow to his head. Dorrington had been following him behind the farmhouse, surely Dorrington hadn't hit him? No, he wouldn't dare, it couldn't be. No, Dorrington himself had been struck down. They must have been seen approaching the farmhouse and an ambush prepared.

Whilst Merriman was thus busy with his thoughts, activity continued round him. The dead bodies were moved outside and in a corner Grahame was in earnest conversation with Moreau. One of the marines with fixed bayonet stood guard over the prisoner.

Jackson re-appeared with a wet rag which, with Merriman's permission, he gently wiped some of the blood off his head and neck.

"Ah-h-h, that's better. Thank you."

"Sir, if you'll allow I've got the piece of Mr St James shirt I used for the signal. It'll make a bandage, sir."

"Very good, carry on, Jackson. Mr St James, where are you?"

The marine officer presented himself. "Here, sir, I was just checking our situation. Apart from yourself and Mr Dorrington, none of our party has been hurt. We have two horses apart from our own, I mean Mr White's horses, sir, which one of the men has gone to collect, and we've found a rough cart or tumbrel that we can carry Mr Dorrington and yourself in."

Merriman noticed that Moreau winced at mention of the word tumbrel. "A word with unhappy memories for you perhaps, m'sieur?"

"Yes, all my family went to the guillotine in those accursed carts. I cannot forget that."

Merriman raised an eyebrow and turned back to the marine officer, replying, "Nonsense, man, I'm able to ride, but we must see if Owen is still alive and pick him up and take him to the doctor. I see that dawn is near so we should start as soon as all is ready. What about the people in the other houses?"

"Only old people, sir, and little ones. They made no trouble."

Chapter Seventeen

Return to Bantry

In the early gloom of that same morning, His Majesty's ship *Lord Stevenage* slowly stole from her anchorage under single topsails and jib and, with Lieutenant Laing in command, crept quietly along the coast to where *La Sirene* was lying.

The previous afternoon, before dark, Lieutenant Andrews had returned to the ship with the seamen and most of the marines, and reported the details of the encounter with the French to an anxious Laing.

"Dammit! I wish I'd been there," he exclaimed. "You've had all the fun whilst we have just been guarding prisoners."

"Yes, sir, but the Captain sends his compliments and you are now required to attack, destroy or capture the French ship *La Sirene*."

"Am I, by God? That suits me well enough. Now that the gale has passed, we may slip down to where she lies and take them by surprise. I think the best time will be just as dawn is breaking."

"Yes, sir, but you should know that some of the French seamen and marines escaped and even now must be trying to reach their ship."

"Did they? Then we must assume that they have managed to do so, although I can't see that it will alter things."

Laing, a careful and deep thinking officer, took a few moments to marshal his thoughts. "Right, David, this is what we will do. Just before first light we will up anchor and proceed under light canvas down to where the Frenchies are and I hope we shall take them by surprise. Since you all left yesterday, I've kept all the guns loaded against the possibility that the French may attempt something against us, so I'll have all the charges drawn and the guns reloaded with fresh powder."

"Aye – aye, sir."

"I think that it would be wise to send one of our boats to try to creep close enough to see what the Frenchies are doing. It might tell us what to expect. Mr Weston has had an easy day aboard the transport vessel, so he can do it. Meanwhile we will prepare for all possibilities. See to it if you please, Mr Andrews," Laing said, reverting back to the more formal wording.

As *Lord Stevenage* crept through the water, there was no sound except the pleasant chuckle of the slight bow wave and the various creaks and groans of the timbers as the ship eased herself over the gentle swells. All the men were alert and armed and Lieutenant Laing had ordered a tot of rum for each of them before the ship moved from her anchorage to approach *La Sirene*.

Ashore, all was quickly arranged. In the cold light of the approaching dawn, Dorrington, still unconscious, was gently laid in the cart, and a horse deftly harnessed to it by Brown, the seaman who had collected the horses.

"That man seems to know his way round horses," commented Merriman to Mr White, watching him.

"I imagine that he was once an ostler or carter or some such, sir, but I agree, he is very capable with the animals."

Merriman was all impatience to know what had happened to his man Owen so he despatched Jackson and a marine ahead of the slowly moving, lumbering cart. When the two men arrived at the cottage where Merriman and Doddington had been attacked, they found the place deserted except for an old woman and Owen. It appeared that the old woman had been trying to tend him as he had been covered with a threadbare blanket and a none too clean rag wrapped round his head, but he still lay where he had fallen and he made no response when Jackson shook his arm.

When the cart and the rest of the party arrived, Jackson was able to report that Owen was still alive and breathing, albeit faintly. "'e's in a bad way, sir. This old woman has tried to 'elp him though she couldn't move 'im by herself."

The arrival of the party of armed men had obviously frightened the woman who tried to creep away, but Jackson held on to her.

Merriman stared at the woman. Dirty and ragged though she was, half-starved and living on the poverty line, she had tried to help and for that he was grateful.

He smiled at her. "I thank you for what you have done for my man," he said, but she shook her head and muttered something unintelligible in reply.

"People round here don't speak English," remarked Mr White. "They have some heathen, outlandish tongue of their own, I can't make head nor tail of it."

"Perhaps if we made a better attempt to understand them we might avoid some of the trouble we have with them," Merriman retorted with some asperity. "Here, you, Brown, give the poor creature some of the food we brought from the other house," he ordered. "We can do no more for her than that."

Owen was laid in the cart next to Dorrington and then, leaving the place, the party slowly began to retrace their steps of the previous day. Merriman led, accompanied by St James and Mr White. Moreau rode behind with Mr Grahame beside him and behind them the two marines rode knee to knee keeping a wary eye on the Frenchman as if expecting him to bolt at the first opportunity. At the tail of the group came the cart driven by Brown, bearing the two injured men with Jackson riding alongside watching over them.

It was late in the afternoon when they reached the house from which Moreau and O'Rourke had stolen the horses. To the profuse thanks of Mrs Charnock they were able to promise the return of her animals after the party had reached Mr White's house.

"What happened to the men who stole them?" she asked with a shy glance at the marine officer.

With a smile St John answered, "Why, ma'am, we caught them. One is our prisoner and the other is dead."

She clapped her hands together. "Will you brave gentlemen not stay for some refreshment?"

Merriman interrupted, "I'm sorry, ma'am, regretfully we must decline. I thank you for your offer but we have two badly wounded men in the cart and must get them to my ship's doctor at Bantry as fast as we can."

"I'm disappointed, sir. Cannot one or two of you stay for a while? It gets lonely here while my husband is away and I lack company. What about you, sir, will you not stay?" She smiled coquettishly at St James.

For his part, the marine turned his shocked face to Merriman. The "get me out of this" appeal in his eyes was unmistakeable.

Merriman grinned at the appalled St James, deliberately delaying his reply. Finally he said, "I must apologise again, ma'am. I'm sure he wishes to stay but I cannot permit it, he is needed aboard my ship."

St James breathed out a huge sigh of relief as they rode away. "For a moment, sir, I thought you were going to deliver me into the hands of the lady and order me stay."

"Believe me, Edward, the thought crossed my mind," replied Merriman with another grin. "But I decided it would be unfair to do that to you. You've had a lucky escape."

Night had fallen by the time they arrived at Mr White's residence, Bantry House. They found that the French prisoners had been forced to carry the French wounded to the stables there where McBride, the ship's doctor, was tending them. All the unwounded and walking wounded prisoners were safely under lock and key in Mr White's spacious coach house, guarded by men of the militia.

The two wounded men were carried indoors from the cart and placed in a downstairs room. Mr White was all hospitality, food was provided for the hungry and exhausted men and all of them found somewhere to sleep. The doctor reported to Merriman that both Owen and Dorrington were still insensible, but he had dressed their wounds and expected that with time they would both recover. With that, Merriman finally allowed McBride to examine his own wound and re-bandage it. That done, he wearily climbed the stairs to the room given to Moreau, Grahame and himself, and collapsed across the bed. He was asleep instantly.

Chapter Eighteen

Arrival of the English Cavalry

Merriman awoke, sleepily staring at the unfamiliar fabric of the half tester over the bed and wondering where he was.

"Sir, sir." Jackson was trying to rouse him. "Sir, can you come? Owen's conscious now and wants to talk to you. The doctor doesn't think 'e's going to live, sir!"

At that moment, though Merriman struggled to collect his wits, he knew. He knew without a shadow of doubt that it really had been Dorrington who had struck him on the head. There had been no Irish ambush. And Owen? Jackson had reported that Owen had been shot. Had Dorrington shot him? Sitting up on the edge of the bed he saw that Moreau and Grahame were already up and gone.

"Very well. I'll come at once."

In the room where Dorrington and Owen were, he found the doctor bending over Owen, re-bandaging the man's head.

"How is he, Mr McBride?"

The doctor shook his head. "It's not good, sir. He pulled his bandage off in the night and tried to get up. Then he must have fallen and hit his head on the table here. He's barely conscious, but he keeps saying that he must tell you something."

Merriman knelt down by the low bed and took the man's hand. "I'm here, Owen, what is it you have to say?"

Owen opened his eyes then closed them again as pain hit him and he groaned. Then, feebly clutching Merriman's hand, he said, "Sir, I saw Mr Dorrington 'it you on the head and then 'e shot me when I ran forward to 'elp."

"Are you sure about this?"

"Yes, sir, I know - know you told me to stay back when you and Mr Dorrington went off to – to look round." His voice faded, making Merriman and the doctor lean closer to hear. "But I didn't trust 'im not to do you some 'arm, sir, not after 'is threats aboard ship, so I followed you." Owen rallied a little and tried to lift his head. "I were near enough to see though, sir, I know he did it." He groaned again and his head fell back.

"Let me see, sir," exclaimed the doctor. "He's still alive, but after that second blow to his head, I don't know if he will live."

"Well do your best for him. He's a good man and has saved my life on more than one occasion. Did you hear what he said?' asked Merriman.

"Yes, sir, I did. But I can hardly believe what I heard. Surely Mr Dorrington wouldn't go that far?" McBride turned to glance over at the other bed where Dorrington lay. "He still hasn't come round, sir. He has three broken ribs and judging by the wounds to his head, he must have been severely beaten and probably kicked."

Merriman rose to his feet. "Keep your eye on him, Mr McBride, and tell me immediately he wakes up, but don't let him or anyone else know what Owen said."

He left the room and went to look for the others. He found them eating a hearty breakfast of eggs and pork with lovely fresh white bread. The smell of food and coffee told him how hungry he was and he eagerly set about the plateful offered to him by a maid. With the inner man finally satisfied, he considered his next move.

"Gentlemen, this is very nice and cosy, but we have work to do. Mr White, your hospitality is overwhelming and I am grateful, but we cannot stay here longer. I must get back to my ship as soon as may be, taking my people with me. Is there any word about the presence of cavalry or any of our military hereabouts?"

"They are not yet here, sir, but my groom who rode off to find them came back not an hour ago and told us that a troop of cavalry will be with us shortly."

"Very good, they can take charge of the prisoners and perhaps they can send a detachment to round up the escapees. Now then, is there any boat available that could take us round to find the ship in Kenmare river?"

"Nothing beyond a few small rowing boats I'm afraid. Nothing that could live in the seas further out."

"Hmm, that won't do. There is nothing else for it but for me to ride back over the hills to see what is happening over there. Then we'll have to bring the ship round into Bantry Bay."

He pondered for a moment. "Mr White, if we may presume on your hospitality further and you are agreeable, I'll leave Mr Grahame, M'sieur Moreau and the men here. We'll be back to pick them up as soon as possible."

"Gladly, Captain. Is there anything else I can do to help?"

"There is, sir, I need to borrow your horses yet again. Mr St James, I'll take you and the two of your marines who can ride. And I'll take Jackson and Brown too, and one of your men, Mr White, to bring the horses back. And you might as well keep those three horses that belonged to the French. You can at least use them to drag the cannon round."

As they made their way into the stable yard to collect the horses, there was a clatter of hooves and the jingle and rattle of equipment as a troop of cavalry arrived. A mud-spattered officer looked over the waiting group, immediately identified Merriman as the one in command, swung down from his horse and saluted.

"Captain Desmond Hall, sir, His Majesty's 3rd Regiment of Lancers. I understand you have some French prisoners to be taken off your hands."

"Captain Merriman, Captain, of His Majesty's frigate *Lord Stevenage* which is presently in the Kenmare River. There was an attempted French landing there and here in Bantry but fortunately the gales drove most of their ships away. We have some hundred and fifty prisoners here of which fifty or so are wounded, some seriously, the others less so. We caught them after a brief fight but unfortunately, perhaps another hundred got away and need to be hunted down. They are mostly unarmed, cold, wet and hungry, so will probably put up little resistance."

"Very good, sir, we'll set off immediately. Have you any idea in which direction they went?"

"Southward, along the west side of the bay, but they will be trying to get back to their own ship which is also in Kenmare River, although I hope my own ship will manage to stop their escape." He turned to Mr White. "Sir, can we depend on your militiamen to stay here guarding the prisoners?"

"I was proposing to keep only one hundred of the best of them, Captain. Well-armed as they now are with the captured muskets and equipment, I don't think they will have any trouble."

"Sir, on the way here we passed two companies of foot marching towards Bantry. They could be here before midday," said Captain Hall.

"Excellent. Even better, perhaps you can leave word for them to follow you. Then, with your permission, Mr White, I'll leave Lieutenant Goodwin and his marines here with the doctor to help in looking after the wounded. I am anxious to get back to *Lord Stevenage* so we must go immediately."

Hastily mounting, Merriman and his party set off, closely followed by the cavalry. When they arrived at the site of the forlorn French attack and defeat, Merriman sent Captain Hall and his men off in the direction which he expected the remaining French to have gone and then he, St James and the others started the arduous journey back over the hills to Kenmare River, passing where the French dead had been hastily buried.

As he rode, he tried to recall detail of the events leading up to Dorrington's attempt to kill him. Of course there was the fact that the youth had been sent to the masthead as punishment on more than one occasion and, when he was found to have beaten young Small with his riding whip, Merriman had had him caned by the Bos'n after which he had threatened to kill his captain. At the time Merriman had considered this to be no more than hot air and an empty threat, but obviously he was wrong.

Dorrington was a violent, sadistic and depraved youth with an inflated idea of his own importance. Arrogant and used to having his own way, his fatherless upbringing and temperament had culminated in the attempted murder of his captain. If Owen died then that would be murder. Merriman shook his head sadly as he mentally castigated himself for underestimating the youth's capacity for evil. Owen had been more aware of it and had been prepared to disobey orders to protect his captain. The loyal man had paid a terrible price. It was one more problem with which Merriman would have to deal when they were all back aboard *Lord Stevenage*.

Eventually they reached a point high up from where they could see down to the place where the ship was supposed to be, but there was no sign of it. The captured French transport ship was still there and the French prisoners were still on the beach where a rough shelter had been erected to protect them from the elements. So where was the ship?

Merriman had to admit that he was shaken, but a few moments reflection told him that his ship must be further down the coast. After all, he had sent his men back to the ship with orders to the First Lieutenant to capture or destroy the French ship *La Sirene*.

"Right then, we will continue along the ridge until we can see something of the ships. Jackson, I want you to scout ahead and keep your eyes peeled. We mustn't forget that the French we failed to capture must have headed for the same place and we don't want to find ourselves ambushed."

But there was no ambush. They had not gone far when the two vessels became visible. *La Sirene* appeared to be aground and *Lord Stevenage* was anchored in deeper water astern of her. Red coats could be seen on the Frenchman's deck which indicated that Lieutenant Laing had succeeded in capturing her.

A flood of relief washed over Merriman at the sight. If anything had happened to his own ship in his absence he would be finished and would never get another command. He looked up as there was a pounding of hooves and Jackson came riding furiously towards them. He hauled his horse to a standstill near Merriman.

"Sir, I've seen the French. There are lots of 'em on the beach and more on the slope of the hill leading down there. Best of all, sir, if you ride another few 'undred yards you can see our cavalry on the ridge above 'em."

They all moved forward behind Jackson who flung out his arm dramatically and pointed. "There, sir, you can see them on the top there."

Merriman pulled his small telescope from his pocket and focussed on the ships first. There was no doubt that *La Sirene* was a prize of war, he saw Lieutenant Andrews striding about the deck as he issued orders to a group of men including Mr Brockle the Bos'n and Mr Green the carpenter. Obviously they were involved in repairs.

Focussing on the men on the beach, Merriman saw that they looked totally dispirited, sitting round in groups on the sand or stamping round slapping their arms round their body in an attempt to keep warm. "Probably the crew," he conjectured, turning his glass on the other men on the hill.

These looked totally exhausted, some of them looking hopelessly at their ship but even in their misery there were some men running about, attempting to form a square to receive the cavalry. By contrast, the cavalrymen sat their mounts quietly, the pennons on their lances fluttering in the breeze.

There was a flurry of activity at the centre of the lancers and Captain Hall cantered towards Merriman and his party. "As you see, sir, we found them and followed to see where they went. Apart from a few with more fight in them than sense, they are beaten men. The ones attempting to form square have only a few muskets and bayonets and must surely see the futility of their position. One charge downhill by my men could scatter them but I hesitated to order more bloodshed."

"That was a kind thought, Captain. I'm in full agreement, but we must herd them together and disarm them. I don't think there will be any trouble, look there, two men are coming towards us waving a white flag. They wish to parley or surrender. Anyway, I'll leave all that to you, I must get back aboard my ship."

The boom of cannon caused them to look at *Lord Stevenage*. A puff of smoke showed where the cannon had been fired and Lieutenant Laing could be discerned on the quarterdeck looking through his telescope at Merriman's party. Laing waved his arm and pointed to where seamen were manning a boat.

"There we are, Mr St James, they are sending a boat for us. We'll keep well away from the French and go to meet it."

Leading their horses down the steep hill they reached the beach. The boat had seen them and changed direction towards them. As it grounded on the sand, Midshipman Hungerford jumped out and raised his hat to Merriman. "Welcome back, sir." He looked round at the rest of them. "Are the others following? Did the French invade?"

"All in good time, Mr Hungerford, all in good time." Merriman handed the reins of his horse to the groom. "You can take the horses back now. Be sure to express my grateful thanks to Mr White and inform him that I shall take my ship round to Bantry as soon as I can. Right, gentlemen, shall we proceed?"

Chapter Nineteen

Capture of a French Corvette

"Good to see you back, sir," exclaimed Laing with a big smile on his face as Merriman climbed aboard. "Mr Andrews told us all about the way you beat the French. Did you manage to catch that fellow Moreau?"

"We certainly did and I'll tell you all about it another time, but now I want to hear what has been going on in my absence."

"Yes, sir. Well, as you can see, the ship is repaired and she is ready for anything. I sent a boat ashore with an old sail out of the transport so that the poor devils there could make some sort of shelter. Other than that trip, I kept the boats with me so as not to tempt any of the prisoners to try to escape, though I don't think any of them would be capable of it. Mr Weston is still aboard the transport with a few men."

"Well done, Mr Laing, and about the French corvette?"

"That is the most interesting part, sir, if I may say so. When Mr Andrews came back with the men and I had nearly a full complement, we sailed down here yesterday at dawn. The French crew were working on the repairs and already had new spars up to replace the topmast and bowsprit, though not all the rigging was finished. She is aground as you can see, sir, on the shore with a kedge anchor out astern."

Merriman turned to look, seeing that Laing's assessment was true.

Laing continued, "We sailed past her and I called on them to surrender or I would fire. They didn't reply, but a warning shot fired alongside soon changed their minds. I could see that they were in no position to fight, so thought it best not to give them a broadside. The stern cabin and the after part of her gundeck are a shambles from our earlier encounter and most of the crew fled ashore."

"A good decision, Mr Laing," Merriman said.

"As you can see, sir, she is slightly canted to starboard and down by the bow. I think her cables must have parted in the gale and allowed her to drift ashore. Evidently she struck a rock and settled on sand and mud. The carpenter and the bos'n report that there is a small hole down at the turn of the bilge just below the waterline on the starboard side. They believe they can patch it at low tide and we could float her off."

"Excellent, Mr Laing. You have done well in my absence and my report to the admiral will say so."

"Thank you, sir," said Laing simply.

"I wonder why they abandoned the ship without making a fight of it?" Merriman mused aloud. "Was there no attempt to destroy her?"

"No, sir, not as far as I know, but here is the most interesting thing. When we boarded her we found the captain and two of the officers dead. They'd been tied up in the ruined cabin and their throats cut. A strongbox had been smashed open and emptied. Maybe it contained money to pay the rebels."

"I expect you're right, Mr Laing. Probably the crew panicked when you approached and stole the money hoping to get ashore and join the fleet which they expected to be in the next bay. Of course, they didn't know that there was no fleet. Anyway, they've been rounded up by our cavalry and some redcoats will be along soon to join them. We'll have somebody go ashore and tell the army captain that some of his prisoners murdered their captain and officers and probably have stolen monies in their possession."

Considering all the recent events, Merriman laughed out loud. "'Pon my word, Colin, this cruise has been most rewarding. We caused two enemy transports to be destroyed, we captured Moreau, and we now have two prizes to find crew for. Were any charts and documents found?"

"Yes, sir, all the usual charts and a folder full of papers. I put them aside for you, sir."

Merriman walked up and down the quarterdeck a few times, tugging at his ear and thinking about what had to be done before sailing to Bantry Bay. He must make sure that the military could cope with all the able bodied prisoners who faced a long walk to wherever they would be incarcerated, and then there were the wounded ones to be dealt with.

Then there was the question of trying to refloat *La Sirene*. Well, no question at all really. The French corvette would be a valuable addition to the navy which was always short of ships. Besides, he owed it to the crew to bring the ship off, they would all welcome the prize money.

His mind made up, he turned to the First Lieutenant and the marine officer who were waiting for orders. "Gentlemen, this is what we will do. Mr St James, will you go ashore again and speak with Captain Hill. Tell him of the murder of the French officers and then ask him if he is content to take the able bodied prisoners back with him. Then see how many wounded will need to be transported by ship. When the number is known, go and see Mr Weston aboard that first ship we captured and have him make arrangements to receive them. Mr Weston can take command of her with a reduced crew and a few marines to keep an eye on the prisoners. We'll take them to Bantry and hand them over to the military to look after. See to it please, Edward, while I go aboard *La Sirene* to see what needs to be done."

Climbing aboard the French corvette Merriman was greeted by a grinning Lieutenant Andrews. "She's a fine ship, sir, we can have her afloat again in a couple of days. The carpenter is below with a working party to try and fix a temporary patch over the hole whilst the tide is falling, and I was planning to move all the for'ard guns to the stern to lighten her for'ard to bring the hole up to where we can put a more secure patch over it."

Andrew checked his enthusiasm for a moment. "That is, with your approval, sir?"

"Of course, Mr Andrews, of course. And I see that the bos'n has men trying to replace the bowsprit we smashed. What is the story there?"

"Well, sir, the Frenchies had made a very good start on the job of replacing the fore topmast with a spare mainyard, in fact it only needs to be swayed up into position and secured. All the stays and yards are ready, but we will need some more time to complete it, sir. The bowsprit is another matter, the French tried to use one of the tops'l yards but the bos'n is of the opinion that it won't be strong enough and there is no suitable spar available to replace it. With your permission, I was wondering if I could take one of the spares off our ship, sir."

"Yes, that seems to be the best solution, take the bos'n with you and have one towed across. I'm going below to see how the patching is going on."

Down below, in the gloom of the hold, Merriman found a bedraggled working party waist deep in icy water hammering at timbers to wedge beams into place to secure a hastily contrived wooden patch. The carpenter saw Merriman and waded toward him.

"Nearly done, sir. I've folded an old sail into a sort of pad and put it behind the patch. I think it will hold until we can lift her and get a patch on the outside. Mr Andrews is having the forr'ard guns moved aft and to larboard so when we pump her out the hole should be just about above water and I can finish the job."

"Excellent, Mr Green. You and your men have done well. As soon as you are satisfied with the work we'll pump her out and kedge her off."

Kedging her off meant exhausting work for the crew but Merriman heard no complaints. First of all, anchors had to be taken out and laid astern of *Lord Stevenage* to hold the ship steady. Then a cable had to be run out of a hawsehole at the stem and secured to the French ship which itself had a kedge anchor out astern. As the tide rose, the ship rose with it and with the men at the capstans keeping a strain on the cables, she floated off as easily as a duck taking to the water.

It took the two days as Andrews had predicted but at the end of that time *La Sirene* floated in deep water again, ready to sail anywhere. A small amount of water still found its way into the bilge but a brisk half hour of pumping twice a day would keep it under control.

Meanwhile Lieutenant Weston had brought his shipload of wounded men to anchor near to the frigate and her prize. He reported to Merriman.

"All ready, sir. We lifted all the dead horses out of her and sluiced the hold down with seawater then pumped her dry." He paused and looked apologetic as he continued, "I used some of the able bodied French prisoners off the beach to do most of that, sir. I thought that as they'd killed the animals they should clear up the mess."

"Well done, Mr Weston, how many have you aboard now?"

"Thirty five, sir. Some of the wounded died. I had the French bury their dead up behind the beach, there where you can see that rough cross. I gave them some of our materials to do it, sir, I hope that was in order."

"It was, the poor devils will have no other memorial." Merriman became aware of Tomkins and O'Flynn trying to attract his attention. "Yes, what have you two reprobates to report?"

"List of what we found aboard, sir, as you ordered. Shall I read it out?" asked Tomkins.

At Merriman's nodded assent he continued, "Sir, we found five more field pieces and over an 'undred boxes of powder cartridges made up ready for them, an' 'undreds of shot, sir, mostly canister and grapeshot with roundshot as well." He paused to draw breath.

"Yes, yes, go on, man" said Merriman impatiently.

"Yessir, there are fifty kegs of salted meat, forty bags of biscuit and a few water barrels with contents intact. A lot of barrels had been smashed open. Nothing else of value, sir, apart from the usual bos'n's stores. Unless you count these, sir."

He indicated the large bundle which Merriman had noticed O'Flynn holding very carefully.

"All right, don't keep me in suspense, what else have you found?"

"Two dozen bottles of French wine, sir, in a locker in the main cabin. Lucky we found them before the other rogues aboard. And then there's these, sir, papers and charts out of the captain's cabin. Mr Weston kept the charts he thought he might need and told us to bring the rest to you, sir. He said they was charts of the French coast and ports."

"Charts and papers eh! Maybe there is something to be learned from them. Put them all in my cabin." Merriman knew that French charts could be invaluable to the Admiralty cartographic department.

"Yessir, and the wine?"

"My cabin too. I expect you've sampled it already, haven't you?"

"Well, sir, Mr Weston took one and there *was* one bottle that got the top knocked off, accidental like, and we thought we should try it to see if it was fit for you to drink, sir."

"Say no more," said Merriman trying to keep the smile off his face. "Get below, the pair of you."

On the evening of the second day, Merriman called his officers to his cabin.

"Gentlemen, may I interest you in a glass of some rather good wine Tomkins liberated from the French captain's cabin? Legitimate spoils of war. Peters, see to it please."

When all had a full glass, Merriman proposed a toast. "I think congratulations are due to us all, officers and men, for our success. Here's to our ship *Lord Stevenage*." He raised his glass and drained it and the others did likewise.

"Now then, this is what we'll do tomorrow at first light. Mr Laing, you will command the corvette and Mr Andrews will remain with me as First Lieutenant. Mr Weston, you will take the transport ship - what's her name by the way?"

"Something unpronounceable, sir," replied Weston. "So the men have taken to calling her *The Fat Frog*. I didn't stop them, sir, it seemed quite harmless."

There was a roar of laughter from the others and Merriman, said with a smile, "*The Fat Frog* it shall be then. All right, we'll proceed round to Bantry Bay to pick up the rest of our men. Mr Laing, and you, Mr Weston, will have to manage with skeleton crews as I must keep enough men here to fight the ship if we are unlucky enough to encounter any more French. Our speed will be limited to that of Mr Weston's *Fat Frog*. Do the best you can, Mr Weston, and I will keep to seaward of you both to screen you. After we leave Bantry, subject to Mr Grahame having nothing more for us to do, I think we might hope to return to Portsmouth."

Chapter Twenty

Triumphant return with two prizes to Bantry

Sailing up Bantry Bay with his small squadron under his lee, Merriman experienced a thrill to see the other ships flying the ensign over the French tricolour which indicated that they were prizes.

"With the two ships and the stores in the hold of *the Fat Frog*, there should be a fair bit of prize money, I shouldn't wonder, sir," said Lieutenant Andrews, rubbing his hands together. "And no other King's ship near to share it with either."

After the ships had been safely anchored, Merriman had himself rowed ashore. He was desperate to see if Owen had recovered and to find out what had happened at Bantry House whilst he had been away. A welcoming party comprising Mr Grahame, Lieutenant Goodwin and Mr McBride, the doctor, met him on the small jetty below the house. Hovering behind Grahame was the tall figure of Moreau, the Frenchman.

"You've been busy, sir, congratulations. All has gone well with you, I trust," were the first words spoken by a smiling McBride, raising his hat to his captain.

"Indeed, yes," Merriman replied, "and how is everything here?"

"Well enough, sir. The army marched the prisoners away, all except the more seriously wounded who are guarded in the coach house."

"And Owen, my cox'n, what of him?"

The doctor glanced at the others then took a deep breath. "I'm sorry, sir, he's dead. He died shortly after you left to rejoin the ship, sir. I did my best but I couldn't save him."

Merriman stared almost uncomprehendingly at the white face of the doctor as thoughts raced through his mind. Owen, the man who had guarded his back through many a desperate fight, who was always there when needed, his shadow, gone, dead, and himself not there at the last. He recovered himself to see that the doctor was still standing in front of him with a look almost of terror on his face.

"It's all right, Mr McBride, I'm sure you did all that could be done," he said quietly, gently touching him on the shoulder. "But damn it, I shall miss that man."

"I know, sir, he'd been with you a long time. But he was lucid before he died and wanted to be sure that you knew that it was Mr Dorrington who had shot him and tried to kill you. I think he was content at the end, sir. We buried him in the little churchyard nearby."

"I take it that you gentlemen know about this matter?" said Merriman turning to the others.

"Yes, sir. The doctor called me in at the end in case Owen had more to say and of course you now have me as another witness to his last words, his deathbed statement if you will," replied the marine lieutenant.

"Yes, James, I was a witness as well and there is more you should know, but may I propose that we move into the house away from this devilishly cold wind?" said Mr Grahame.

Once settled in the warmth from a roaring fire in Mr White's house, and with a glass of mulled wine in hand, Merriman looked round the serious faces in front of him.

"Well then, what more is there I should know?" he demanded harshly.

Grahame gestured to Moreau, who spoke up. "Captain, I saw all that happened the night you were captured. I was in the stable and I know it was your midshipman M'sieur Dorrington who struck you down. Also, I saw him shoot the other man that I now know to be your man Owen." He paused. "It was I who hit M'sieur Dorrington from behind, but I could not save him from further harm at the hands or boots of the Irishmen."

"Why did you not say anything of this before, M'sieur?"

"I did not wish to burden you with further problems. I thought that M'sieur Dorrington was going to die and, had he done so, there would be no need to refer to the affair again. It would be over."

"I see. Mr McBride, how is Dorrington now?"

"He regained consciousness a few hours ago. He's very weak, but he is young and I expect he will recover fairly quickly. He has broken ribs and multiple cuts and bruises, and he has lost two or three teeth, but from what Mr Moreau has told us it could have been a lot worse. He asked about you, sir. I simply told him that you had been attacked and taken prisoner also and that you had both been rescued when we caught Mr Moreau."

"I suppose it would have been better for him if he had died. As it is, he stands accused of murder and an attack on a senior officer. Both of these offences require him to face a court martial from which there can be only one result."

"What will you do with him, sir?" asked St James.

"I believe there is no option but to confine him under guard, once he has recovered sufficiently. Meanwhile, no word of what we know should reach him in case he does something desperate. If he enquires about my cox'n, simply tell him that Owen was killed in the rescue. Are we in accord on this, gentlemen?"

All signified their agreement. Merriman stood up. "Now to other matters, what about the wounded French prisoners still here?"

"When the army marched the able bodied of them away to Cork, sir," reported St James, "they took most of their wounded with them. We organised litters for the more seriously hurt of them and of course there were plenty of their fellows to carry them. As for the rest of them, sir, perhaps Mr McBride would be the best one to tell you."

"Those two men who gave themselves hernias when they were hauling that damned cannon uphill are up and about again. I fitted them with a sort of truss," said the Doctor. "Jack is a hardy fellow and copes with physical damage which would probably kill lesser men. I expect them both to recover in time. As for the French, there are ten or twelve who are almost fit to travel. One other of them will die for certain and two others will probably not survive."

"Very well, Mr McBride, apart from those three, can the rest of them be moved to *The Fat Frog* to be taken to Cork by sea?"

"Well I suppose so, but *The Fat Frog, s*ir? I don't understand."

"Of course. That is the name given by the prize crew to the transport ship we took." He looked at Moreau. "My apologies, m'sieur."

Moreau inclined his head in acknowledgement. "No need to apologise, m'sieur, I know that we French are named Frogs or Froggies by the English, but," and here he laughed. "It would be better that I not tell you what the French call the English."

"Then, gentlemen, there is no reason why we cannot get back to sea. I think it would be for the best if Mr Dorrington is taken back on board the frigate where he can be put in Mr Weston's cabin. As soon as he is able to understand his situation we'll tell him what he is accused of and I'll have a marine sentry on his door."

Whilst the arrangements were being made to put the wounded Frenchmen aboard and prepare for sea again, Merriman and Mr Grahame went in search of Mr White. They found him in his stable yard supervising the last few men of the militia preparing the wounded for travelling.

"Mr White, I wish to express my thanks for all you have done to help and for allowing your home to become our temporary headquarters."

"My dear, sir, say no more about it. I have enjoyed our adventures immensely and I'm only too pleased to have been of service in helping to thwart the damned French, although I must say that that fellow Moreau seems to be a likeable chap."

"Nevertheless, sir, I *will* say more about it," said Grahame. "I shall commend your assistance in the warmest possible terms to my superiors in London. We would have been unlikely to have caught Moreau without your help. And that of your militia."

Back at sea, aboard *Lord Stevenage,* Merriman's satisfaction at the outcome of the last few days was tempered by the loss of Owen. Owen had been his cox'n for the last four years and knew his ways like no other except Peters his servant. He sighed deeply. He was still pondering when the marine sentry knocked on the door and announced, "Mr Grahame, sir."

"James, why the long face? Everything we planned for has concluded well. I have Moreau as a prisoner and he has given me much valuable information, although he will only tell me what he knows about the Revolutionary Council and their plans and spy network. Which reminds me, James, I owe you an apology."

"Good heavens, sir, what on earth for?"

"I apologise for losing my temper when you accepted Moreau's parole. You were quite right to do so and I regret the harsh words I said to you."

"Mr Grahame, say no more. I had quite forgotten the incident."

"Another matter should be mentioned, James. The documents and papers found aboard *La Sirene* contain some very interesting information. Most of them are only routine orders and records concerning the day to day matters of the ship, as indeed are the ones from the aptly named *Fat Frog.* However, there is also a list of French contacts in Ireland which will be invaluable. Moreau currently believes that his papers had been destroyed by the French captain, so I have not told him what we have. There are others but I have not yet had time to decipher them."

"That is excellent news, sir. And now, I have some excellent wine discovered aboard one of the prizes which I urge you to try. Peters, where are you, man? Ah there you are, we'll have some of that new French wine you liberated, lively now."

When Peters had finished serving and disappeared into his own little hidey-hole in the pantry, Grahame raised the matter of Dorrington again.

"Tell me, James, where will you have him tried? Could it perhaps be done at the military garrison at Cork?"

"No, sir, it's a matter for the navy to resolve, not the army, and there are not enough naval officers in Cork to form a court martial. There must be at least three Post Captains."

"I see. The fellow is undoubtedly a bad lot and fully deserves all the punishment he gets. From the beginning he antagonised everybody with his sneering and arrogant ways and then his treatment of young Small, followed by his attack on you and the murder of your man Owen, well really, he will be lucky to escape the noose."

"Yes, but I feel sorry for his mother. Apparently, since his father died she has tried to control him, but there was some trouble with a servant girl and as a last resort she asked Admiral FitzHerbert at Portsmouth, who is her brother, to find him a place in the navy. She had hoped that some discipline would do him good. And now it has come to this."

Both men sat lost in thought for a while as they sipped the wine, then Merriman roused himself, saying, "My long face as you called it, was because I was trying to decide who I can find to replace Owen."

Over the next day or two, he gave the matter of a new cox'n more thought but in the end had decided that it had to be either Matthews, the seaman whom Dorrington had tried to have flogged, or Jackson, the man whose efforts had been so helpful in capturing Moreau. Eventually he decided to have Jackson rated as a petty officer and Matthews as his cox'n. He called for the First Lieutenant.

"Mr Laing, I have decided that after all his sterling efforts Jackson must be promoted. I think with a bit of reorganisation of the watch bill you can find room for him as a petty officer, especially as we lost so many men recently."

"Excellent idea, sir. I've had my eye on him for some time and I am sure he will be suitable."

"And further, I think Matthews would be a good replacement for Owen. What do you think?"

"He's a good steady man, sir, should fit into your routine very well."

That settled, Merriman informed a grateful Matthews of his decision and informed him what his duties would be.

The next day, as Dorrington was recovering well, Merriman could procrastinate no longer and decided that Dorrington must face his accusers. To that end he called for Mr Grahame, Mr Laing, Doctor McBride, M'sieur Moreau and the two marine officers to come to his cabin.

"Gentlemen, I intend to inform Mr Dorrington what his position is, what he is accused of, and present him with the evidence. All of you know what has happened so I require you to be present. We'll make this a formal affair and so I would be obliged, Mr St James, if you would take a marine guard and bring him here. And I'll have a guard over him from now on. Thank you."

An apprehensive looking Dorrington walked in flanked by two marines with the marine officer leading. He stood in front of the other men, casting anxious eyes over the serious faces of the officers and others present. Merriman opened the proceedings.

"Mr Dorrington, you have been brought here to face various charges about your conduct during our recent excursion ashore. The main charges are as follows: Item one, that you did strike me, your commanding officer from behind. Item two, that you then shot my cox'n Owen, resulting in his death. Item three, that our attempt to capture some Irish rebels and M'sieur Moreau here, was seriously impeded by your actions. There are further charges which can be made concerning your sexual proclivities and your treatment of Midshipman Small, but these first three will suffice for the present. What have you to say?"

During this recital of the charges against him, Dorrington's face had turned deathly white and then a fiery, angry red. "It's a lie, I did none of those things. What proof have you?"

"We have plenty, Mr Dorrington. You were seen when you struck me and when you shot Owen when he tried to help me."

"It's a lie! Who saw me? We were ambushed by the rebels, and beaten, you know how I was injured."

M'sieur Moreau saw you, he was in the stable and..."

"Lies I tell you," interrupted the youth, "The damned Frog is trying to cause trouble, that's what he's doing! Can't you see?"

Merriman ignored the wild outburst and continued, "There was another witness, Mr Dorrington. Owen saw you and lived long enough to tell me, the Doctor and Mr Goodwin what you had done."

"He couldn't have lived, I shot him in the he..." Dorrington stopped as he realised that he had convicted himself by his own words. Then he muttered, "Damn you, Merriman. You've had your knife in me since I joined this blasted ship. I should have shot you when I had the chance."

There was a stony silence in the cabin, then Merriman, forcing himself to remain calm said, "You will return to your cabin and there will be a twenty four hour guard outside. When we arrive at Portsmouth, you will appear before a court martial which will decide your fate. Should you attempt to leave your cabin I will have you in chains for the rest of our journey. Take him away, Mr St James."

There was one last despairing cry from the miserable Dorrington as the marines dragged him out, struggling and screaming. "You can't do that, I'm a gentleman, you can't chain me like a common felon!"

"I'm glad that's over," remarked Mr Grahame once the door closed on Dorrington. "I hope not to see him again until his trial."

"Yes, an unpleasant business altogether. Thank you, gentlemen. Of course you will all be required to give evidence at that court martial."

Chapter Twenty-One

Ships prepare to sail for Portsmouth

In spite of the lumbering slowness of *The Fat Frog,* they made good time and arrived in Cork on the early morning flood tide and anchored. There the last of the surviving wounded French prisoners were put ashore into the hands of the military garrison whose commanding officer already knew that the other prisoners were on their way.

The cutter *Tiny* with Lieutenant Hetherington arrived shortly after them and immediately Merriman sent for the lieutenant.

"What happened to you after you left to warn the garrison here?"

"Well, sir, I did call here and then left to find Commodore Pellew as you instructed. I didn't find him but I met with one of our brigs which had been sent from the fleet to warn the garrisons here. I told the captain that Cork had already been warned so he ordered me back here whilst he went to find Captain Pellew."

"Very good, Lieutenant, there is nothing more for you to do here so I think you had better return to Portsmouth as your previous orders required. I will write a report for you to explain to the Admiral what you have been doing. You can also take some letters for me and advise the Admiral that my full report will follow."

"Yes, sir, thank you, sir. I'll go as soon as your correspondence is ready."

As soon as Hetherington had gone, the marine sentry knocked and announced, "Mr Grahame, sir." Grahame entered with a satisfied, almost smug smile on his face.

"James, I have some excellent news! You will remember that Lieutenant Hetherington brought me a letter on his first visit to this ship? It was from Lord Stevenage but because the contents were not directly concerned with our present commission, I did not confide in you at that point. The letter concerned reports from agents of ours indicating that the French are proposing to increase their network of agents in Portugal and in the Mediterranean, more particularly in the Kingdoms of Sicily and Sardinia, and there were some notes about agents in India."

"That hardly seems to be good news, sir, but I assume there is more?"

"Indeed so, James. As you know, we recovered papers from *La Sirene* which belonged to our friend Moreau and there is clear evidence in them that, once he had finished his work in Ireland, he was to go to Sicily to assist their agents in fomenting revolution there. Better still, I just found a list of people there who would be prepared to turn their coats and spy for France, for money I assume."

"Well it certainly would give us an advantage to know who these people are and give us a chance to do something about it, sir."

"Yes, James, it also means that I must return to London as soon as possible to acquaint his Lordship with our new findings. I imagine it will be quite likely I will have to go to Portugal or Sicily, or even India, and I shall ask for your services again."

"Thank you, sir, but before then I hope that I shall have the opportunity to go home and get married. I understand that all arrangements have been made, only the date has to be settled."

Grahame grinned at Merriman. "Ah, the delightful Miss Simpson, I expect. Well, I think you have waited long enough. I'll see what I can do to help. I remember that his Lordship wanted to be invited to the wedding although I cannot understand why."

"No, sir, neither can I."

"It will be a damned uncomfortable journey, but I think I should go back to Portsmouth in *Tiny,* as it will be quicker than this ship. Perhaps you would be kind enough to ask Mr Hetherington to make room for me? I'll leave Moreau with you for the time being. As Mr White said, he is a likeable fellow and has given me plenty of information."

"Of course, sir. *Tiny* will be sailing as soon as I have completed some letters and reports."

"Ah, I do not envy you in writing the difficult report for Admiral FitzHerbert concerning his nephew. Your letter to Miss Simpson can contain better news, at least."

Chapter Twenty-Two

Merriman reports to the Admiralty

For most of the voyage the weather was favourable and progress was brisk but then a gale came out of the north which cost them two days, plus another day repairing the *Fat Frog's* rigging. It had been found unequal to the strains put upon it. The leak in the corvette's hull also became markedly worse and required almost constant pumping to keep the water at bay.

During this time, Merriman found himself spending more and more time in the Frenchman's company and, little by little, learned more about his past. The luxurious life he had led in the family chateau, then the increasing tension between himself and his father which resulted in him leaving home with only a horse and his father's sword.

Moreau was a good raconteur and the time passed quickly as he told of his adventures with the Marquis de Lafayette and his French volunteers during the American War of Independence. He had been a soldier of fortune, known simply as Charles Henri Moreau instead of his true and grandiose title of Count.

Most of his experiences had been serious but he had Merriman and other officers laughing helplessly when he related some of his more hilarious exploits.

He also spoke sadly of his horror on his return to France to find that his entire family, even his young sister, had perished beneath the guillotine and of how he had had to conceal the fact that he was an aristocrat and remained Charles Moreau.

By now he and Merriman had become friends and on first name terms. Merriman told him of his forthcoming marriage and spoke of his fiancée, Helen, in glowing terms.

Charles remarked, "I can see, James, that you are a fortunate man and I wish you every happiness. I only wish I could meet the lady."

Their arrival in Portsmouth should have provided an enjoyable experience for Merriman as the *Lord Stevenage* entered the harbour. Spontaneous cheering broke out from other ships at anchor when the two other vessels following were seen to be displaying the Union flag over the Tricolour, clearly indicating that they were prizes. He raised his hat in acknowledgement, but in spite of the excitement, he was too involved in the procedures of saluting the flag and anchoring where the harbour master's boat indicated.

"Signal, sir," reported Midshipman Small. "Captain to report to Flag immediately."

Merriman's stomach gave a lurch as he realised that the dreaded moment had come. Now he would have to face the Admiral and tell him all the details of his nephew's crimes. But he had no choice. His full report was written, explaining all, he was wearing his best, new uniform, and was as prepared as he could be.

Matthews was watching the lowering of his captain's boat like a hawk and, as soon as the keel touched the water, the crew leapt in. Merriman climbed down into the boat to the accompaniment of the usual ceremony of bos'n's whistles and the presenting of arms by the marines. He seated himself in the sternsheets, clutching his report beneath his cloak to keep it dry.

The same harassed Lieutenant Williams met him on the quayside, imploring him to hurry. "Please, sir, the Admiral is impatient and he wants to see you in his quarters, not his office. Without delay, sir, and I'll be in trouble if you take too long, sir."

"We certainly don't want that to happen, do we, Lieutenant? Please do lead the way."

"Captain Merriman, sir," announced the Lieutenant, ushering Merriman into a room which displayed little elegance but nevertheless showed a woman's touch in the draperies and cushions.

"Come in, Captain. Lieutenant, take the captain's cloak and note well that I do not wish to be disturbed for anything short of a French invasion. See to it."

The Lieutenant fled, closing the door after him. On Merriman's first acquaintance with him, Admiral Sir George FitzHerbert had been every inch the fiery and stern martinet but on this occasion he quietly indicated that Merriman should be seated.

Then drawing a deep breath he asked, "Now, Captain Merriman, what is all this about my nephew? That fellow Grahame told me something of it before he shot off to London but I want to hear the details from you."

"It's all in my report here, Sir George," replied Merriman, handing the papers over.

"I know it is, but I want it straight, not cluttered up with the usual jargon."

As Merriman recounted the various events since Midshipman Dorrington had joined his ship, from the first rudeness to Mr Grahame and mastheading, to his arrogance and repeated attempts to have seamen flogged, the Admiral's face grew longer and longer. When Merriman reached the episode of Dorrington's whipping and beating of Midshipman Small because Small wouldn't accommodate his depraved wishes, the Admiral was white faced and aghast.

"My God, I knew he was a bad lot, but this is beyond belief. Is there more, Captain Merriman?"

"Yes, sir, I'm afraid the worst is yet to come."

"The worst? Wait a moment, I need a drink, and I'm sure you do, Captain."

Turning to the door he bellowed, "Williams!"

The Flag Lieutenant almost fell through the door in his haste. "Yessir?"

"We need a drink, fetch some of my best claret. No, damn it, I need something stronger. Fetch the brandy. Quickly, man, quickly."

The Admiral's perturbation was evident in his attitude after Williams brought the wine and brandy and left them to it. He mopped his brow with a kerchief clutched in a trembling hand and almost whispered, "What can I tell my sister? She'll be distraught, she thinks the world of the boy."

Merriman kept silent, not knowing what to say. The Admiral composed himself, took a long drink, then said, "Tell me the rest of it."

"Yes, sir. There's no way to break this gently, sir. I regret to have to tell you that your nephew stands accused of striking down a superior officer and the murder of my cox'n," said Merriman bluntly.

"Oh my God, is there no doubt about his guilt?"

"No, sir. There are several reliable witnesses."

Merriman went on to recount briefly the events leading up to the point at which Dorrington struck him down.

"He was behind me, sir, and knocked me unconscious, then he shot Owen, my cox'n, when he tried to help me. This was witnessed by our French captive, M'sieur Moreau, a gentleman on parole to me. Owen did not die immediately but told me what had happened. He lived another two days before regaining consciousness again. And also he told Doctor McBride and my marine Lieutenant before he died. Not until then did M'sieur Moreau tell what he had seen."

"This is unbelievable, Captain, unbelievable," said FitzHerbert. "Who knows about this?"

"Well, sir, all the ship's company knows about his ill treatment of Mr Small and of course his attempts to have men flogged. They also witnessed the caning I awarded him, twenty strokes it was, laid on with a will, but only a few of us know of the worst, although they all know he is confined to a cabin under guard."

Merriman paused, "I think it was the caning that did it, sir. He didn't seem to realise that the world about him was real. He thought himself above it. I think the punishment unhinged his mind in some way. He threatened my life afterwards and that was heard by all on the quarter deck, though I took it for no more than bluster at the time."

He paused. The Admiral was staring unseeingly before him. The news seemed to have aged him in some way. Merriman coughed.

"Sir, although the Admiralty will have to know, as yet I have only sent to them a brief and preliminary report in the hands of Mr Grahame concerning the success of our commission. It mentions nothing about your nephew."

Fitzpatrick looked up. "Why have you not told them, Captain?"

"Well, sir, as I said, I have to send them a full report, which I have written, but I have written a second report detailing your nephew's behaviour. The officers comprising the court martial will need to see that one without them needing to know all the details of the commission we were on. I am sure that you understand that those details are confidential for the eyes of Lord Stevenage and the Admiralty only."

FitzHerbert nodded.

Merriman continued, "I thought I should tell you first so that you are prepared for the inevitable announcement of his court martial. And there's his mother, sir. I can see no way of hushing up this matter. The whole service, if not the whole country will soon know what he has done."

"Thank you, Captain Merriman. As you say, this cannot and must not be covered up, indeed, my nephew must stand trial and punishment, God help him. Naval discipline and regulations demand it."

He brightened a little as a thought struck him. "Captain Merriman, you said that you thought his mind was unhinged in some way, do you think that would form a defence? Would you be prepared to say as much at his trial?"

"I'm not a lawyer, sir, and know none of the intricacies of the law, so I don't know if that defence is possible. I believe you should consult a doctor as to the state of his mind but if needed I would be prepared to say that I thought he was not himself."

"You are right, of course. Now I have the awful task of telling his mother. Where is the boy now?"

"Still under guard aboard my ship, sir."

"Right, send him ashore under a marine guard. We have quarters here where he can be kept secure. And, Captain, I am very grateful for your actions and consideration in this matter, I do not see what else you could have done. Send the complete report to the Admiralty and let the cards fall as they will. I have much to think about. Please leave me now, return to your ship and wait for further orders. I'll speak to you again tomorrow."

"Yes, sir. I'm sorry, sir."

Merriman returned to *Lord Stevenage* with a mixture of relief and sadness. Relief that the Admiral now knew the truth, and sadness that he had not seen into Dorrington's character earlier. If he had, he might have prevented the matter going as far as it did.

He spent a miserable evening and sleepless night shut alone in his cabin, trying to think of what else he might have done. But the die was cast and it was now out of his hands.

Next morning, as he waited in his best uniform for the summons from the Admiral, he could still not stop thinking about the miserable youth, Dorrington, and the awful fate ahead of him. His thoughts were interrupted by a knock on the door. Midshipman Small tumbled in, out of breath, and squeaked, "Mr Andrews' compliments, sir, there's a signal. Captain to report to flag immediately."

"Very good, Mr Small, thank you. And, Mr Small, don't rush about so, remember you are an officer."

"Aye – aye, sir, I mean yes, sir."

Once again Merriman was greeted by the harassed Lieutenant Williams.

"Good morning, sir. Sir, I don't know what you told the Admiral yesterday, but whatever it was he has not shouted at me since. He has been uncommonly quiet and there are all sorts of rumours spreading since his nephew arrived under guard."

"All in good time, Mr Williams. You will know all about it eventually."

Admiral FitzHerbert was indeed a changed man, although his grasp of the situation and his orders were as crisp as ever.

"Captain Merriman, I have received orders that you are to proceed directly to the Admiralty in London. I myself am going to London to see my sister and give her the awful news, so I would be pleased to share a post chaise with you."

"Thank you, sir, I'm very grateful."

"Before we go, I have to tell you that I have ensured that your two prize ships will be accepted by the navy board. The cargo of the transport will also be purchased, the field pieces going on to the army. I hear that your crew renamed her the *Fat Frog*, very apt, if I may say so," he said with a wry smile.

"Yes, sir, it was some wag on the lower deck with a sense of humour. They couldn't pronounce the French name."

"Then there is the matter of the French warship. I have ordered her to be moved into the dockyard for a complete repair. I'll have the damned French name *La Sirene* painted out and replaced with the English form of the name." The Admiral paused for a moment. "D'you know, Captain, come to think of it, I like that better. We'll call her the *English Mermaid*. A fast ship like that will be an invaluable addition to the fleet."

Merriman smiled.

"As you are aware, it falls to my prerogative to find an officer to command her. After the affair with my nephew, I am reluctant to make a personal recommendation, so do you think your first Lieutenant is suitable?"

"Indeed, Sir George, I could think of none better. He is an excellent officer and a fine seaman. He deserves this opportunity, sir, although I shall miss him."

"That's settled then, Captain. He can take command when she is ready. Your second can move up and I'll see to it that you get another junior. Meanwhile he can stay aboard *Lord Stevenage*. Be on the quayside at first light tomorrow morning."

On board his ship, Merriman lost no time in calling the officers down to his cabin.

"Gentlemen, I have to go to London to the Admiralty. The court martial will be convened when I return. Our repairs will be checked by the shipyard and the ship prepared for sea again. I look to you all to keep the men hard at work. I expect to return in a few days with new orders. I hope we may go to warmer climes."

The journey to London was uneventful. The post chaise was a four wheeled carriage with seating for two or three people and with a window at the front. The post boy or driver rode one of the two horses. Built for fast, long distance travel, the horses were changed regularly at post stations along the way. There were no difficulties with footpads or highwaymen, both common in that day and age, although Merriman had brought a brace of pistols with him just in case.

The Admiral repeatedly stuck his head out of the window shouting to the post-boy for more speed, and, once more the irascible martinet, chivvying the ostlers at each change of horses. In truth Merriman was glad when the journey was over, for the Admiral was not a good travelling companion, being sunk in gloom about his task of telling his sister that her son was a murderer. Conversation was brief and when the Admiral deposited him outside the Admiralty all he could say was, "Doubtless we shall meet again in Portsmouth, Captain, goodbye!"

Inside, Merriman asked a lieutenant to inform Admiral Sir David Edwards of his presence and with little delay he was ushered into the familiar room.

The Admiral was alone and greeted Merriman cheerfully, "Good to see you again, Captain Merriman, your latest venture was very successful, I hear. Mr Grahame was here two days ago with Lord Stevenage to tell us all about it. His Lordship is mightily pleased that you captured Moreau the spy and again Mr Grahame spoke highly of you."

"Thank you, Sir Edward. We were fortunate."

'Fortune, good or ill, had nothing to do with it, I hear. Now, Mr Grahame hinted at another matter, of murder in fact, but I saw no mention of that in your very brief report."

"No, sir, but I have here my complete report on the whole affair. I wrote a second report for Admiral FitzHerbert as it concerns his relative, but I omitted details of why we were in Irish waters. I hope that is in order, sir."

"Probably, Captain, probably, but we'll talk further when I have read your report. Come back in..." he consulted his pocket watch, "in two hours from now. I'll give orders for you to be brought straight in."

Precisely two hours later, Merriman was again in the presence of the Admiral but this time both Lord Stevenage and Mr Grahame were there, all with serious faces.

"This is a bad business, Captain, did this Midshipman really do all that you say, strike you and murder a seaman?" asked Lord Stevenage.

"Yes, my Lord, there is no question about it, and the report does not give all the minor events leading up to it which I considered at the time to be only shipboard matters."

"Mr Grahame told us most of it a few days ago," said the Admiral, "and we have read your report which is clear and concise and confirms all he said. In the circumstances I cannot see that you could have acted other than you did. Naturally there will have to be a court martial and you must return to Portsmouth for it."

"Of course, Sir Edward."

"And now, Captain, we will go on to the future," interrupted Lord Stevenage. "I believe Mr Grahame hinted that your next enterprise could be Portugal or possibly Sicily, but we do not yet have all the information we need to have before sending you and Mr Grahame on another adventure. So, Captain, it has been decided that you will return to Portsmouth immediately."

Here he smiled a surprisingly warm smile at Merriman, "And as soon as the damned trial is over, which should take no more than a few days, you may take time to go home and get married. Don't forget, I will be pleased to be invited to the event."

"Thank you, my Lord. From the last letter I received from home it seems that all is ready for the wedding. It only requires me to let them know when I shall arrive. May I suggest a week from today, my Lord?"

"Indeed you may, Captain, and I shall be there. The Admiralty has approved this, subject to your being prepared to return to your ship at short notice should you be needed. The ship will remain in Portsmouth, such repairs as may be required will be done, and she will be supplied for an extended voyage. If you are not recalled earlier, you must be back with your ship in, what shall we say, Sir Edward, three weeks from today?"

"I think that should do nicely, my Lord. As you said before Captain Merriman arrived, it will take that long for more news to reach us from your people over in Portugal and elsewhere."

"Thank you, gentlemen." Greatly daring Merriman asked, "My Lord, I would be pleased if Mr Grahame could be spared to attend the wedding as well, he knows the lady and it was he who encouraged me to ask for her hand when I was too hesitant."

"A matchmaker too, are you, in addition to all your other talents?" said His Lordship to Mr Grahame with a laugh. "Yes, Captain, I believe he will be able to travel to Cheshire in my coach unless anything untoward turns up."

"Thank you. There is one other matter to which I wish to draw your particular attention, my Lord. It's all in my report but I cannot stress too highly that our success was due in no small measure to the actions of Mr Richard White of Bantry House and the militia of the district. He put his house and buildings completely at our disposal and furnished the horses which we needed."

"Yes, Captain, Mr Grahame has already impressed on me the value of Mr White's services. I shall mention this in the right quarters, you may be sure."

On his arrival back in Portsmouth, Merriman immediately reported his return to Admiral Sir George FitzHerbert who had arrived back before him, and showed him his orders from the Admiralty.

"Going to get married are you, Captain? I suppose congratulations are in order." The Admiral rose and shook Merriman by the hand. "I hope all will be well for you and your lady in the future."

"Thank you, Sir George, but I can't go until after the court martial of your nephew."

"That's true, but it won't take long," he said sadly. "I think you can be on your way in two days, or three at the most. I have sufficient Post Captains to form a court and it will convene at eight o'clock tomorrow morning. Obviously with me being the boy's uncle, I cannot be in attendance officially, but I will be there. You will come ashore with all the witnesses and present yourselves here."

"Aye – aye, sir," was all Merriman could reply.

At precisely ten minutes to eight the next morning they were at the rooms reserved for the trial. There had been frantic brushing of best uniforms, washing of shirts and white stockings and polishing of shoes going on for most of the night and all were as clean and smart as they could be. The two Midshipmen, Small and Hungerford, were almost terrified by the ordeal awaiting them and the others, Lieutenants Laing and Goodwin with acting Lieutenant Shrigley and the doctor were equally nervous. The most composed of them all was Moreau who was looking about him with interest at the bustle of activity in this, one of Britain's principal seaports.

Merriman had brought along seamen Matthews and Jackson in case the court wished to question them also.

"Do you think we shall have to wait long, sir," asked Goodwin. "I've never been a witness before."

The others also admitted that this was the first time they had been involved.

"It's my first time too, gentlemen. All that is required from you are clear answers to the questions asked you. And you two boys, remember to speak out loudly enough for everyone to hear you."

In the event it did not take long for the proceedings to get under way. Merriman's report had been read by the officers of the court and he was called in to take his place as the first witness. A white faced Dorrington was escorted in by a marine guard and placed in a chair where he would be facing toward where his accusers and the witnesses would stand. Surprisingly, his defending officer was a very nervous Lieutenant Williams, Admiral FitzHerbert's Aide. The prosecutor was an elderly lieutenant.

The trial proceeded on its inexorable way with Merriman being questioned closely by the prosecuting officer. Then, in turn, the witnesses were brought in, Seaman Jackson first, followed by Shrigley, Laing and the doctor. The doctor was given permission to stay when Midshipman Small was called in. The boy was questioned briefly and Mr McBride was asked to remove Small's coat and shirt. The marks of the whipping had faded somewhat but were still visible and there were still scabs over the worst. When the boy's back was seen, a disgusted murmur ran round the people who had been allowed to watch. The President of the court banged on the table with his gavel and demanded quiet before conferring briefly with the other officers.

"I believe the court has heard enough evidence with regard to the first charge. We shall move on to the more serious charges, that the accused did strike his senior officer and murdered a seaman. Are we all prepared?"

Once again the parade of witnesses followed one after the other. Jackson first who described the event as he saw it, then the Doctor again and Lieutenant Goodwin who had heard Owen's deathbed statement. Finally M'sieur Moreau was called.

His appearance caused a flurry of excited interest among the people attending, especially the ladies who seemed impressed by Moreau's dark good looks.

Moreau was questioned by the prosecuting officer who asked him to tell the court why he, a Frenchman was here giving evidence.

At this point, Williams the defending officer made another effort to do something for his client. "This man is an enemy of our country, how do we know we can trust him?"

Moreau looked him up and down. "It is true our countries are at war, but I do not lie. I am a gentleman, sir, Charles Henri Moreau, formerly Count of Treville and Beaupreau, paroled to Captain Merriman. I witnessed the cowardly attempt on Captain Merriman's life and there is no question that I saw that man there, M'sieur Dorrington, shoot the English seaman."

To be fair to Lieutenant Williams, he did his best, but the evidence against his client was overwhelming and so damning that he stood little chance of affecting the result of the court's findings.

The members of the court retired to another room to consider their verdict but there was really only one verdict they could bring in. They filed back in after only a very few minutes and took their places. Then Dorrington was brought in and told to stand facing them. It was immediately obvious to him what the verdict would be as his midshipman's dirk was placed on the table with the point towards him. He stood there trembling as the President of the court spoke.

"Mr Dorrington, you have been found guilty of all the charges placed against you. Have you anything to say before I pronounce sentence?"

Dorrington stood looking at his feet and shook his head.

"There is only one punishment this court should award. You are an evil, depraved man found guilty of serious charges, each of which calls for death by hanging. However, with regard to your parentage, and the distinguished career of your late father, this court does not wish to add further to the dishonour you have brought to the family name and so you will not be hanged as a common criminal. The court has decided therefore that you will be deported in chains to the new penal colony, Botany Bay in Australia, there to stay for the rest of your natural life. Take him away."

Two marines moved forward and took Dorrington's arms, whereupon he roused himself and looked round at his accusers. "Damn you to Hell, Merriman, you bastard. I should have slit your throat when I had the chance. I hope a French cannon ball tears you apart, I hope you…"

His cries and shrieks faded as a marine clamped his hand firmly over Dorrington's mouth and he was forced, still struggling and kicking, out of the room.

Merriman and his party, a sombre group, returned to the ship, each busy with his own thoughts. The only one to say anything was Midshipman Small who whispered to Merriman, "I hated him for what he did to me, sir, and wished him dead, but deportation is terrible. He'll never see England and his home again and I helped to send him away."

"Don't dwell on this too deeply, Mr Small. Mr Dorrington had his chances to reform, but instead he chose to commit murder. His own actions brought him to this. You did your duty and I am proud of you. You'll make fine officer one day, I'm certain," said Merriman with his hand on the boy's shoulder.

He turned to address the group. "Now, gentlemen, we must be about our duties, but first I would like you and all the other officers to join me in my cabin."

When they were assembled, some seated and some standing, and each with a glass of wine in his hand, Merriman dismissed Peters and Tomkins. The buzz of conversation died and all the officers looked expectantly at him.

"Gentlemen, this sorry affair has affected us all deeply and I hope that we can put it all behind us. I want to hear no more about it. And now I have something more pleasing to tell you. We are to lose Mr Laing. Congratulations, Colin, you have been selected to command the corvette which is to be renamed the *English Mermaid.*"

There was a chorus of congratulations and everyone wanted to shake Laing by the hand.

"Thank you, thank you, gentlemen. Sir, this is rather sudden, did you have a hand in giving me this command?"

"Well, the Admiral asked if I had a recommendation and I could think of no-one better. Mind you, it won't be easy. She will be in the dockyard for some time yet and you will take command of her when she is repaired. Of course you will have to find a crew. David, you will be First officer when Colin leaves."

"Again thank you for giving me this chance, sir, though I'll be sorry to leave this company," said Laing.

"Peters," shouted Merriman, "we need some more wine. Gentlemen, I know you'll join me in a toast to the new captain of the *English Mermaid.*"

When the hubbub and backslapping had died down, Merriman said as gravely as he could, "There is one other *very, very* serious matter, gentlemen," said Merriman. The officers looked apprehensive but broke into spontaneous laughter when Merriman announced, "I am to be married."

There was immediate uproar with all of them wanting to offer him their congratulations.

When peace and quiet were restored, Lieutenant Laing said, "Sir, if Peters will fill our glasses once again with your excellent claret, may I propose a toast?"

The glasses were hastily filled by Peters and Tomkins.

"Gentlemen, please join with me in wishing Captain Merriman and his lady health and every happiness in their union." The glasses were drained at a gulp.

"Sir, am I to understand that your bride is the lovely lady I met at your house all those years ago, Miss Simpson?" asked Andrews.

"Correct, she did me the honour of accepting my proposal before we left for the West Indies. I shall be going home in a day or two, once I'm certain that the work on our ship is progressing well, and I propose to take you, Mr Andrews, Mr Shrigley, Mr St James and the doctor with me. All know the lady and I am sure she will be pleased to see you again. I'm sorry I can't take you all, but somebody must remain aboard to oversee the final repairs. That will be you, Colin. Also I have requested that M'sieur Moreau go with us. He is paroled to me and I should keep an eye on him."

Eventually the time arrived for Merriman and his party to leave for Chester, near to where the Merriman family home was situated in the village of Burton.

St James, Andrews and Midshipman Shrigley, Mr McBride, the doctor, and Moreau climbed down into the cutter to wait for him. Merriman turned to his first Lieutenant, "I leave the ship in your hands, Mr Laing, the others will be back as soon as possible but I'll be a few days longer."

Laing grinned. "Aye - aye, sir, I won't let the deck fall overboard. Enjoy your wedding, sir."

Merriman descended to the boat to the usual ceremonies and had hardly settled himself and his sword before the boat pushed off. Part of the way to the harbour wall, his new cox'n, Matthews called, "Avast rowing," and swung the tiller over to point the boat back to the ship.

"What the devil…" Merriman started to say, then he saw that his whole ship's company was clinging to every conceivable vantage point and cheering lustily. Merriman raised his hat in acknowledgement. The officers were smiling and the boat's crew were all grinning like Cheshire cats.

"Did you know about this, Mr Andrews?"

"Yes, sir, we all did. Mr Laing's idea it was. Even the men knew about your wedding."

"I'm gratified, gentlemen, 'pon my word I am. Now, Matthews, put the boat about and we'll be on our way. When you return to the ship I want you to thank Mr Laing for me and tell him he is to issue a double tot to every one of the men and be damned to what the Purser says."

"Aye – aye, sir," responded Matthews enthusiastically. "And be damned to what the Purser says!"

Chapter Twenty-Four

A long-awaited return home

As the day of the wedding drew near, Helen Simpson found herself becoming more and more apprehensive and agitated. As usual for brides-to-be, she was afflicted with various doubts and emotions. The letters sent by James from London had indicated that he would be home in time for the ceremony to take place no later than a week from the date on the letters. That was nearly a week ago, five days to be exact, and he could be home tomorrow, even today if the weather permitted and the roads were passable.

The four years since she last saw him on the day of their betrothal had seemed like a lifetime and now, finally, after all the waiting, he was coming home. After four years, would he have changed, would he still really want to marry her? After all, she was now twenty five years old which he may think was too old for a wife. But he was older still, although she hadn't considered that fact before.

A call from her father downstairs brought her out of her thoughts.

"Helen, my dear, are you coming? Your aunt and I are waiting."

It had been arranged that she and her father, together with his widowed sister Jane Prentice, should stay at the Merriman residence until James arrived. They would then return home to prepare her for the wedding. Her aunt and Mrs Merriman had become great friends and arranged everything beforehand so everybody knew what to do. Annie, Mrs Merriman's friend and housekeeper, was in her element, preparing for a great feast for the wedding breakfast.

The family sat before a huge fire. Of course the main topic of conversation was the wedding, with Mrs Merriman worrying as all mothers do about last minute arrangements. "Joseph, are you certain that the church is ready and the reverend knows it will be tomorrow or the next day? And have sufficient rooms been prepared for the officers James is bringing with him?"

"My dear Elizabeth, do stop fussing and relax. There is nothing more to be done until James gets here. You and Emily, with the help of Mrs Prentice and Annie, have dealt with everything. You've been over the arrangements time and time again and yes, accommodation is arranged at the inn in Neston for James' officers," said Captain Merriman, James' father.

"I can't help it, Joseph. It's the first wedding we've had in the family, and don't forget that Lord Stevenage is coming as well. Nothing must go wrong, nothing."

At that moment a servant announced that Doctor Simpson, his sister and daughter had arrived.

"Bring them in, girl, bring them in, don't leave them to freeze outside."

The new arrivals were soon settled by the fire and all the ladies began chattering away like magpies, going over details again and again. The men, that is Merriman's father, James' younger brother Matthew, and Doctor Simpson, kept themselves to a separate group, talking quietly.

Merriman and his companions arrived at the Merriman residence in the pale sunlight of the fine February afternoon. The stage had brought them as far as Chester from where Merriman had hired a carriage to take them to the house.

There was instant pandemonium. The family came to the door to greet them, dogs came rushing round from the back of the house with servants trying to catch hold of them without getting in everybody's way, while other servants unloaded the travellers' baggage from the back of the carriage.

Merriman's father roared for quiet. "James my boy, I'm glad to see you and your companions again, you are all most welcome. 'Pon my soul, Mr Shrigley, you've grown since we last met. Still eating well, I trust? Now then, come in out of the cold, all of you. James, where is your man Owen? I expected to see him with you."

"He's dead, Father, murdered by one of my midshipmen. It's a long story which can wait 'til later." He paused, "Father, where is my old dog, Jack?"

"He died, James, last year. He was a very, very old dog, you know. He must have tried to be near you at the end because we found him beside your bed. Knowing how much he meant to you, we buried him in the orchard. There's a stone with his name carved on it."

Merriman was upset, no doubt about it. Jack had been his constant companion from his youth and to realise that the poor old dog had gone affected him deeply.

"Come, James, there is someone here you must be dying to see."

Helen had not come out to the step when the family rushed out. Instead she had remained in the warm room with her father and aunt, waiting for James to come in. She was desperately trying to remain calm but the butterflies in her stomach and the thumping of her heart threatened to overwhelm her. She greeted the officers she had met before, and then suddenly he was there in front of her.

Some women would rather die than let outsiders know or see their innermost thoughts and emotions and Helen was just such a one. Coolly and calmly she extended her hand, "Welcome home, James," was all she said, but the look in her eyes and the trembling grip of her hand said so very much more.

"Helen, you are just as I remember you, except that you look even lovelier than I remember."

She blushed. "Oh, James, that cannot be true. I'm years older, but it is obvious to anyone that you have been under a tropical sun, you're as brown as a nut."

Both were trying to appear composed in front of the others when all either wanted was to be in each other's arms. Servants dispensed drinks and refreshments and the noise level rose with all of them talking volubly. As most of those present had met before, few introductions were needed. Only Moreau needed to be introduced to everyone and he very quickly charmed the ladies with his courtly manner.

Amongst all the chatter, old Captain Merriman was somewhat reserved and a bit put out at having a Frenchman under his roof, but when his son had briefly related why Moreau was there he became more affable and welcomed him. His son handed over to him the sword surrendered by Moreau on his parole.

"One more for your collection, Father, although I promised him it would be returned to him after the war, if we survive that is."

"It's a fine weapon, monsieur. Well used and cared for, I see."

"Yes, Captain Merriman. It was carried with honour by my father before me and, as he is now murdered by the revolution, it is now mine."

Merriman's sister, Emily, was surrounded by the young officers with St James relating a story which caused loud laughter from the group, but James and Helen were oblivious to the turmoil around them.

Merriman finally released Helen's hand to be able to speak to the family. His mother was sitting in an upright chair near the fireplace with Captain Merriman's hand resting on her shoulder. Now that he had the chance to pay more attention to them, Merriman was dismayed to see how much they had aged over the last four years. His mother was now completely grey haired and even his normally bluff, energetic father looked somehow smaller than Merriman remembered him.

Merriman bent over and took his mother's hand and kissed her on the cheek. "Mother, how are you? Still keeping Father in his place, I hope?"

"Well enough, James, well enough. I have been living for this day, to see you married, I didn't think I…"

"James, you should know that your mother has been quite poorly for some time," interrupted her husband. "In fact I am certain that if we had not had your future father-in-law to look after her, she would not be with us now. She has been abed for some time but insisted on being down with us when you came home."

"What is the matter with you, Mo…"

"I don't want to talk about it now, James. Seeing you and Helen together has done me good and did you know that Emily is to marry your friend Robert? They insisted on waiting until you were home, so we have arranged a double ceremony."

"That's wonderful, Mother, but where is Robert?"

"He will be here any moment now. He has been with Emily and us every day for the past week."

As if on cue, a servant came in and announced, "Major Saville!"

Merriman stepped forward to shake the newcomer's hand. "My dear Robert, it's good to see you again after so long. I hear that there is to be a double wedding for Helen and I and you and Emily. Congratulations again. Mind you take good care of my little sister though, she is very dear to me."

"Oh, I will, James, I will. Be in no doubt about it. As soon as we met we knew we were made for each other. And may I congratulate you, James, on your promotion to Post Captain."

"Thank you. Congratulations are flying round like bees round a honey pot. I hear that you also have also moved up, to Major, I see."

"Yes, a lot of men died to give me the chance. Indeed, I myself was so ill with fever that it was touch and go if I would survive. Excuse me, James."

Robert turned to Emily who was watching him with shining eyes. It was so obvious that she was happy, that Merriman couldn't resist hugging her and giving her a big kiss, before turning back to Helen and his parents.

"Have you heard from Lord Stevenage yet, Father?"

"Yes indeed. His man came with a message from him to say that he and your friend Mr Grahame have secured rooms at the White Lion in Chester, and will wait there until told that you are home and when and where the wedding will be. I'll send a note to him right away. Hoskins can take it."

"What exactly are the arrangements?"

"Of course, you don't know. Well, Helen, you tell him."

"My father, my aunt and myself will go back home now, and the wedding is set for eleven o'clock the day after tomorrow. Robert's father has come up for his son's wedding and they are both staying in Chester in a rented property. Robert's father came here yesterday to meet the family, especially Emily."

She laughed and went on, "Emily had him eating out of her hand in no time. Anyway, we will all meet in the morning at the church in Burton. Matthew has asked to be your groomsman which I hope is agreeable to you. Other arrangements have been made which I am not supposed to know about."

Conversation then became general until Annie, Mrs Merriman's housekeeper and friend, announced that a meal was prepared. Afterwards, Helen, her father and aunt left for home. Merriman's officers, Moreau with them, left for their respective lodgings and Robert left for Chester, leaving the five members of the family alone and quiet with their thoughts.

Well-fed, warm and comfortable, Merriman stretched his legs out towards the fire with a satisfied grunt and a feeling of relief. At last the time had come. For four years he had dreamed of it and now it was here.

"You and Emily are very quiet, James. Having second thoughts, either of you?"

"No, Father, I'm not. Just thinking how lucky I am."

"The same for me," said Emily. "I once thought Robert was dead and now here I am, ready to marry him the day after tomorrow."

"Your Father and I are very pleased and proud of you both," said their mother. "And now I must go to bed and rest. Come with me, Joseph, and help me."

When they had said their goodnights and gone upstairs, Merriman turned to his siblings and asked, "What's wrong with mother? Father told me that he hadn't believed she would be still alive now and only Doctor Simpson saved her."

"We don't know, James," replied Matthew. "They won't tell us, either of us. She has been ill for nearly two years and in some discomfort. I even asked the doctor but he wouldn't say."

"Well, I'll find out before I go back to my ship. Matthew, have you decided what you want to do with your life?"

"Indeed yes, Father bought me an ensign's commission in the Cheshire Regiment and Robert has promised to keep an eye on me."

"Good for you, brother, we all seem to be well settled in our future plans. And now I think we should all retire. We have a busy time ahead of us."

As he climbed the stairs he paused for a moment and raised his candle higher to better see the portraits lining the walls. Yes, there was his uncle Nathaniel, who had been killed with so many others of his regiment in the Americas. So, Matthew was to follow in his footsteps. Merriman noticed a new portrait of his mother but as yet there wasn't one of his father. He shook his head sadly and headed for his room.

Chapter Twenty-Five

Merriman marries but learns some sombre news

The following morning, Merriman awoke to a bitterly cold, wet January day with the wind howling round the house, rain lashing at the windows and black clouds racing overhead. He was the first of the family down and, as he watched the servants bustling round, lighting fires and preparing for breakfast, he wondered again about his mother's illness. He had little knowledge of medical affairs, but if Dr Simpson, his future father in law, thought it serious then it must be. *I must have a serious talk with the good doctor*, he mused, staring into the flames of a newly lit fire.

Suddenly he shivered, the room was not yet warm but it was more than that, he felt a horrible apprehension that something would go wrong over the next few days to interrupt the wedding. He shook off the mood as his father came into the room.

"Morning, James, a cold one again," said the older man, rubbing his hands together and stretching them out to the blaze in the hearth.

"Good morning, Father. It's certainly cold and with this wind it'll be a bad one at sea."

"That's true, but it's no worse than many another gale we've seen, eh?"

"I suppose not, but listen, please tell me what is the matter with mother. Neither Matthew nor Emily know and I think you should tell us the truth."

His father passed a shaking hand over his face and stared ahead of himself with a sombre look on his face. "You're right, of course, you should know, but let it wait until after breakfast when I'll tell the three of you together."

Silence fell, each of them busy with his own thoughts until a noisy Matthew burst into the room closely followed by his sister.

"I was hoping to go riding with you again, big brother, like we did last time you were home. I know I can beat you now if we have a race."

"Very likely, Matthew, very likely," laughed Merriman. "I've hardly sat a horse since then but I expect you have. Anyway the weather's too bad today."

At that moment a servant announced that breakfast was prepared and so the four of them went into the dining room and seated themselves, eyeing the various dishes on the side table. Some were steaming, some not, and a mouth-watering aroma filling the room. As they helped themselves to the food, Merriman realised that his mother wasn't with them and asked where she was.

"She has a light breakfast in her room nowadays. Annie takes it to her and helps her with it," said Emily. "She doesn't get up every day and never before midday."

Merriman looked at their father but the older man avoided his eye and said nothing, picking at his food without enthusiasm. Matthew noticed nothing, being totally absorbed in his meal, but Emily was aware of the strained atmosphere and looked from her brother to her father. She was about to ask what was the matter, but Merriman gave a little shake of his head and she remained silent.

When they had all finished their meal, the old man, and with surprise Merriman realised that their father really was an old man, asked them to gather in another room. There, with the door shut behind them, he motioned to them to sit down. He stood with his back to them for a few moments before speaking and when he turned to face them there was such misery on his face that Emily impulsively jumped up and flung her arms round him.

"It's time I told you what is wrong with your mother. I know you, Matthew, and you, Emily, have asked many times but now that James is home I can tell you all together."

He cleared his suddenly hoarse throat and continued, "As you know, she had a severe fall last winter. Hoskins was driving her in the light carriage over to see Helen and her aunt when something startled the horse, a wheel dropped into the ditch and the carriage overturned, throwing her out and knocking her unconscious. Hoskins tried to revive her and when he couldn't he ran off to get assistance. It was pouring with rain and mother was soaked through before he got back with help. She was brought home and put to bed and the doctor called for."

He paused before continuing. "Unfortunately Doctor Simpson had been called away to another patient and it was many hours before he came here. Your mother was never very strong and she caught a chill that day which very quickly turned to pneumonia. The doctor hardly left her side and I don't think she would be alive now but for him. The poor man was completely exhausted but he pulled her through, although the worst was yet to come."

The three siblings waited in silence except for Merriman who leapt to his feet and in his agitation paced back and forth exclaiming, "That's not the worst, you say, what could be worse?"

"Sit down, James, and I'll tell you. It seems that mother's heart was weakened and she has never been the same since." The older man closed his eyes, swallowed and cleared his throat again. "Your mother is dying and Doctor Simpson gives her no more than two or three weeks to live. Several times we thought she had gone but she has an iron will and I think it's been the determination to see you all married and settled that has kept her going."

Silence enveloped them. Emily was weeping quietly and Matthew, white faced, was shaking his head slowly from side to side. James went to his father and put his arm round the older man's shoulders.

"Thank you for telling us, Father. It must have been dreadful for you keeping it all to yourself and, now that we do know, you have all the love and support we can give you."

The four of them stood for a while in a group embrace before their father, never one to show his emotions openly, said, "Right that's enough of that. I know it will be difficult to proceed as if everything is normal but we must put on a brave face in front of your mother and make sure that the festivities continue as planned. Come now, Emily, stop blubbing, time for that later. You're being married tomorrow. You don't want to show a swollen blotchy face to your new husband, do you?"

Merriman, trying to help break the sombre mood, asked about the arrangements that Helen had told him she was not supposed to know of.

"Well, James, we all gather at the church at eleven in the morning and after the ceremonies are over everyone's coming back here for the wedding breakfast. The Simpsons have agreed to this as their place is just not big enough to find room for all the people coming."

"How many are coming then?"

"At the last count the number was forty five, including your aunts, uncles and cousins on your mother's side and my side of the family, the officers you brought with you, Moreau, Robert and his father, Lord Stevenage and Mr Grahame, though why His Lordship wants to come, I can't imagine. The rest are friends of ours from the district."

"Ye gods, so many."

"Yes, and the arrangements for after the wedding are all in hand. Robert is to take Emily back to Chester where his father has rented a house for them and you and Helen will have the old dower house down by the river."

"That old place? I can't take Helen there, it's dirty, damp and totally unsuitable."

"You're wrong there, James," laughed Emily. "Father has had the entire place rebuilt and extended. We've all had the most fun finding carpets and furniture for you. Even Matthew was helping the men to clean up the grounds."

"That's right, James, I have. It was your mother's idea and it's our wedding gift to you both. Annie has even engaged servants for you. A woman who will be your housekeeper and Helen's maid, and her husband will look after the place for you. How does that sound?"

"Wonderful, I can't thank you enough for all you have done, all of you. I must go up and thank mother as well."

"Not yet, James, leave it to the afternoon."

The rest of the day was spent in last minute preparations for the big day. Merriman's uniform was sponged, washed and pressed, his shoes polished until they shone like glass, and Matthew insisted on being the one to clean and polish his sword. Members of the family turned up and the place was alive with aunts, uncles and cousins, most of whom Merriman couldn't remember. Annie stood guard over his mother's room and allowed in only a few people at a time to ensure that her charge was not overtired.

The great day dawned at last, cold and overcast but at least the rain and wind had ceased. Lying in bed, staring at the ceiling before getting up, Merriman admitted to himself that he was nervous but once he was downstairs and surrounded by all the activity going on he soon forgot that anxiety.

The family gathered in the hall ready to go to the church and Mrs Merriman appeared in a wheeled chair pushed by a footman. She looked bright and cheerful and Merriman could only guess at the effort it must have been to appear so.

As they arrived at the church in Burton village, they were amazed at the number of carriages assembled there amongst which Merriman could see the elegant travelling coach used by Lord Stevenage, easily identifiable by the coat of arms painted on the doors. They made their way inside; Merriman's mother disdained the use of the wheeled chair and, leaning heavily on Matthew's arm, walked slowly to the front of the church with James following. Captain Merriman would follow with his daughter Emily. All Merriman could see was a sea of faces, but one or two stood out from the rest. There were his officers in a group by the door and halfway up the aisle he saw Lord Stevenage and Mr Grahame. Robert and his father were already seated and waiting so James and Matthew joined them. The army officer sitting next to Robert was evidently his groomsman.

They had not long to wait before the sound of carriage wheels outside caused everyone to turn round for the first sight of the brides to be. Steps sounded at the entrance and all rose to their feet in anticipation. The first to appear was Doctor Simpson with a radiant Helen on his arm. They were closely followed by Captain Merriman and Emily.

Merriman had eyes for nobody but Helen while beside him Robert murmured, "By Heaven, James, we are a fortunate pair. Sink me if we're not."

Both girls looked absolutely gorgeous and were dressed in the height of fashion, each bearing a small posy of evergreen foliage. Merriman found a great lump in his throat at the sight. As they all took their places in front of the congregation, his heart was thumping fit to burst but then a strange calm came over him and he was able to think and see clearly again as the parson began the ceremony. Their responses were clear and unhesitating with no trace of shyness or nerves from either Helen or Emily. After signing the register, the two couples emerged from the vestry to face the smiling, laughing crowd.

It was so cold that nobody lingered outside the church and it wasn't long before the newly married couples were gratefully back in the warmth of the Merriman family home, lining up with their parents to welcome the guests. Lord Stevenage made no effort to claim any privileges of his rank, introduced himself only by the name of William D'Ablay, and lined up and took his turn with the rest. When Merriman introduced him to Helen, who gave him a deep curtsey, he said only that he wished them well and would speak with them later. When Mr Grahame appeared he winked at Merriman, leaned forward with a twinkle in his eye and whispered, "Congratulations, James. Remember that you have me to blame for the situation you are in now."

He was referring to the fact that four years ago it was he who had encouraged Merriman to ask Helen to marry him.

Servants circulated with glasses of wine and sherry and soon the noise of chatter rose as people got to know one another and renewed old acquaintances. They all wanted to shake the men by the hand and to kiss the brides, an opportunity taken enthusiastically by Merriman's officers who had all met Helen and Emily before.

A magnificent feast followed. Annie, Mrs Merriman's housekeeper and friend, had made a supreme effort and, although she had been given a place at the table with the other guests, nevertheless she managed to keep an eagle eye on the servants, many of whom had been hired for the occasion.

The time flew by and when the senior Captain Merriman rose to his feet to speak, several of the guests, both male and female had been so overcome by the warmth, the wine and a surfeit of food that they were fast asleep, a not unusual occurrence in that age of gluttony. He spoke of how happy they were to welcome Helen and Robert into the family, and Doctor Simpson replied in a like manner. Some other guests made sometimes clear and sometimes unintelligible speeches and proposed toasts to the happy couple leading to more hilarity and uproar, but eventually Captain Merriman rose to his feet again, pounded on the table and called for silence.

"Ladies and Gentlemen, we have a very distinguished guest in our midst who has asked that he may speak. May I introduce to you Lord Stevenage. My Lord."

There was an immediate buzz of comment, a Lord no less, which was quickly stilled when His Lordship stood and looked around.

"Captain Merriman, I wish to thank you and your delightful wife for inviting me to this occasion and for the overwhelming hospitality I and everyone here have received. I know that there must have been intense speculation in your family as to why I wished to be invited to James and Helen's marriage. I first met James when he and his ship were instrumental in saving my life and those of others aboard an East Indiaman attacked by Algerian corsairs. The name Merriman attracted my attention and I made discreet enquiries into your family and background. I must tell you, Ladies and Gentlemen, that James Merriman is one of the most able of His Majesty's officers in the service today, with, I am sure, a brilliant career ahead of him. I see no reason why he could not attain Flag rank in due course. And now he has made another brilliant move, he has married the lovely Helen. I tell you, James, if I were a younger man I would have been in competition with you for the lady's hand."

The guests clapped and cheered, those that were still awake and able that is. Merriman grinned, somewhat bemusedly, while Helen clutched his hand and somehow contrived to curtsey whilst seated in response to the compliment.

His Lordship continued, "I simply wish to add my own congratulations to those already expressed. To you, James and Helen, and also to you, Emily and Robert, may I wish success and happiness in your lives together. Ladies and Gentlemen, another toast to the happy couples."

When the guests were noisily seating themselves again, his Lordship leaned towards Captain Merriman and whispered, "I would very much like to speak to you and all your family in private, Captain, if I may. After the celebrations are over, of course"

"Certainly, my Lord. I don't think we shall be missed if we slip away into another room now. James, will you push your mother in her wheeled chair while the rest of us follow. Helen, take my arm, my dear, Emily and Robert you must come as well. Matthew, you too."

And so, settled comfortably in another room, the family waited to hear what Lord Stevenage wanted to say. He smiled as he looked round at their faces.

"I know you are all wondering why I asked to speak with you. I wanted to be here at James' wedding of course but there is another reason why I wished to be here. As I am sure you know, Captain Merriman, your father, the late Admiral Josiah Merriman, married a lady whose family wished to have nothing further to do with her for marrying against their wishes."

He paused for a moment before making a startling announcement. "That lady was my favourite aunt, Henrietta, of whom I have only fond memories."

There was a stunned silence before he went on, "Of course, Captain Merriman, you will have realised that that simple fact makes us cousins and James is also related."

At last it became clear to Merriman why Lord Stevenage had taken such an interest in him and done so much to further his career in the navy.

James looked across at his father. The older man was sitting there with a dazed look on his face, staring at his new found relative in astonishment, almost at a loss for words.

"I had no idea, sir, I mean, that is ... my father never told us who my mother was, only that she had married him against her parents' wishes. We had speculated, of course, but it never occurred to us that she was from such an illustrious and noble house."

"Well, cousin, she was. I knew that she married a naval officer named Merriman, but as a boy I was forbidden to talk about her. I always thought how brave she was to defy the family in that way. After I encountered James the first time, the name Merriman interested me and I had enquiries made. After all, it is not a very common name and I wondered if it was possible that I could contact my aunt again. Sadly I learned that she had passed away some years ago."

"Yes, that's right, but neither she nor my father, who died soon after, would tell us anything about her family, although I had the impression that she thought they had treated her badly."

"They did," said Lord Stevenage bluntly. "I had hoped to be able to make amends for what my grandparents did, but I was too late, too late," he repeated sadly.

"We must talk further, sir, but I am sure that you appreciate that James and Helen want to be back with their friends and then be away as soon as they can, and I must play the host to our guests."

"Of course, and we will meet again in time but I must return to London as soon as I can in the morning." He turned to Merriman. "James, with your permission, Mr Grahame and I will take your M'sieur Moreau back to London with us tomorrow."

"Permission, sir?" faltered Merriman.

"Certainly. He is paroled to you but will be more use to us there. We will look after his interests, you may be sure."

"You have my permission, my Lord, willingly given."

"Thank you. I'll take my leave now. Cousin, it has been an honour to be under your roof." Lord Stevenage took Mrs Merriman's hand, bowed deeply and said, "Ma'am, I cannot recall having been made more welcome in any house in the land, thank you for your hospitality."

"My Lord, you are too kind, it is we who are honoured," she said in reply.

After he had gone, with his farewells still in their ears, the family sat in awed silence for several minutes before rousing themselves and joining the guests.

In due course the gathering broke up in the early hours of the morning to send the young couples on their way. Emily and Robert disappeared in a carriage in the direction of Chester and a small decorated carriage was waiting outside for James and Helen. He handed her in but, before climbing in himself, he turned to his parents and hugged and kissed his mother who was looking very tired but trying not to show her discomfort.

"Bless you, James, I can't tell you how happy I am for you and Emily, it was my dearest wish to see you married and Helen will make you a wonderful wife," she whispered in his ear.

Entering the carriage, Merriman was startled to see that the horses had been replaced between the shafts by his officers and friends, Andrews, St James, Shrigley and the ship's doctor McBride, Matthew, his brother, and even Moreau and some of the servants.

"Sit down, sir," yelled an intoxicated Shrigley. "We're off."

To a cheer from the remaining guests, the men set off at a run to the old dower house. Soon they were puffing and blowing, having eaten and drunk too much, but they carried on gamely and delivered Merriman and Helen safely to the house where the two servants were waiting. Moreau, who had absorbed more than a little good French brandy, leaned forward conspiratorially and said, "Go and uphold the honour of the family, James. I don't exsh – exshpect to see you again before tomorrow, oh, it's tomorrow to day, I mean ... er, what do I mean? Anyway I'm off, off to L-L- London with Mr Grahame so I won't she- she- see you again for some time."

"Don't suppose you'll need any help up there will you, sir?" said St James, slowly swaying on his feet supported by Andrews who was in no better state. Shrigley grinned foolishly as he slid down the carriage wheel to end up sitting on the ground. He peered owlishly up at the rest of them as he struggled to get to his feet, but gave up the attempt and subsided to the ground again, snoring gently.

Merriman and Helen entered the house, Helen still blushing from overhearing the comments. The maid, an elderly woman, quickly showed them to their room which was made warm by the large fire burning in the grate. She curtseyed and said, "Sir, Ma'am, I hope you will be very happy, goodnight."

Left alone together for the first time that day, they stood for a long moment just looking at one another before she came to his arms and they kissed longingly.

"Oh, James, how I've longed for this moment. I thought it would never come."

"And I too, my love. Oh, Helen, I do love you so."

"Wait a moment, James, wait for me."

She moved away from him into the shadows by the big four poster bed. He heard the rustle of clothing and then she stood before him with the lamplight making intriguing shadows and highlights over her naked body. Merriman could do no more than stand transfixed looking at her beauty in the amazing knowledge that she was all his.

She held out her hand. "Come, James, come to me now," she whispered, as she slipped into the bed.

He needed no further encouragement. His clothes joined hers on the floor and in a moment their bodies were clasped together. She moaned softly as he entered her and they became one.

Chapter Twenty-Six

An Admiralty dispatch arrives with new orders

The courier pounded up the gravelled carriageway and hauled his sweating, blowing, mud-spattered horse on to its haunches. Leaping off, he thumped on the door of the house for attention. When a servant answered he gasped, "Urgent despatch for Captain James Abel Merriman… is he here?"

"Well I could say yes, but then again, I could say no."

"What is it, girl, what's the problem?" said James' father, coming to the door behind the girl.

"Urgent despatch from London, sir, for Captain James Merriman," repeated the man.

"Very good, I'm his father, also Captain Merriman. He's not here at the moment but I'll see he gets it. Now then, take that animal round to the stableyard for attention and then find the kitchen. They'll give you something to eat."

The servant shut the door and disappeared into the depths of the house. Captain Merriman senior retreated into the hall and studied the superscription on the package. He had seen enough of Admiralty despatches to know that it needed immediate action. He sighed, then bellowed for a man to take it down to the dower house where James and Helen were staying.

For ten wonderful days and nights they had hardly left the house, totally engrossed in learning as much about each other as they could. They had also been making love, repeatedly, Helen with a wild abandon and enthusiasm which surprised James and caused him to respond equally enthusiastically.

When the maid knocked and passed in the Admiralty despatch, Merriman knew immediately that their idyll was over. Harsh reality had intervened and duty called. Reading the letter, quickly cutting through the wordy preamble, he saw that he must return to Portsmouth and his ship without delay. Further orders would await him there. He showed the letter to Helen.

"Oh, James, I don't want you to go. It's too soon. Can't you stay longer, when will I see you again?" she wailed.

"I don't know, my darling. Possibly weeks, months, years even, like it was last time. I don't know where they will send me."

As the tears coursed down her cheeks he held her tightly to him, whispering the things lovers do on parting, before holding her at arm's length and looking deep into her eyes.

"We knew this moment would come, my love. I have to go but the memories of you and these wonderful days will sustain me wherever I go and through whatever happens. And the wonderful nights too," he added as an afterthought.

"Whatever happens to you? Nothing will happen to you, will it?" she cried. "What will I do without you?"

They clung together for a while before making love again, with a frenzy and deep passion, knowing it would be the last time for who knew how long.

As he packed his things ready for the journey, Merriman had to admit to himself that he was eager to get back to his ship and the sea again. Helen was wonderful and he loved her dearly, but the sea was his life. At his parent's house, as he said goodbye to his tearful mother and sad eyed father, he wondered if he would see them again. It was most unlikely that his mother would live much longer and he couldn't imagine his father surviving for long after she was gone. The whole family had split up - Emily away with her new husband and Matthew, a newly commissioned ensign, had recently joined his regiment. Only Helen was left to comfort his parents in their old age, but she had her father and aunt to consider too. He sighed, embraced them and Helen for the last time before climbing into the small family coach which would take him to Chester on the first part of his journey.

Chapter Twenty-Seven

Dorrington kills a marine guard

Portsmouth was the usual bustling place he remembered and when the coach deposited him with the other passengers at the Eagle and Crown near the dockside, he breathed in the smell of the sea overlaid with the aroma of coffee from the inn behind him. There were also the scents of tar and of wet canvas, hemp cordage, and the animal odour from the sweating horses pulling great carts loaded with provisions and supplies which would be taken out on barges and lighters to the ships at anchor.

Immediately he felt at home, then reminded himself that his home was back in Burton and that he had a wife waiting there for his eventual return. Then, guiltily, he realised that he hadn't given her a thought since the coach approached Portsmouth and he caught sight of the tall masts of the warships. He was back where he belonged.

The first thing he must do was to make his presence known to the Port Admiral before going out to his ship. Sir George FitzHerbert was still the stern martinet who had his staff officers jumping at every command, yet as his aide Lieutenant Williams showed Merriman into his office he rose to his feet and greeted him cordially.

"Captain Merriman, I'm pleased to see you here again safe and sound. You'll join me in a glass of something, I'm sure. Williams, where are you man? Fetch us some drinks, wine for you, Captain?"

"Thank you, sir, that I shall enjoy."

In spite of the friendly welcome he had received, Merriman had an uneasy feeling that the Admiral had something more serious on his mind and when the two of them were seated, each with a glass of good red wine in hand, he was proved right. Sir George took a deep draught and then contemplated the dregs left in the glass with a frown on his forehead.

"I've some bad news for you, Captain Merriman, very bad. It concerns my nephew, Midshipman Dorrington. Oh dammit, he's not a midshipman now but he is still my nephew, Arthur."

The Admiral took a deep breath before going on to say, "He escaped from custody three nights ago. He was in leg irons so how he did it I don't know, but he killed a marine guard and took his uniform. Then he inflicted a severe head wound on another marine. The irons were found beside the second man, obviously they had been used as a weapon. The second man died yesterday without recovering consciousness so we could learn nothing from him."

Merriman sat there aghast, his brain working feverishly. "Has he not been seen since, sir?"

"No, Captain, not so much as a hair. Search parties have scoured the town, but to no avail. He's completely disappeared and from that we deduce that somebody is giving him shelter. What particularly concerns me is the fact that he was so vindictive towards you. It may be that he is just waiting somewhere for his chance to kill you."

Merriman said nothing, his mind in a whirl. That Dorrington was dangerous, they already knew, and now he had three dead men to pay for. Surely he would want to be as far away as he could go, abroad if possible. There would be many captains of trading vessels who would welcome another hand without looking too closely into a man's reasons for leaving the country.

Merriman voiced these thoughts to the Admiral. "Surely that's what he would do, sir. If he's caught, he'll hang this time for certain."

"I know, Captain, I know, but I can't rid my mind of the thought that he'll seek revenge against you or even against me. He must be unhinged to do what he did and not thinking clearly."

"Yes, sir. I wondered why there was an increased number of marines outside."

"Can't take chances, Captain, and I urge you to be careful. I've issued orders for him to be shot on sight if he won't surrender."

"I'm sorry to have to say it, sir, but I think it would be better all round if he were to be shot. If he escaped again, God alone knows how many other men he would kill."

"You're right, of course. All we can do is to be on our guard. Anyway, enough about that. You'll probably find Mr Grahame aboard when you rejoin your ship and I believe he has orders for you. *Lord Stevenage* is fully provisioned and you can go when and where he directs. Oh, by the way, your first officer Mr Laing, I've promoted him to take command of the *English Mermaid* and he will be leaving soon to join the fleet in the Channel. Still short of a full crew though, the usual problem, the press can't find men."

Still deep in thought about Dorrington, Merriman engaged a waterman to row him out to join his ship. The man, a short muscular fellow with arms like tree trunks, was assisted by his wife who was scarcely less muscular. They both stared at him when he announced that he should be taken to *Lord Stevenage*.

"That's the old *Thessaly* ain't it, sir? I was cap'n of the foretop before I lost me leg, sir."

Being so lost in thought, Merriman hadn't noticed the man's wooden leg which he kept braced against a wooden block to support him.

"Yes, that's so. She was," was all he said in reply.

The man glanced over his shoulder at his wife who merely shrugged her shoulders. They were quite used to uncommunicative officers and, after all, to them he was just another such. As the boat neared the ship, a hail woke Merriman from his dark mood and he flung open his cloak to reveal his single epaulette. That immediately caused a flurry of activity as preparations were hastily made to welcome the Captain.

He climbed aboard to the usual ceremony of bos'n's whistles, the marine guard presenting arms, and the assembled crew. The officers, all with wide smiles on their faces were waiting to greet him.

"Welcome back, sir. I trust that you and your lady are well."

"Indeed we are, Mr Andrews, indeed we are," he said. "I'm pleased to see that you all got back here safely."

"Yes, sir. Mr Laing has left us and the ship is in all respects ready for sea. Sir, may I present Lieutenant Merryweather, Henry Merryweather. He is our new third officer. Came aboard not an hour ago."

"Welcome aboard, Mr Merryweather. I hope your name means that we shall have good weather in future."

Merryweather, a lanky young man, as dark as a moor, grinned embarrassedly at Merriman's feeble joke which he had heard so often before, whilst the others laughed dutifully.

"Very well, gentlemen, I'll have you all in my cabin in half an hour. Is Mr Grahame aboard?"

"He was, sir, but he has gone ashore again. Are we to wait for him?"

"We are, Mr Andrews, we are," said Merriman as he went below to his cabin to find Peters and Tomkins waiting.

"Welcome back, sir," they chorused together.

"Your baggage is aboard, and I've started to unpack it," added Peters. "Is there anything I can get you, sir?"

"Not at the moment, thank you. Tomkins, is there much paperwork for me?"

"Nothing out of the ordinary, sir, just the usual reports and the ship's books to see, and the master's log of course. There are also the ship's accounts too, sir."

"Very well, I'll attend to those later. The officers will be down shortly and we'll have some of that French claret if there's any left. Or have you two rogues drunk it all?"

"Oh no, sir," said a shocked Peters. "We wouldn't do that."

"No? Perhaps not." Since Tomkins had come aboard to be his captain's clerk, the normally reticent Peters had thawed somewhat and the two men were now good friends and as thick as thieves.

"There will be some boxes and things coming aboard soon, they contain some glassware and bottles and a few fripperies from my wife, make sure there is no damage. Now off you go."

With all the officers except Shrigley, who was the officer of the day, were assembled, Merriman looked round at the eager faces of the men he had come to know so well over the last four years or more. The elderly Master, Mr Cuthbert, with his lined and weather beaten face, Andrews, Weston, the two marine officers, the two remaining midshipmen Hungerford and little Gideon Small, then Doctor McBride and the new man, Merryweather.

"Gentlemen, before those of you who were at my wedding ask, yes, all went well and my wife wishes me to extend to you all her regards and best wishes for our next venture."

He held up his hand to quell their noisy appreciation before continuing in a more serious vein. "Are you aware that Dorrington has escaped from custody and killed two men to do it?"

"We have heard rumour and counter rumour, sir. Some say that he must have fled and joined the crew of some trading ship, others that he must be in hiding somewhere, but there is nothing certain. Some of us were ordered to join the search parties because we could recognise him, but we found no trace of him."

"Well, gentlemen, Admiral FitzHerbert is convinced that Dorrington will try to revenge himself on him or more likely on me. He must be quite mad and there is no telling what he might try to do."

In the shocked silence Midshipman Small whispered, "I thought we had seen the last of him, sir. Do you think he will try anything here?"

"I cannot say, Mr Small. The Admiral has increased the marine guard round himself and his wife and I think we can do no less. Also bear in mind that the Admiral has ordered that Dorrington is to be shot if he is found and won't surrender."

This news elicited a murmuring from the assembled men.

"Mr St James, until we sail, I want our marine sentries doubled and you, Mr Andrews, will see to it that extra hands are allocated to guard duties during the night. See to that if you please, gentlemen. Before you go, is there anything else?"

"Yes, sir, if I may ask, who was this Dorrington you spoke about?" asked Merryweather.

"Of course, you don't know. However, I'm sure that one of the other officers will be pleased to tell you the whole sorry story."

Merriman sat down at his desk and called for his clerk, Tomkins, to bring all the reports and papers which had accumulated in his absence. Tomkins had prepared most of them ready for his signature but he still had to read them all to bring himself up to date with all that had happened.

He was completely immersed in the task when the sound of cheering, becoming louder and louder, brought him out on deck to find almost the entire crew hanging over the side listening to news shouted out from a boat being rowed round the anchored ships. They too burst out into excited cheering, the officers no less than the men.

"What the devil is going on?"

"Something about Sir Edward Pellew, sir, and a great victory for us."

"We need to know more about this. Mr Weston, take a boat and go ashore and see what you can find out."

"Aye - aye, sir." Weston shouted for a boat's crew and, in no time at all, they were pulling lustily for the harbour steps.

Merriman and the rest waited in anticipation for Weston's return but it was almost two hours before the boat was seen approaching.

"Well, Mr Weston, what's the news?" asked Merriman impatiently, the other officers gathering round to hear.

Weston was so excited that he could hardly speak coherently.

"Incredible news, sir, a great victory. It's unbelievable. How he did it, I don't know, but the news is all over Portsmouth. They probably don't know yet in London."

"Calm down, Mr Weston, calm down and tell us what has happened."

"Yes, sir, it seems that a brig arrived here this morning carrying despatches from the channel fleet and it's true, Sir Edward, in the frigate *Indefatigable* caught the French warship, a three decker named *Droits De L'Homme,* on its own, attacked it and drove it ashore."

"A three decker, by God. What else do you know? Was Pellew's, I mean Sir Edward's ship the only English warship involved?"

"No, sir, another frigate, *Amazon,* came up later and between them they engaged the French. There was a full gale blowing and on the evening of the first day the French lost their mizzen mast. Then, on the second day, in the early morning, land was seen and Sir Edward broke off the action as they were on a lee shore. Because of damage, *Amazon* and *Droits de L'Homme* couldn't beat to seaward and both went aground, sir. Oh, and apparently the despatch mentioned that the French ship was carrying a large number of troops."

"Do you think it could have been a part of the fleet trying to invade Ireland, sir?" asked Shrigley.

"It might have been, Alfred, but we may never know. It was a remarkable action all the same, the more remarkable when you consider the difference in size and firepower between the ships. Normally a frigate would never dare to engage a three decker."

It was later confirmed that the action took place in Audierne Bay south of Brest. *Droits De L'Homme* was indeed part of that ill-fated French fleet and was one of the last to leave Bantry Bay. She had over seven hundred soldiers on board. Due to the severity of the gale, the French warship had been unable to open her lower gunports for fear of being swamped which reduced the weight of her broadside to no more than that of *Indefatigable*. A total of more than nine hundred men, soldiers and sailors, died, many of the rest being left aboard the wreck for four or five days before rescue. The *Amazon* lost only a few men, most of the crew managing to get ashore on rafts, although there they became prisoners of war.

Chapter Twenty-Eight

The final accounting, Dorrington is shot

Two weeks later the ship was still lying at anchor in Portsmouth harbour while they waited for Mr Grahame to return. So long after Dorrington's escape nobody now really expected anything to happen. At first there was great interest and wagers were made as to how long it would be before he was caught, but as time passed most people presumed he was far away.

As ordered, extra guards had been posted but as nothing out of the ordinary happened, the men and marines were beginning to lose their earlier keenness and it took repeated threats from the marine corporals and petty officers to subdue the sulky mutterings of the men about the extra duty.

Sam Gibbons was a 'good enough' sort of man. His marine uniform was always just good enough for inspection, his equipment was always just good enough for inspection, and his musket was the despair of the sergeant and corporals. When the marines were paraded, the sergeant made him stand in the rear rank in the hope that he would not be noticed.

"Out of sight, my lad, but not out of my mind, you lazy bugger," was the sergeant's repeated comment.

In short, Sam Gibbons was far from the smartest man, either mentally or physically. True, he had twice reached the dizzy heights of corporal's rank but had very quickly lost his stripes due to drunkenness and disorderly conduct. If there had been such a thing as a bad conduct medal, he would have won it several times over.

On this particular night, an extra swig of illegally hoarded rum on top of what he had absorbed earlier meant that he was finding it increasingly difficult to keep his eyes open. He was posted on the quarter-deck and had heard the sounds coming from the great cabin as Merriman entertained his officers. Now all was quiet below as they had retired for the night.

Gibbons bitterly resented the fact that he had to be on guard at all and with the old soldier's ability to sleep on his feet, he did just that, leaning against the rail.

A faint bump against the side of the ship below him roused him enough to peer over the side but all he could see in the dark was an old boat with what appeared to be a bundle of canvas on the bottom. The only thought that passed briefly through his fuddled mind was that some careless fool had lost his boat, and then he was asleep again.

He never saw the shadowy figure clad in marine uniform climbing aboard and he never felt the bayonet thrust up through his stomach and into his heart. One brief convulsion and he was dead.

Dorrington smiled to himself. He had felt an almost sensual pleasure as the man died. It had been so easy and he blessed his forethought in grinding and sharpening the bayonet to a needle point so that it could slide into flesh without difficulty. He stood still for a moment looking down at the corpse, his clouded mind wondering why he had killed the man. It was evident that neither the marine on the other side of the quarter deck or anyone else had heard the disturbance, but the sound of a man coughing brought him to his senses. Quickly and quietly he pushed Gibbons' body into the deep shadows behind the loops and coils of rope hanging from the fife rail at the foot of the mizzen mast where it would not be seen until daylight. Then he picked up the man's hat and musket and stood in his place, staring out at the lights ashore.

He was just in time, for the corporal of the guard was making the rounds of the sentries. Fortunately for Dorrington the corporal was drowsy and, seeing a figure in marine uniform, contented himself with a quick glance. He asked merely, "Alright, Gibbons? Keep yer bloody eyes open."

Dorrington simply grunted an unintelligible reply and the corporal moved on and disappeared below. The murderer relaxed, knowing that he had at least half an hour before the corporal came up again. He stood awhile, marking in his mind where the other sentries were. He recognised the officer of the watch, Weston, who was on the fo'c's'le talking with Midshipman Hungerford. The two of them were faintly illuminated by the light coming from the fo'rrard companionway.

For a moment Dorrington savoured to himself the thought of the pleasure he could have from sliding his bayonet between Hungerford's ribs, but he was after bigger game. Captain Merriman was below, probably fast asleep by now, and he was the one that deserved to be killed, preferably slowly and while suffering great pain. Dorrington sighed, knowing that he would have to content himself with a simple thrust of the bayonet because he must make no noise if he wanted to escape again, although he had given no real thought to escaping after the deed was done. He was sane enough to know that he would probably be caught sometime and would hang, but somehow he didn't care, his crazed mind concentrating on a single thing: to kill Merriman.

Completely unobserved he moved down the steps from the quarter-deck to the main deck and in through the door leading to the flat outside the Captain's and officers cabins. In the half light and shadows cast by a single lantern, the marine on guard outside the captain's quarters noticed nothing wrong when another marine in full uniform approached him.

"You're early, mate. I thought I had another hour to go."

"No you haven't, you've no time at all," whispered Dorrington as he thrust the bayonet home once more.

The man collapsed. Dorrington held him but was unable to catch the man's musket which hit the deck with a clatter. Surprisingly nobody was disturbed by the noise and all remained quiet. He slid the bayonet back into its scabbard without even wiping off the dead man's blood. Taking a chance, he cautiously opened the door to the Captain's quarters, listened for a moment and then slowly dragged the body inside, picked up the fallen musket and closed the door behind him.

He was in a sort of lobby with the door to the great cabin ahead of him. A light shone from underneath that door, and the door to the captain's sleeping quarters stood open on his right. No sound came from the small cabin, neither snoring nor even breathing, so Dorrington peeped round the doorpost. Even in the gloom it was obvious that the cot was empty. He turned back to the other door, slowly turned the handle, and pushed the door open, startled to hear Merriman's voice as he stepped inside.

"Ah, Mr Dorrington, I've been expecting you. Do sit down while we talk."

Merriman was sitting behind the table in the centre of the cabin, holding a large book in front of him. Obviously he had been reading. The captain's calm acceptance of his presence bewildered Dorrington.

"But, but I've come here to kill you, you bastard, not talk."

"Oh yes, I know all about that, Arthur, but we must talk first."

The casual use of his Christian name un-nerved Dorrington even more and, before he knew what he was doing, he sat down.

Merriman continued, "How about a glass of claret to steady your nerves?"

Dorrington nodded dumbly and accepted the glass offered to him. Merriman leaned back in his chair and raised his glass. "Your health, Mr Dorrington."

Dorrington giggled before he drank. Surely the fool didn't think talking would save him. It would all be so easy, all was quiet aboard and the captain was sitting there defenceless.

"D'you know, Arthur, your mother loves you still. Your uncle tells me that she is heartbroken, knowing what you have done."

Mention of his mother roused Dorrington to anger.

"I wouldn't have done any of it if you'd treated me and my title with respect. You forced me to do it with your stupid rules and regulations, so I've you to blame for ruining my life."

He snorted with laughter as he realised he had outwitted everybody and had the captain at his mercy.

He stood up and tugged at the bayonet at his belt. He giggled again as he anticipated thrusting the weapon into Merriman's stomach, but the weapon resisted a little due to the drying blood on the blade. The door to the pantry crashed open to reveal Tomkins with a carving knife in his hand.

"I 'eard it all, sir. Dorrington, you evil bugger, I'll 'ave you." Tomkins moved forward.

Dorrington turned towards him, looked down at the bayonet, momentarily perplexed, then tugged harder. Out it came just in time to deflect Tomkins' blow and, with a quick stab, Dorrington pierced the man's arm. He turned back to see Merriman still sitting there but now he held a pistol, aimed at Dorrington's heart.

'Don't force me to use this, Arthur. Put that down and surrender to me."

"Surrender, surrender to you? I'll see you in hell first, damn you."

He lunged forward, Merriman fired and the heavy pistol ball flung Dorrington backwards and he dropped. His last thought was disappointment that he had failed, then he thought nothing more. He was dead.

The other door was flung open and Lieutenants Andrews and Weston, each with a pistol at the ready, burst in and stopped dead at the sight of Dorrington in a crumpled heap before them.

"It's all right, gentlemen, it's all over now," said Merriman calmly.

"My God, sir, he got to you, when did he – I mean how did he, has he - ?" Andrews stopped, aghast at the thought that in spite of their precautions Dorrington had so nearly succeeded in his aim of murdering their captain.

"I'm unharmed, David, but I fear that poor Tomkins received a nasty wound in the arm when he tried to help me."

As the other officers crowded into the cabin to see what had happened, Merriman continued, "Ah, Doctor, I fear that Mr Dorrington is beyond your help but please see to Tomkins if you will. Now, Mr St James, how did Dorrington get past your marine guards and sentries?"

The horrified officer could do no more than gasp, "I don't know, sir, but we have two dead men. One on deck and one outside your door. I'm very sorry, sir, that we were found wanting in our duty to protect you."

"Very well, I'll speak to you later. Mr Weston, you are officer of the watch, I believe? I'll speak to you later as well. In the meanwhile be good enough to have some men remove the body. I'll take it ashore in the morning."

Andrews was bursting with questions. "Sir, were you expecting Dorrington, I mean, obviously you had not retired as you are still dressed. Did you know he was aboard?"

"No, David, I didn't, but I'm not surprised. I knew how much he wanted to kill me so I thought it wise to take precautions. That's why I had a pistol primed and ready. And now, if you'll all leave, I think I'll try and get some sleep."

However, sleep would not come and Merriman tossed and turned in his cot with the thoughts of how near he had come to being murdered in his sleep keeping him awake. So in the morning it was a very tired and angry man who gave both St James and Weston the biggest dressing down either had ever received in their career. Neither man could offer a defence and Merriman dismissed them with a few more well-chosen words of censure.

Later Merriman had himself rowed to the landing steps in the cutter with Midshipman Hungerford at the tiller. It was an uncomfortable journey with the canvas swathed body in the bottom of the boat to remind them all of what had happened.

Before Merriman climbed the water worn steps, he cautioned Hungerford and the men not to gossip with any of the loungers on shore. "I'll see that someone comes down to take the body but I want no wild stories spread around."

At Admiral FitzHerbert's office he had to wait no more than a few minutes before he was ushered in by the same harassed Lieutenant Williams as before. The Admiral greeted him warmly.

"Captain Merriman, this is a pleasure. Williams, wine for the Captain."

"Thank you, sir, but no, I think you should hear what I have to tell you first."

"Oh, indeed," said the Admiral with a raised eyebrow.

"Yes, sir. It's about your nephew, Arthur." Merriman drew a deep breath. "He's dead, sir. I shot him last night."

"Oh my God, how did this happen?"

Merriman told the full story, how Dorrington must have climbed aboard, the murder of two marines and the confrontation in the great cabin with the wounding of Tomkins when he tried to defend his captain. "Really, sir, I believe I had no option and I'm sure that he was quite mad at the end. He must have known he was doomed and would hang when caught. It was fortunate for me that I was still awake and reading, otherwise I don't think I would be alive now."

"You're right, Captain. There will have to be an enquiry but as he was an escaped murderer it will only be a formality. I'll send somebody down to collect his body which can be disposed of quietly." The Admiral sighed. "I'm sorry I inflicted him on you in the first place. It's probably for the best that it fell out this way, if he had been captured there is no doubt that he would have hanged. No blame will be attached to you but I shall require your written report of course."

"I have it here, sir."

"Very good, Captain. I understand that you will be leaving soon. Your friend Mr Grahame was here only yesterday and he told me that he will be joining your ship today and expects to leave immediately. Where for, he wouldn't say, so may I wish you good fortune and again offer my thanks for the way you acted in this whole sad business."

Mr Grahame was aboard when Merriman returned to *Lord Stevenage*. Later that day, having discussed plans and studied charts, Merriman ordered the ship on a course for the open sea, bound for the South, on its way to new adventures.

THE END

Historical notes:

It is a matter of historical fact that the French attempted an invasion of Ireland in 1796 but were defeated by the gales which scattered the fleet before any troops were landed. The fleet did not reassemble.

It is also historically true that Sir Edward Pellew's frigate *Indefatigable* and the frigate *Amazon* did defeat the greatly superior French warship *Droits De L'Homme,* driving her ashore with great loss of life. The *Amazon* was also lost in this action.

Further attempts were made by the French in 1797 and 1798. In 1798 they actually did manage to get a force ashore which was defeated at the battle of Vinegar Hill. They never tried again.

Wolfe Tone, the Irish patriot or rebel (depending on one's point of view), was captured and only escaped hanging by committing suicide in prison.

All characters are fictional except for the French generals and admirals who really existed and were in command of the French forces at the time. Mr White also existed and was knighted for his services to the crown. The White family still live at Bantry House where there is a small museum with artefacts from this event.

Author Biography
Roger Burnage (1933 to 2015)

Roger Burnage had an eventful life that ultimately led him to pursue his passion for writing. Born and raised in the village of Lymm, Warrington, Cheshire, United Kingdom, he embarked on a journey of adventure and self-discovery.

Roger's life took an intriguing turn when he served in the Royal Air Force (RAF) during his national service. He was stationed in Ceylon, which is now known as Sri Lanka, where he worked as a radio mechanic, handling large transmitters.

After his release from the RAF, Roger went on to work as a draughtsman at Vickers in Manchester. Through dedication and hard work, he eventually climbed the ranks to become a sales engineer. His job involved traveling abroad to places like Scandinavia and India, which exposed him to new cultures and experiences.

It was during this period that Roger Burnage stumbled upon the Hornblower novels by C. S. Forester. The captivating tales of naval adventures ignited a spark of interest in the historical fiction genre within him.

Eventually, Roger settled in North Wales, where he focused on building a business and raising a family. Throughout his professional and personal life, the desire to write for himself never waned. However, it wasn't until retirement that he finally had the time and opportunity to pursue his dream of becoming an author.

Despite facing initial challenges and enduring multiple rejections from publishers and agents, Roger persevered. He refused to give up on his writing aspirations. Even when he underwent open-heart surgery and had an operation for a brain haemorrhage, he continued to work diligently on his craft. Typing away with only two fingers for months on end, he crafted "The Merriman Chronicles."

In 2012, with the support of his youngest son, Robin, Roger self-published his debut novel, "A Certain Threat," on Amazon KDP, making it available in both paperback and Kindle formats. His determination and talent began to bear fruit, as his fan base grew, and book sales remained strong.

More information about
The Merriman Chronicles is available online

Follow the Author on Amazon

Get notified when a new books and audiobooks are released.

Desktop, Mobile & Tablet:
Search for the author, click the author's name on any of the book pages to jump to the Amazon author page, click the follow button at the bottom.

Kindle eReader and Kindle Apps:
The follow button is normally after the last page of the book.

Don't forget to leave a review or rating too!

For more background information, book details and announcements of upcoming novels, check the website at:

www.merriman-chronicles.com

You can also follow us on social media:-

https://twitter.com/Merriman1792

https://www.facebook.com/MerrimanChronicles

Printed in Great Britain
by Amazon